Scratched Off

By Julie C. Gilbert

Aletheia Pyralis Publishers

For information about special discounts available for bulk purchases, sales promotions, fund-raising and educational needs, please email: devyaschildren@gmail.com

http://www.juliecgilbert.com/
https://sites.google.com/view/juliecgilbert-writer/

Love Science Fiction or Mystery?

Choose your adventure!

Visit: http://www.juliecgilbert.com/

For details on getting
Free ebooks.

Foreword:

Dear Reader,

I typically don't like forewords, yet here I am writing one. Personally, I'm like "give me the story, you fiend," but I write in a wide variety of genres, including squeaky clean Christian mysteries. If that's more your thing, please go check out the Heartfelt Cases series. The first in the series, *The Collins Case* (and much of my backlist) should be free.

This is also a contemporary mystery story, but it's quite a bit more intense than Heartfelt Cases. While still free of curse words and "adult" scenes, it's about a serial killer, so there are definitely some disturbing scenes. For what it's worth, if it were a TV show, I'd rate it TV-14.

Thanks for your time. If you're still invested in checking out the story, welcome and I hope you enjoy *Scratched Off*.

Sincerely,

Julie C. Gilbert

Dedication:

To Erin Finigan for being one of the first readers.

And to murder mystery fans everywhere, those lovely, morbid
people.
(I'm right there with you.)

Disclaimer: The events and descriptions herein are the product of my
imagination.
They should not reflect poorly upon any entity, state, or company.

Fair warning: some descriptions are of a disturbing nature.
Reader discretion is advised.

Table of Contents:

Prologue:
Luck of the Draw

Hillsborough High School
Hillsborough, New Jersey

Melissa Novak stood with a few thousand strangers and tried to remember what it felt like to not feel disgustingly sweaty. Breathing had been a chore since she had exited her tiny apartment hours earlier. Her ancient little Civic had not pumped air conditioning in years, but at least it had the decency to not break down on her too often. The humidity played havoc with her long dark hair, so she confined it to a messy, bun-like thing at the back of her head.

Music filled the thick air as the graduates slowly filed in. Melissa pitied the poor band students, especially those wielding a trombone or a trumpet. Her brass instrument career had ended in the eighth grade when her mom entered round one of her lung cancer battle, but Melissa still remembered how much effort it took. With almost six hundred graduates to accompany, the students would be playing for a while.

"Here they come!" a nearby woman exclaimed, swatting her husband's arm to catch his attention.

That's usually what "Pomp and Circumstance" means.

Aware the heat made her cranky, Melissa concentrated on not rolling her blue eyes at the woman. She watched in amusement as parents, grandparents, siblings, and really good friends whipped out phones, cameras, and other recording devices to preserve the moment. She'd have to make do with memories. She doubted her phone would have done anything but blink at her if she tried to take a picture with it. Besides, she was out of minutes and couldn't afford to pay for more right now. Dinner would about kill her credit card, but it would be worth every penny. She could worry about the mounting debt crisis later.

Rank upon rank of red-gowned graduates shuffled by. Her brothers, Josh and Andy, were surprisingly close to the front, so she did her sisterly duty of waving like mad then let her mind wander.

Too bad Josie couldn't make it.

Despite the thought, Melissa couldn't help but feel an immense sense of relief that Josie's coworker at Paul's Coffee Café had called in sick. Josephine Miller, their neighbor, had practically grown up with the twins. She'd even dated them both off and on throughout high school. Being two years older than the boys made her two years younger than Melissa. The age gap had never mattered much to Melissa, who counted Josie as one of her best friends. If Josie had come, she naturally would have been invited to the celebratory dinner. She probably would have offered to pay for dinner too, but Melissa couldn't allow that. This way, the entire awkward situation was avoided.

Mom would've loved to be here too.

The thought sent a jolt of guilt through Melissa. If she'd fought harder, maybe the doctor would have signed off on Elena Novak undertaking such an excursion. Dragging around the oxygen tank would have been hard work, but the bigger issue would have been her mother's energy level. Dinner would be out of the question. Melissa would barely get to greet her brothers before having to dash back to the hospital to return their mother.

Maybe Dad got the easier end of the deal.

She didn't mean that. Her father had died of a heart attack about a year before Elena's diagnosis of lung cancer. The numerous health issues made Melissa grateful she was adopted. Better to have family health history be a big question mark than worry about a weak heart or the possibility of cancer. Still, the boys seemed healthy, and that was reason enough to celebrate.

Tuning out the speeches, Melissa craned her neck to study her baby brothers. From this distance and with the cardboard caps on, she had to squint carefully to decide which was which. They weren't identical twins, but from this distance, they might as well have been. Without the caps, it would have been easy. Josh kept his dirty blond hair cropped short, while Andy usually needed several reminders his hair needed cutting before he dealt with it. Josh was an hour older and had bushier eyebrows, a broader forehead, steady blue eyes much like Melissa's, high cheekbones, a subtle nose, a deep tan, and wider shoulders. Andy was slighter with green eyes, thinner lips, and a paler complexion.

Young men.

At eighteen, they'd reached the threshold of adulthood, but they'd probably forever be "boys" in Melissa's mind. She tried not to think about it. If she got too sentimental, she'd turn into a blubbery mess. Even now, she sniffled and tried to blink back tears. They'd made it, thanks in no small part to her. When she'd graduated high school, their mother had suffered a serious relapse, changing Melissa's college plans. She'd attended community college for three years so she could work and keep the boys on a halfway decent schedule. All that hard work finally paid off. This graduation didn't quite mark the end of her self-imposed duties, but at least now she could see light at the end of the long tunnel.

In a few months, Josh would enter Raritan Valley Community College to take health and emergency medical training classes in order to prepare for a career as a fireman. She was proud of him. He'd always enjoyed rescuing lost cats, and besides, he had a service-oriented heart.

At least I have a couple of months to adjust to the idea.

Not so with Andy. In a matter of days, he would move to California to work as an intern for a professor he'd been corresponding with for months now. Melissa's heart ached at the thought of him moving so far away, even though she knew the partially needs-based, full-ride scholarship to the University of California—Berkley meant the world to him. This was one instance where the financial struggle had actually worked in their favor. The meager government aid and insurance paid most of the hospital bills, but everything Melissa made got sucked into the never-ending cycle of bills.

She refocused when the graduates started filing forward to receive their empty diploma folders. Because of the sheer number of students, the school had arranged for two different vice-principals to read the tiny scraps of paper upon which the graduates had scrawled their names. The ingenious system kept the line moving forward without having one of the readers pass out. Still, whole minutes ticked by while 577 names were read in a respectful, yet steady, pace.

Melissa's ears perked up when she heard one of the VPs call Joshua Gordon Novak. Leaping to her feet, Melissa clapped hard and cheered. Luckily, she wasn't the only one. Several sharp whistles rang out both from the grandstands and from the ranks of graduates.

Josh had always made friends easily. Ever the showman, he went down the line shaking hands enthusiastically, like a politician greeting big donors. When he finished, Josh held both hands up, waved quickly then executed a full theatrical bow. Straightening, he waved again and danced off the platform.

Another name got called from the other vice principal before the second name Melissa had been waiting for rang out: Andrew Frederick Novak.

Once again, Melissa jumped up and clapped like crazy. A few scattered, half-hearted cheers joined her, but this time, she was definitely the most enthusiastic one. She chalked it up to Andy liking his alone time more than Josh. She didn't care. The difference had earned Andy a golden ticket out of this small town life. He'd worked hard, and she determined not to begrudge him the freedom.

Unlike Josh, Andy chose to mark the moment with firm handshakes and curt nods, moving as quickly down the line as he could.

The rest of the commencement ceremony dragged for Melissa. She couldn't wait to take the boys out to dinner, even though it was barely past 4:30. They'd hang out and have ice cream sodas if they needed to wait. She'd opted to take them to The Riverview Diner, which they all enjoyed. When she'd asked for their suggestions, Andy had shrugged and Josh had chosen a steakhouse that would have required a second mortgage on the house. Selling the house would be the next big hurdle for Melissa. She didn't want to kill the mood, but she'd have to discuss that with her brothers at some point. Andy's pending journey sort of put a timer on that conversation. A lump formed in her throat when she considered this might be the last family dinner outing for many years.

A massive cheer momentarily drove away gloomy thoughts. A torrent of red hats went flying, and then the graduates promptly scrambled to grab a new one. Melissa smiled, recalling the rule that one didn't receive the actual diploma until they traded in both the flimsy cap and the blood-red gown. She lost sight of Andy as he headed in to get his diploma. Josh bounded up the bleachers toward her and swept her up in a huge hug.

"You made it!" Josh cried. Sobering, he set her down, and asked, "How's Mom?"

He towered over her.

"I wouldn't miss it," Melissa said. She reached up and patted Josh's cheek. "Mom's same as always. She wishes she could be here."

Melissa hadn't gotten to talk to their mother, but she knew the sentiment would hold true, even if she'd not actually heard the words. These days, Mom spent most of her time sleeping to escape the pain.

"Where's Andy?" Josh scanned the nearby bleachers.

"I saw him headed back to the school," Melissa said, hesitating this time. She sensed the shift in Josh's mood.

"He didn't even stop by to say 'hi'?" Josh looked offended on her behalf. "What's wrong with him?"

Sometimes Melissa asked herself that very question. Her brothers might look similar, but their eating habits and attitudes could hardly be more different.

"He probably just wanted to get out of the sun." Melissa shrugged and masked the tinge of hurt. "Don't worry about it. He'll meet us by the car when he's ready." She grinned. "Having the only set of car keys is good for something."

After soothing Josh's ruffled feathers, Melissa sent him in to exchange the cap and robe for that all-important piece of paper. She spent the waiting time by the car, eager to get to an air conditioned restaurant. The wait gave her a moment to move the carefully wrapped gifts to the trunk where they would be out of sight until the appropriate time.

The twenty-minute drive to the diner was somewhat tense. Josh sat in the front passenger seat, having flat-out sprinted to obtain the honor, while Andy sulked in the back. Melissa could tell they were still miffed at each other, but she didn't try to moderate. Deep down, they loved each other, even if they did turn everything into a competition. She figured it was just as well Andy's love for computers set him on a different path. If he and Josh both became firemen, they'd likely get hurt on the quest to outperform each other.

Once the drinks arrived, the ride was forgotten, and both boys chattered about past events, present plans, and future dreams. The diner held many families celebrating graduations. Some parties were huge, spanning several tables. These also tended to feature hundreds of dollars in pricey balloons. From time to time, Melissa would notice Andy's eyes flicker over to the shiny balloons. She wished she could have afforded some for them, but she thought they'd enjoy her small gift more.

She didn't have to remind them they could order what they wanted; they exercised the privilege with ease. Melissa ordered a burger. Andy chose the Hungry Man breakfast—three eggs over easy, two sausage links, two strips of bacon, and two pieces of toast. Slightly more health conscious, Josh went with a chicken Caesar salad. Both brothers cleared their plates and helped her with half her burger and the fries. Living in her apartment with three other girls the last six months, Melissa had forgotten how much boys could eat. It was one thing to do the weekly shopping and another to actually watch her brothers consume food.

They dragged out the meal as long as possible, ordering a round of coffee and cherry pie. By this time, a new round of guests had arrived, and Melissa caught the waitresses holding a conference over how to speed them along. Waving for the check, she dug out her credit card, not even wanting to see the damages done. It wasn't as bad as she'd feared, but the bill still hurt. She hurried over to the cash register and paid as quickly as possible, wanting the pain over and done with.

Once outside, Josh and Andy thanked her for the great meal.

"I've got one more surprise for you," said Melissa, walking past the driver's door toward the trunk. She stabbed the open trunk button and was delighted to see the back pop open. Reaching in, she plucked up the two tiny, identically wrapped packages.

"What is it?" Josh said, making his tone childish. His eyes sparkled. He knew exactly what the packages contained. It was family tradition, after all. "Which do you want?" he asked Andy. Receiving a shrug, Josh took the left package and ripped into it. "This one feels lucky."

Melissa handed the other package to Andy, and then dug out a quarter for each of them. Josh was right. His lottery ticket proved to be a winner to the tune of $5.00, the price of the actual ticket. Andy tried to stuff his into his back pocket, but neither Melissa, nor Josh, would accept that. Reluctantly, he opened the package, took out the ticket, and scratched off the play area with infuriating slowness. The meticulous work paid off, however, revealing a win of $500. The win resulted in a brilliant smile and good-natured teasing from Andy. His mood was so good he let Josh claim the front seat for the ride home. Josh bore the ribbing with grace.

Melissa decided to put off the "sell the house" and "mom's current health" conversations for a few hours. She was enjoying the carefree moment where everything looked like it would work out for her little brothers.

Chapter 1:
Fortune and Glory

About eleven years later ...
The Killer's Lair
Undisclosed Location
Gloves, mask, and apron. Check.

The list amused him because it sounded like the equipment needed for life-saving surgery, not the things needed to deal death. His body trembled with anticipation as he donned the items one by one. The victim was primed and ready, chained to the wall as planned. The things one could buy on the internet amazed him. In addition to the chains on the wall, he also had a modified dental chair. He looked forward to testing that out, but this occasion called for more traditional symbolism.

The tarp was already in place, eager to do its job, and the GHB—Gamma Hydroxy Butyrate—should be wearing off soon. He had plenty of bleach and running water available for the cleanup.

Scalpel, kitchen knife, or hunting dagger?

Andrew Novak frowned. So many decisions needed to be made. There ought to be a manual about how to kill people most efficiently. It wasn't a bad idea. Perhaps he would jot down some thoughts after dealing with Old Jimbo out there. He understood that it wasn't wise to kill someone he knew, but this man so richly deserved it, he just had to make an exception. Besides, few people knew of their real relationship anyway. To them, he was simply one of the hundreds of students who passed through Professor James Lurch's classroom every year.

Investigators would also need to find enough of him to identify the body before digging deep into the man's past. They wouldn't have to dig far to find evidence of shady dealings. Lurch might fancy himself a mastermind, but his work was more consistent with a third-rate hack. His main advantage was unbridled access to a horde of talented but naïve young people trying to make it somewhere in the virtual world.

Within a month of Andrew's arrival in California, Lurch had approached him with a special opportunity to earn some money. The job involved hacking into several large credit card companies and planting a spy program that reported customers' spending habits. Sixty-seven percent of the customers paid their bills online, so they also had the opportunity to use a second program to track back to each person's home IP address. Once on the home computers or laptops, they had carte blanche to steal whatever information they desired. The plan had worked like a charm, probably earning Lurch millions, but the helpers earned only a pitiful flat fee and a stern warning to keep their mouths shut.

You should have paid us fairly.

He flung the thought at the man chained to the wall and waited impatiently for him to awaken. Spotting a lottery ticket over on one of his work benches, he picked up the scalpel, perched on a stool, and gently scratched the surface with the dull side of the blade. His heartrate quickened with anticipation as he slowly revealed the player's cards.

"Where am I?" The chains rattled as the victim suddenly realized his plight. "Who are you?" The tone sat somewhere between plea and demand.

Abandoning the lottery ticket, Andrew stood and watched the man's blindfolded head swivel back and forth as he attempted to gather information through his ears.

"What do you want? Is it money? I have money! Lots of it. Millions. Let me go and it's yours!"

"It's already mine."

"Mr. Novak? Is that you? What's going on?" For a moment, the questions sounded hopeful before the man's addled brain gathered the pieces to the puzzle and started compiling a picture. "Talk to me. Let's make a deal." The words were soothing.

The blindfold didn't seem necessary anymore. Three long strides closed the distance between them. The smell of sweat and fear struck him as he got within inches of the man. Pressing one hand firmly over the blindfold, Andrew swiped the scalpel through the thin straps on either side. The victim yelped as the blade inflicted two shallow cuts on either side of his temple and down each cheek.

"Are you insane? You can't treat—"

Andrew buried the scalpel in the man's right side, ending the righteous speech.

The man moaned and muttered some curses.

Breathing hard, Andrew leaned close, keeping the mask in place so he wouldn't be tempted to spit on the man. The inside of his nitrile gloves felt slick with sweat, but he gripped the handle of the scalpel and yanked it free, eliciting a grunt of pain.

"You asked me what I want. Do you still want to know?" Andrew asked. Without waiting for a reply, he said one word. "Erin."

The man's eyes watered with tears, and his body stiffened with recognition.

"That wasn't my fault," he protested.

Massive willpower kept Andrew from striking with the blade again. He would finish the job, but not before the man confessed to all his sins. He didn't want the professor too delirious with pain to appreciate what was happening to him and why.

"How many did you hurt?" he growled the question. Behind the mask, his cheeks flushed. He couldn't even bring himself to say the word for what Lurch had done to Erin Thompson.

"I didn't kill her," whimpered Lurch.

Andrew slapped the man with his left hand, trying to get him to focus.

"No. She took care of that after you ruined her life." Tucking the scalpel beneath Lurch's chin, Andrew applied gentle pressure and repeated his question. "How many?"

"Four? Five? I can't remember! You're making me nervous!"

"Sixteen," Andrew supplied. "And those are only the ones I know about. What'd you do? Sleep with every female student who needed a grade boost?"

"Please. I have a wife and three kids."

Andrew laughed bitterly.

"You haven't been home in weeks. When I contacted you to discuss an 'exciting deal,' you were 'touring' Thailand."

"I have a problem. I admit that, but my family doesn't know." Lurch fell quiet for a moment. "Will you tell them?"

"Your wife sends her regards," said Andrew. It was a lie, but the shock and horror on Lurch's face justified it in full. In truth, Andrew had had no contact with Rebecca Lurch, but he made a mental note to send her an insurance payout to make up for her years of suffering at the hands of this louse.

"I'll change," Lurch promised. "Please. Let me go."

The scalpel wasn't cutting it for him anymore. He needed something stronger, more decisive. Walking over to the dental chair, Andrew considered the tools available to him. A kitchen knife would make a nice statement, but his patience was waning. The man's evil presence was tainting the air down here. Andrew would have to address the ventilation issues before the next job. Selecting the hunting knife, Andrew tested the blade's sharpness on a scrap of paper kept for that purpose. It sliced cleanly into the flimsy sheet.

"I'm glad you feel remorse for your actions," said Andrew. "Killing you is 'just a matter of practicality though. You see where I'm coming from, don't you?'"

The man paled as he recognized the words. It was the same speech he gave to each student he roped—or duped—into criminal activities then cheated out of money or success.

"I made you what you are," said Lurch softly. "You lacked direction when I first met you. I honed your skills and taught you a better way to use them."

"You showed me how to make money," Andrew admitted. "But you don't get to claim anything else." He studied the dagger. The short blade gleamed in the harsh fluorescent lights. "I'm going to end your reign of terror once and for all." He locked eyes with the man. "Right now."

***

Day 1: Early morning.

I killed for the first time today. It was messier than anticipated, but nothing a good amount of bleach and water couldn't handle. The tarp wasn't necessary until it came time to remove the body, and by then,

I'd washed most of the blood down the drain.

He deserved it. I ought to carve that message into his body, but I guess it's too late for that. The dogs have disposed of most of him, but I'll have to bury the bones somewhere. If I leave the body in an open field in the middle of these woods, nature will reclaim its own if given enough time. The hard work still lies ahead of me, but I must endure. Dragging the bones about won't be easy, especially since I'll need to drive them far away from here.

I rid the world of one piece of refuse, and it felt great. Scary, but great. I was once his victim. This brand of scum had a definite preference for female company physically, but he was equal opportunity cruel when it came to taking advantage of lost college kids. My early works disappeared only to reappear under his name. When I confronted him, he laughed and told me I was paying my dues and would reap the rewards one day.

He was right.

I'm now in control of his extensive secret bank accounts. There's freedom in financial security, but I cannot spend the money as I wish. When the work is complete, I will retire to a warm, comfortable place where I can be at peace.

But there's still work to do.

I would do it again if I could. It's his fault. If he'd left me alone, I probably wouldn't have even known of his crimes.

I'm not a monster. I didn't make him suffer to the extent he deserved. I might have to be a monster one day. One cannot fight monsters without risking a walk in their shoes. Vigilantes have a code, but it's not perfect.

I'm not perfect yet, but I will be.

I don't think one can truly prepare the mind to end another. There's intoxicating power in the idea and euphoria in the process. Watching life flicker, then slowly fade is almost … magical. There's no other word for it.

I'm a killer, a murderer, a marked man.

But I don't care.

It's addictive.

I must do this again, but I'm not sure knives are the way to go. They're slow. It's not about the pain. It's about justice. The weapon this round was a hunting dagger. I started with a scalpel, but that wasn't satisfying or quick. I would have been at it for hours, unless I went straight for an artery. Next time, I'll try the guns. They seem too easy though, like cheating. A knife forces one to get up close and personal and earn the kill. This kill was personal. The next will likely not be, but I need to make it so.

I should make the rest of the body disappear, but what would that accomplish? There's no risk. I will gather a following and be worshiped, if only from afar. Maybe I'll send the head to the police. A head will keep them busy. They must have something. I can't work in anonymity forever. On the other hand, I can't make it too easy for them so early in the game. Maybe just a finger? Can they work with that? I'll have to see if there are any left.

What's a show without an audience?

The world needs me.

I'm a hunter, a fixer, a warrior. If I have to take down the deserving one at a time, I'll do it. It's the ultimate man vs. the universe story. People are horrible to each other. The news is filled with tales of hardship and tragedy. I know I'll add to that, but it's for the greater good. People need to be purified.

How do I know?

I won on a scratch-off ticket today. The amount was just $5.00—the price of the ticket—but the win proves I'm on the right track. The ticket was called Fortune and Glory. You can win a trip to Hollywood or up to $50,000. I've never won that big, but the amount doesn't matter. It's the principle. Most of the good things in my life have been marked by a win.

The difficulty will be in choosing only one victim at a time. There might be some innocent blood shed along the way. I can't make this too easy on the police. They can't learn I have a type or a pattern. But I definitely do.

Evildoers will die.

Chapter 2:
Mystery Dust

State Game Lands Number 219
Warren Township, Pennsylvania
A cool breeze carried the scent of blood, smoke, and vomit to Sheriff Cayden West. The drive up from Towanda had taken him a little over a half-hour. The unusually pleasant late October air had lured him into riding with the windows open for the last leg of the trip. He scowled, closed the windows, and climbed out of his truck. He was getting too old to be tromping around forests to find dead bodies, not that he would ever admit such aloud. If his wife had her way, he'd be living the boring life in Florida. That plan would have to wait. He had a job to do. The unlovely scents told him he didn't have far to go. The sound of retching also led the way. Following his senses, the sheriff made his way over to the others.

It didn't take much to tell what had caught everybody's attention. A clear plastic bag had been nailed to the trunk of an American beech tree. Condensation obscured the view slightly, but Sheriff West had no trouble seeing that it held a head. Below the bag, words had been carved into the tree trunk with crude block letters.

HE DESERVED THIS!

I'm not sure anybody deserves to wind up in a bag on a tree.

He stepped on a stick as he approached.

The deputy whirled.

"Sheriff!" The one-word greeting from Deputy Amos Pitts

broke into the sheriff's thoughts. The young man sounded about ready to cry with relief.

At the deputy's feet sat a sullen man smoking a cigarette. From the amount of butts piled up next to him, the man had probably been chain smoking since calling in the gruesome find.

That explained the smell of smoke. Sheriff West considered scolding the man for smoking in a wooded area but doubted he would hear any of it. A few steps closer revealed the source of the vomit smell.

"What do we have?" West asked the deputy.

A quick survey of the surrounding area revealed the blood source to be a dead turkey.

"Heck of a thing to find on Halloween, sir," said the deputy. "It's a head, but it gets worse."

The sheriff fixed the deputy with a pointed stare.

"Worse than a head in a tree?" he inquired.

"Yes, sir," answered Deputy Pitts. "I think we have most of a body—or more, but whoever left us the gifts wanted us to work for it."

West was about to voice another question when it died on his lips. A new sight caught his attention as he got close enough to touch the plastic bag with the head. He blinked, then stared, and blinked some more.

The trees on either side as far as he could see held more plastic bags. The nearest one on his left held a hand and part of an arm, but no fingers. Morbid curiosity made him walk over and peer closely into the bag. Most of the flesh was gone, and what was left showed teeth marks.

Bile rose inside him.

No wonder the man had lost his breakfast.

"Take the witness to the parking lot and interview him," the sheriff ordered, stabbing a finger toward the civilian. "And call the State Police and the FBI."

Deputy Pitts hustled to obey. He helped the man up and led him away. Seeing the pile of cigarette leavings, the sheriff snapped a picture of them with his phone and pulled out a sealable sandwich bag from his pocket to preserve them in. He highly doubted the man was their perpetrator, but stranger things had happened. Normally, he would leave possible evidence in place, but not when it might spark a forest fire if left unattended.

This is way beyond us.

Placing hands on hips, Sheriff West scanned the trees left and right of the one featuring the head. He had never seen a body dump in person, let alone one so bizarre. The only dead bodies he'd seen were at motor vehicle accidents or in funeral homes. In this state, the sheriff and his deputies were little more than glorified court employees there to serve bench warrants and transport prisoners around the county. His department had made about three arrests in the course of the last five years, and those were for crimes that happened in his presence or that of a deputy.

West shook his head. He would gladly hand this case off to somebody with greater resources. Processing the evidence on this case was going to cost that somebody a bundle. Nevertheless, before that handoff could happen, the sheriff and his people were in for a long day. He checked his cell phone for a signal and found none. The troops would have to be rallied from his radio.

The sheriff took one last look at the ominous plastic bags marking dozens of trees in the area. Then, he headed for the parking lot. The State Police could probably send help within the hour, but he didn't know exactly how long it would take the FBI people to arrive. If he remembered correctly, they had a field office in Philadelphia on the lower east side of the state. This being the upper east side of the state, it could take three and a half hours or more for them to show up, assuming they could dispatch an agent immediately.

He made a mental note to call his wife too. Charlotte would want to help once she realized he would be stuck in the forest most of the day. She and her quilting club could at least provide food for the law enforcement personnel who descended upon the land today. He wanted her nowhere near the sight of the plastic bags, but the parking lot below should be safe enough.

***

FBI Special Agent Samuel Kerman unfolded his long legs from the passenger space and hoped they would hold him once he exited the white Ford Focus. He couldn't really complain about the amount of legroom up front, but the long drive from Philadelphia left him stiff. It would have been nicer if they had stopped once or twice or if he could have pushed the seat back all the way. The amount of stuff in the back prevented any seat movement except forward, and the driver was too excited to stop along the way.

Mira Stratham bounded out of the car like a caffeinated cat, ripped open the back door, and rummaged through the tools of her trade.

For the hundredth time this morning, Sam wished he hadn't taken the train to work today. If he had driven, they might have added a half-hour to their travel time, but it would have been a much more enjoyable experience. He ran a weary hand down his face to boost the circulation and studiously avoided leaning down and checking his reflection in the rearview mirror. He wished he'd remembered his sunglasses. The sun felt great shining down through his close-cropped brown hair, but it was murder on the eyes. Midway through a luxurious stretch, a pair of pale blue cloth booties sailed over the car's roof and struck him on the chin. He caught them as they bounced off.

"Put those on," ordered Mira. In response to his expression, she continued, "I know they're not stylish, but if you're coming with me, you're doing so on my terms. And lose the tie, even if it does match those lovely sea green eyes."

At first, Sam had been ecstatic to work with the prominent forensic scientist. He loved crime shows that glorified the trade, even though he understood that most of the "facts" presented on those shows were complete
nonsense.

"You know a dozen locals have probably already tromped the place to pieces, right?" Sam asked, loosening the knot of his tie and slipping it over his head. He considered taking off the jacket too, but decided against going that far.

"That's no excuse for sloppy work on our end," she countered.

Knowing he was going to look like an idiot, Sam donned the Smurf shoes and sighed. Blue shoe covers did not go with a black suit.

"Oh, it's not that bad," said Mira. She flashed him a bright smile that reached her cool gray eyes. "You're lucky I don't carry lab coats in your size." As she spoke, the petite woman donned a white lab coat and plucked a pair of blue gloves from the pocket. After pulling the gloves on, she dove back into her car and came up with a fresh box of gloves. The box was promptly hurled over the car.

Ready this time, Sam caught the box with ease and glanced down, pleased to see they were size extra-large.

"Wear a pair and stuff a bunch in your pockets," instructed the scientist. "I'm without a technician today, so you're going to fulfill that role, if you're willing." The words floated to him slightly distorted as she was still digging around in the guts of her car. Popping her head up so she could make eye contact, she asked, "You're not squeamish, are you?"

"I don't faint at the sight of blood," Sam said, squaring his shoulders.

"How are you with foul smells?"

He didn't know how to answer her. Nobody had ever asked him such an oddball question.

"Um, fair, I guess." Sam prepared to catch something else and wasn't disappointed. A tiny container of pale yellow gel sailed his way. He cautiously opened the lid then made a face when a strong chemical odor crawled
up his nose.

"It's better than what we're about to find," said Mira cheerfully. "Rub that under your nose. You can wash it off when we're done. I have baby wipes for just that purpose."

Sam wondered if there was anything the scientist didn't have packed into the back of her car. He waited a beat, just in case she wanted to chuck something else at him. When nothing else came, he applied a small amount of the yellow gunk just above his upper lip. The minty chemical scaled the hairs in his nostrils. The stuff had the consistency of melted lip balm. Wiping the excess on the back of his other hand, Sam sealed the rest and pocketed the container. Then, he took a handful of gloves and stuffed them into a different pocket. He didn't want to put the gloves on until the last moment. He remembered the feeling from high school biology class, just before dissections. Those had smelled nasty, especially the shark.

"Do you have the Vicks?" asked Mira, breaking into his memories of bio class.

"The what?" he responded.

"The smelly goo that looks like Vaseline," she clarified.

"Sure." Sam retrieved it from his pocket and gently tossed it her way.

Snatching it out of the air, Mira thanked him and applied some to her face. She now wore a heavy-duty digital camera around her neck. The accessory made her look more like a tourist than a scientist, but the lab coat, booties, gloves, and hairnet spoke otherwise. Sam silently thanked the universe she hadn't made him wear a hairnet. Once the ritual was complete, Mira leaned down and picked up a giant toolbox Sam hadn't even seen her take out of the car.

Hurrying around the car's rear, Sam reached for the case.

"Here, let me get that for you."

"It's heavy," Mira warned.

Sam grunted when the full weight transferred to him.

"What's in here?" He adjusted his grip to better facilitate carrying the bulky container.

"Too many things to list," replied the scientist. She grinned. "Now you know why I like to travel with a strapping young tech—or a federal substitute." Her gaze swept over him, and her eyes were filled with mirth. "You'll do." With that, she spun around and headed for the nearest uniformed trooper.

Setting the box down, Sam quickly pulled on a pair of gloves. This gave the scientist the chance to reach the edge of the woods. The trooper gestured and explained something to her. She nodded and marched in. Sam scooped up the toolbox and hurried after her.

He arrived as Mira lined up the first shot of a plastic bag hanging from a tree. Without looking up, she motioned for him to stop. He did so, unwittingly becoming a part of a somber semi-circle of uniformed men and women that had gathered to watch the scientist work. One man made the sign of the cross on his chest. Sam didn't see what the big deal was until he looked closer at the bag and saw the lifeless eyes staring at him. He flinched, but nobody mocked him for it.

After taking dozens of pictures, Mira reached up and gently removed the long nail holding the bag in place. The head shifted, but Mira caught the top of the plastic bag and held it in place.

Everybody drew a sharp breath.

"Is there anything we can do to help, ma'am?" asked an older man wearing a sheriff's badge.

Mira glanced at the man.

"No offense, but you're not properly geared to help, Sheriff," Mira said.

"I am," Sam reminded her, suddenly grateful for the stupid blue booties. "What do you need me to do?"

"Who are you?" demanded the sheriff.

"That's Agent Kerman with the FBI. The rest of the proper introductions will have to wait until the tricky part's done, but I'm sure we'll be here a while," said Mira, lifting her chin to point to her right.

Following the motion, Sam saw that this wasn't the only tree bearing a bag. He stared.

"Sam." Mira waited until she had his attention. "Please take the bag and lower it gently to the ground. I want to take a few more pictures. Then, you'll need to extract the head so I can examine it."

Swallowing hard, Sam carried out the instructions. He opened the bag as wide as possible and considered his options. If he used two hands, his sleeves would definitely brush the sides. If he used one hand, he risked dropping the head. Aside from being disrespectful to the dead, the scientist would have his head should that happen. Reminding himself he loved his job, Sam steeled his nerves and reached into the bag, keeping his elbows as close together as possible. With a few awkward maneuvers, Sam managed to extract the head and place it on top of a plastic sheet Mira laid out for that purpose.

The scientist worked in silence for several long minutes.

Sam moved back to the semi-circle to keep out of her way. The only sounds that could be heard belonged to the creatures around going about their daily lives. The occasional far-off gunshot could also be heard. One of the hunting seasons must have opened, but he couldn't remember which one.

Finally, Mira Stratham stood, wearing a puzzled expression.

"What'd you find?" asked the sheriff.

"I'm not sure," the scientist admitted. "It's a gray, flaky mystery particle of some kind. It looks sort of like greasy dust. I'll know more when I get to test it properly." She reached into her toolbox and selected a swab and a tiny plastic bag. After brief consideration, she threw the swab back into the box and chose a small metal scoop. Holding the bag at an angle, she brushed some flakes in. Picking up a new swab, she rubbed it along the edges of two shallow cuts running down the man's face. She secured the new swab in its own plastic bag and stood up, examining the two prizes.

Chapter 3:
Good Brothers

The Killer's Lair
Undisclosed Location

Six monitors flashed images in front of Andrew Novak. The top three were tuned to various national news providers covering the grim Halloween discovery of a body in an area preserved for hunting. Serious-faced beautiful people silently spoke of what had first been pegged for a disgusting Mischief Night prank. He didn't have to hear them to know what they were saying. Their stories had altered only minutely for hours.

The bottom three screens held home security footage from various places around his sister's house. He hadn't pegged Mel for being quite so sentimental until he discovered she was renovating their childhood home.

Getting unobtrusive security cameras in place had been child's play. He had simply waited for her to go to work then strolled right in. She couldn't take enough time off to supervise every workman who came and went for the better part of three months. Her patients would miss her too much. A swell of pride filled him as he thought of her accomplishments. Their mother's death had devastated her, but when she bounced back, she also redirected her life, choosing to treat pediatric patients suffering from cancer. The road to getting a medical degree had taken her longer than other people, but she'd made it. Andrew had helped with an anonymous—and rather generous—"scholarship," but the brainy stuff was all Mel.

Two years ago, when he decided to launch a crusade against evildoers everywhere, Andrew had cut off most contact with his sister. He expected to make enemies along the way, and Mel was perhaps the only person he still cared about. He'd lost touch with Josh during college, mostly because the jerk had married Andrew's ex-girlfriend without telling him.

Each November first—Mel's birthday—Andrew always made an exception to his self-imposed no-contact rules by sending her a large bouquet of purple amaryllis flowers. She had always had a thing for the pricey flowers. Now that he had money, he enjoyed indulging her, even from a distance. He never signed the card, but she would know it was from him.

Movement on the bottom left screen made him frown. Tapping a few keys, Andrew spread the image over the six tightly arranged screens, so that they formed one image. A man in firefighter gear stood on Mel's front stoop holding a bulky bakery box in one hand and a bouquet of flowers in the other. The camera sending the image was too far away to offer many details, but Andrew recognized the figure.

His blood pressure spiked.

Josh.

A few more key strokes switched the view to a different camera. This one offered an excellent view as Mel greeted Josh with a warm hug. Jealousy gripped Andrew as Josh lowered the bakery box to the ground and picked Mel up with one arm, spinning in a complete circle once, twice, and then a third time. Hating himself for not being there, Andrew added sound so he could hear their conversation.

"Put me down!" Mel ordered, laughing as she playfully swatted Josh's head. "And watch your step or you'll be headed to work with cake on your boots. Won't you stay and have some?"

Setting her down, Josh shook his head.

"Sorry. Duty calls, so I have to jet. Must earn the big bucks if I want to see the 49ers trash the Seahawks in person this year."

"You've been saying that for years," said Mel.

Andrew could tell from her expression that she wondered if Josh would let her pay for such a trip. For all his complaints about money, their brother took enormous pride in providing for his family. "Go for it. Eddie's old enough to appreciate it."

"Maybe we will," Josh murmured. He shook off the thoughtful expression like a dog casting off water. "Anyway, happy birthday, Sis. Josie said she and the kids would help you with the cake problem when they get here. Gotta go." After one more, brief hug, Josh turned around and headed for his Expedition. Midway down the walk, he turned, and said, "I'll call later if it gets slow. How's two-thirty sound?"

"Sounds great!" Mel called back. "But remember Josie and the kids are camping here for a few days. If you wake one of the little ones, you'll answer to her."

Josh gave a mock shudder, threw Mel a casual salute, and climbed into his vehicle.

Their ease with each other bothered Andrew. He indulged in a few moments of regret at having lost touch with his siblings, before sighing and releasing the feelings. Family was a sacrifice necessary for his crusade. Watching over Mel from afar would have to suffice in lieu of a real relationship.

Mel picked up the cake box and brought it into the kitchen along with the flowers. Seeing her put the cake into the refrigerator required yet another camera switch. When she started unwrapping the bouquet of roses Josh had given her, Andrew switched back to Camera-2, the one that viewed the front door.

Backing up the image, Andrew froze Josh's face at the instant before he turned to leave. It was the first real glimpse of his brother in years. The physically demanding job had strengthened Josh's body. His shoulders were broader than Andrew remembered, and his muscles appeared more defined through the thin, white undershirt.

For one second, Andrew considered killing Josh, but he dismissed the idea for several reasons. First, in the grand scheme of life, his crimes were petty. Marrying Josie might have been a low move, but if he were honest, Andrew knew he had no real claim over her at that stage in their lives. Second, killing Josh would draw attention to their family. If the investigators were thorough, they might seek him out. He had a lot to accomplish before letting them get that close. Third, it would make Mel sad. She'd suffered enough in her thirty-four years of life. Even if it meant letting Josh play the part of the good brother, Andrew would let her keep him as an emotional support.

Setting the cameras back to normal status, Andrew turned the news stations back on and unmuted the middle one at random.

The reporter peered into the camera and nodded in response to whatever the anchor had just said.

"That's right, Al. The FBI has just released a statement saying that due to the violent nature of the crime committed, they're working closely with the Pennsylvania State Police to get answers as soon as possible. This is Channel Thirteen's Natalie Carmen reporting live from Bradford County."

Muting the news before it could switch back to the studio people, Andrew rubbed his hands together in anticipation. He'd been without a true challenge for a long time. He wasn't certain what law enforcement would do next, but he wanted to find out. Once he knew the key players involved, he could monitor the situation and manipulate them as necessary. The media might prove useful too. Hacking into the FBI might be tempting, but he refrained. That could come up later, but he'd start off easier. The news people were social media divas. Finding one to suit his purposes would be a simple matter of some Google searches. He needed somebody young, ambitious, and beautiful but not too high up the food chain.

***

Super-Saver Motel
Bradford County, Pennsylvania
Midnight had come and gone by the time Sam Kerman checked into the questionable motel. He would have preferred to drive through the night to get back to Philadelphia for the privilege of sleeping in his own apartment, but once again, Special Agent in Charge Louis Hatcher had overruled him. They had a meeting tomorrow afternoon to discuss the case, but the SAC wanted Sam and Mira close to the scene just in case something new developed.

If the phone conversations Sam had overheard panned out, Mira would be sticking around the area to oversee the evidence team being dispatched from Quantico. That would mean waiting around until he got a ride or renting a car. Kicking off his shoes, Sam laid back on the bed, being careful not to land on his gun, and closed his eyes, dreading how soon morning would come. He didn't even have a toothbrush to perform proper bedtime rituals.

A brilliant idea sailed into his head, causing him to sit up. Maybe he wouldn't have to wait around after all. Digging out his phone, Sam checked his text messages and voicemails. His kid sister had called three times and texted him about eight times, demanding updates. Jenn had been incredibly jealous of him meeting Mira Stratham. Apparently the tiny woman was a superstar in the forensic science world. Sam couldn't remember the details. He'd sort of blocked out Jenn's glowing report when she started spewing facts like normal people give baseball statistics.

Knowing he should clear his idea with the lady scientist first, Sam forced his body up and stumbled over to the phone. After muddling through the room to room instructions, he placed the call. Mira answered on the third ring sounding wide awake. Sam wasted no time in stating his proposal. Mira asked some probing questions, and then granted his request. Lest Sam get too comfortable, she reminded him that he ought to clear it with SAC Hatcher.

Once he hung up, Sam sat on his bed and pulled his sister's number up on his phone. He hesitated only a moment, deciding that she'd get over her crankiness in a hurry once she heard him out.

"Did you get it?" Jenn's question caught him off guard.

"Hey, Squirt. Nice to hear your sweet voice. How was your day?"

"You forgot," Jenn accused.

"I forgot," Sam admitted, remembering her ridiculous request for an autograph. "But you're going to forgive me in a moment because I got you something far better."

"Oh, yeah? Like what?" Jenn's tone made her skepticism clear.

"The opportunity to play hooky and let me borrow your car."

"What's in it for me?"

Sam let a few beats pass just to make her suffer. That was his job as her older brother.

"You get to spend all day—and possibly multiple days— shadowing Mira Stratham and her team while they work to catalogue the evidence out here in the Pennsylvania sticks."

"Really?" Pure elation filled her tone. She was mere weeks from completing her forensic science degree with a double major in that and chemistry.

"I still have to clear it with my boss," Sam cautioned, "but Dr. Stratham's on board with the idea. Can you afford to miss a few days?"

"Of course! Most of my classmates would practically kill for an opportunity like this."

Sam enjoyed the irony of her statement.

"Who's the best brother ever?"

"This time, you definitely are," Jenn replied. "This is awesome! I've got to go pack. I'll be there in a few hours."

"Whoa. Slow down, Squirt. The dead guy's still going to be here whenever you arrive."

"Dr. Stratham's going to want to get an early start," Jenn argued. "They're predicting rain in that area for tomorrow afternoon."

"Nerd."

"Ignoramus," Jenn returned with ease.

It was a familiar exchange.

"See you in a few hours," said Sam. "Drive safely."

She sighed but promised to do so.

When the call ended, Sam stared at the phone for a moment, wondering at the wisdom of involving Jenn. Sure, she'd be knee deep in muck and never far from a dozen like-minded science freaks, but he didn't like the idea of exposing her to the sights and smells he'd seen today. Given her career choice, she would see the dark side of humanity sooner rather than later, but Sam still felt mildly guilty for bringing her anywhere near this case. It gave him a bad vibe.

People who hacked up others and carved messages into trees typically weren't one-shot wonders. Even if this was the perpetrator's first kill, it would probably not be his last.

Chapter 4:
The Big One

FBI Field Office
William J. Green, Jr. Federal Building
Philadelphia, Pennsylvania

Luck finally favored Special Agent Samuel Kerman as he reached the City of Brotherly Love. A car pulled away, leaving Sam a parking spot within sight of his destination. After expertly parallel parking his sister's Hyundai Elantra in the space, Sam checked for traffic and leapt out as soon as the coast was clear. Both knees cracked as his feet hit the pavement. Self-respecting men taller than 5' 5" should never drive an Elantra for more than an hour at a stretch, especially cherry-red ones with Hello Kitty bumper stickers.

All 6' 2" and 180 pounds of Sam were grateful to escape the small car. Jenn had terrible taste in music too. That left the scratchy radio as the only means of breaking up the monotony. He made a mental note to get his sister a subscription to one of those satellite radio programs for Christmas. She would probably fill the memory buttons with country music channels, but if he was ever forced to borrow her car again, he'd have palatable options.

After checking through security, Sam headed up to his cubicle. He needed to find his spare suit before meeting his boss. Stopping at his apartment would have been nice, but that would have made him late. Sam was still too new in the building to take liberties with the SAC's time. His first three-year stint had been at a resident agency in Elk City, Oklahoma. Being an East Coast boy, Sam had returned as soon as possible. He really wanted to work in New York City, but he'd been recruited from the Newark, New Jersey field office. Career goals aside, Sam had no complaints about Philly so far. The cheesesteaks that could be found were always amazing. Thinking of cheesesteak made his stomach grumble.

The reminder of skipping lunch made him dig around in his desk until he found a power bar. Hopefully, the meeting with Special Agent in Charge Louis Hatcher would be relatively quick, so Sam could go out for a proper meal. After changing, Sam strode briskly toward the real offices.

"What's your secret, Kerman?" Thane Joseph Newhouse asked. The agent leaned casually against the left side of the threshold to his cubicle, sipping from a large cup of coffee.

"What are you talking about?" Sam inquired, pausing long enough to toss his go bag into his office.

"Rumor mill says you've landed The Big One. Is that a fact?" T.J. kept his tone even, but the unmistakable glint of jealousy shone from his eyes.

"I don't know," said Sam. "Guess I'll find out soon. I've got a meeting with Hatcher in a few minutes." Grateful for the excuse, he resumed his quest to reach the SAC's office fifteen minutes before the meeting was set to start.

"If it's true, I want in!" T.J. called after Sam.

For his part, Sam waved to acknowledge the request. He wasn't sure why T.J. thought he'd have any say in the matter. Thane wasn't a bad sort, but in Sam's humble opinion, the older man came across as too ambitious and career-oriented to really be a good agent. Pushing T.J. from his mind, Sam finished the trek to the suite of real offices and checked in with the SAC's administrative assistant.

"Have a seat, Agent Kerman," said the woman. "I'll let Agent Hatcher know you're here, and I'll call you when he has a moment to see you."

Catching sight of her nameplate, which read: Dawn Hopper, Sam thanked her by name and took a seat. His father had always stressed the importance of being polite, especially when it came to people who had the power to make one wait. His fingers itched to check his phone, but he resisted the temptation. He did not need the SAC to come out and see him fiddling with a cell phone.

When twenty minutes had dragged by, Dawn waved to catch

his attention.

"Agent Hatcher is on an important conference call, but he said it should wrap up soon," she reported. "Would you like some coffee while you wait? There's a fresh pot in the back."

"No, thank you, ma'am."

"Suit yourself," she said with a shrug. "It's really good."

"I plan to have a late lunch after my meeting," Sam said, wondering why he felt compelled to explain himself.

A red light blinked on Dawn's phone, snapping the woman to attention.

"That might be him now, perhaps you won't have to wait," she commented, picking up the receiver and pressing the red button.

A short conversation later, Dawn smiled at Sam and told him his wait was over.

Soon, Sam was shaking hands with a man he'd only met once in his life. Louis Hatcher had a large, slightly crooked nose, big ears, and a forehead that seemed to go on forever due to the prominent bald island at the top of his head. Sam liked him. He had a gruff Brooklyn accent, scruff on his chin and above his lips, and a straightforward approach to everything.

After quick pleasantries, Hatcher got to the point.

"You got one heck of a fairy godmother looking out for your career, Agent Kerman. I've got a U.S. senator asking me to make you the poster boy for our forensic lab cleanup."

Sam wasn't quite sure how to respond to that. Hatcher's glare could have melted steel if it were
weaponized, but he didn't think the ire was directed at him.

"Sir?" Sam's inflection made it a question. "I'm not sure what you're referring to."

Hatcher sighed.

"All right. Quick history lesson. A couple of years back, the head of the Quantico lab goes on record saying innocent people wound up wrongly convicted 'cause a few agents got overzealous and fudged some things." Hatcher's expression told Sam what he thought about the whistleblower. "You can imagine the fallout that followed. Credibility goes to crap, funding gets cut, convictions get overturned, bad guys walk, and the people with nothing better to do cry for a zillion reforms."

Sam thought reforms were probably a good thing, but he had

enough sense to keep the opinion in.

"Normally, I don't give a rat's tail what any senator wants, but we work for one of the largest political beasts out there," said Hatcher. "Long story short, part of the reforms involves showing that the Bureau as a whole is keeping a close eye on the lab people. That's where you come in."

"What do you need me to do, sir?" Sam asked, trying to keep an open mind.

Hatcher wasn't exactly painting a glorious picture of his new assignment.

"I need you to be my liaison with Dr. Stratham's people, so I'm giving you the go on heading up this park killer case."

A thrill ran through Sam. The assignment also reminded him that he needed to ask the SAC for a favor.

"Speaking of Dr. Stratham, do you mind if she hires my sister as a temporary intern? Jennifer's almost finished with her forensic science degree."

One of Hatcher's eyebrows took a higher position on his forehead.

"I already gave the scientist permission for that this morning," he said. His tone implied: *what took you so long to ask?*

"She called?" Sam asked, before he could stop himself.

"Of course, she called, first thing this morning. You're gonna have to work on your communication with the lady if you intend to take this assignment."

"Yes, sir," Sam said, trying to look contrite. He was too relieved for the expression to stick well.

"You're probably wondering 'why me?' right about now," predicted Hatcher. He sat back in his expansive black leather chair and regarded Sam carefully.

Sam had been trying to find a tactful way to put the question for several minutes now. He confirmed his curiosity with a nod.

"I'll be honest with you. A high profile case like this would typically go to somebody with more seniority. I won't pretend to know every reason, but whoever made the call did their homework well," said Hatcher.

Sam leaned forward a little, not wanting to miss a word. His boss didn't seem like the type of man to exaggerate, so what would follow could probably be taken as a fair assessment of where he stood in the hierarchy.

"The fact that you're new to this building means you haven't set down deep roots. You also haven't been around long enough to make many enemies. The Behavioral Science Unit people will appreciate that if and when they become involved. Besides, your background means you can probably understand the forensic scientists without hovering too much. You already have at least one fan in the Newark office, and you can thank Dr. Stratham for backing the recommendation. She's the one that's gotta stand you in the long run." Hatcher leveled a serious gaze at Sam. "People have high hopes for you, but the good fortune comes with a warning."

"People aren't going to appreciate me cutting the line, so to speak," Sam said.

"Field agents call a case like this 'The Big One.' It's got the power to make or break your career. I know that's a lot of pressure for a young agent. Are you up to this?"

"I'm ready, sir," said Sam. He met Hatcher's gaze.

"Good. Then, take that file and study it. Pack a bag and return to Bradford County. Help Dr. Stratham as needed, but your first priority will be to work up a victim profile. Get me some notes by tomorrow. You'll probably have to wait until after the autopsy to know much, but write down as many questions as you can think of. I need to know this guy inside and out. Once we know him, we'll be better able to say who wanted him dead and on display all over those hunting grounds."

***

Joe's Steak & Soda Shop
Philadelphia, Pennsylvania
Who was the victim?

Sam usually tried to keep meal time separate from work time, but he was too excited to wait. He wolfed down a giant cheesesteak in four minutes flat, then washed his hands and dove into the case notes while he leisurely finished off a Dr. Pepper. He could take or leave soda, but there was something about a greasy cheesesteak that made a carbonated beverage a requirement. Jenn would yell if she knew of his eating habits, so he made it a point to avoid discussing meals with her.

Grabbing a pen and his pocket notebook, Sam started listing things he wanted to know about the John Doe found in plastic bags yesterday. He would have preferred to work on his laptop, but the act of writing the questions out gave him time to consider each. Every question rolled around his head a few times before he jotted it down.

Physical: tall or short, slight or muscular? What would it take to overpower him? Ask Dr. S. about drugs.

Mental: intelligence level? What could he have gotten into that got him in trouble?

Emotional: nice or mean, helpful or hurtful, compassionate or selfish?

Other: What is his family situation? Is he married? Does he have kids?

Random victim or targeted victim?

Sam really hoped the victim was targeted because that would give him something to work with. If he was just a guy in the wrong place at the right time to cross paths with the killer, the investigation would be much more difficult.

Motive for murder?

Motives tended to fall into two broad categories: love and money. Without even knowing the man's name, it was hard to predict which motive happened to be more likely. Getting cut into tiny pieces meant somebody was plenty upset with him. That was a vote for this being personal, but said nothing about the question of motive.

Having exhausted his initial questions, Sam moved on to the finer details of motives. Odds were better that if love was the ultimate motive, the killer could be a woman. The man must have done something pretty rotten to end up in his current state. A jealous man would be more likely to beat the offender to a bloody pulp and move on with his life. Slicing, dicing, and packing took a lot of effort.

Money opened up more possibilities. Somebody cheated in some significant way could be angry enough to put in the work necessary to make such a statement.

Perceived wrong or real wrong?

Sam couldn't rule out the idea of the victim's crimes being figments of the killer's imagination, but he leaned toward "real wrong." Gut instinct came back to the notion that somebody who put in that much effort to kill probably had a reason, whether justified or not.

Chapter 5:
Good Guys are Gone

Melissa Novak's Private Residence
Hillsborough, New Jersey

The delicious smell of garlic greeted Melissa as she entered the house. She let the scent relax her. The musical clatter of moving pots and pans combined with the hiss of steam to tell her someone was hard at work in the kitchen. Tossing her coat and briefcase onto the couch, Melissa kicked off her shoes and padded toward the activity in her stocking-clad feet.

"Honey, I'm home," Melissa joked, crossing the threshold into the kitchen. Two steps in, her right foot came down on something small and hard. "Ouch!" she cried, lifting her foot to peek at the offending block.

"Watch your step," Josie warned belatedly.

"Mine!" declared an unseen voice from beneath the table.

"Edwin David, what did I say about your toys?" asked Josie.

"Mommy's," answered the voice.

"That's right," Josie replied in a sing-song tone. "So play with them nicely."

"And don't leave them in the walkway," Melissa added, crouching down so she could see the child. "Hello, Eddie."

"What's your name?" asked Eddie.

"You know me. I'm your Aunt Mel."

"That's his new favorite question as of this morning," explained Josie. "Expect it at least a dozen times this evening. You can thank *Felicity's Furry Friends* for that." Josie stopped her dinner preparations long enough to give Melissa a long-suffering look.

Melissa chuckled. She knew of the TV show both from her work and from exposure to her three-year-old nephew. Some weeks she couldn't go one day without seeing a *Felicity's Furry Friends* T-shirt, sneaker, sock, pencil, or other kid paraphernalia. Whoever did the marketing for that show sure knew how to milk the popularity.

"What's your name?" repeated Eddie.

"Eddie, please!" begged Josie. "Enough with the question. Play with the blocks."

"Hey, don't I get a hug?" Melissa asked. Her knees were starting to get stiff, but she wanted to draw Eddie out from under the table. She couldn't safely sit down at the kitchen table without stepping on him in his current position.

The boy scrambled to his feet, slammed his head on the table, and burst into tears.

"Oooo, that's gotta hurt," Melissa said sympathetically.

"What happened?" Josie asked.

"He hit his head on the table," Melissa explained. "Don't worry about it. I've got this." Reaching in, Melissa gripped Eddie's arms and carefully extracted the boy from the space beneath the table. "You're all right," she assured the boy, wrapping him in a tight hug. She kissed the tender spot on his head.

Eddie wailed for about a minute before subsiding into moody sniffles. The lack of screaming allowed Melissa to hear faint crying from a different room.

"Uh-oh. Carley wants to cry too," said Melissa to Eddie. "Shall we go visit her?"

The boy shook his head emphatically, smearing snot and tears over a wider section of Melissa's nice suit jacket. It didn't faze her. Snot and tears were occupational hazards. She probably kept the local economy afloat through the power of her dry cleaning bills.

"How much time do we have?" Melissa inquired.

"The salad's already done, but the chicken will take another ten minutes," said Josie. "You've got time to collect the other loud one, if you're willing."

The whine of a dog reached Melissa's ears. She had almost forgotten about the Dalmatian puppy.

"Where's Sal?"

"See Sal!" exclaimed Eddie, meaning he wanted to see the dog.

"Maybe later," said Melissa.

"Porch exile." Josie's narrowed eyes and tone told Melissa there was a story behind the two-word answer.

"What'd he do now?" Melissa asked. She thought of how un-kid-and-dog-proof her house was and winced.

Carley's cries intensified.

"Hold that thought," said Melissa. "Carley duty calls."

Shifting her grip on Eddie, Melissa wound her way through the hallway leading toward the front door. She would have hurried except she wanted to avoid any more building block incidents.

"Whew, you're a workout," she said to Eddie once they were midway up the stairs.

They reached the guest room holding the crying infant and entered cautiously. Melissa was grateful Carley's cries were normal fussy noises and not screeches yet.

"Hush!" ordered Eddie. He clapped both hands over his ears and growled at his sister.

"Eddie! We do not growl at the baby," Melissa scolded, trying not to laugh.

Somebody's picked up a bad habit from Sal.

"Let's go see what she wants."

It didn't take long to ascertain the disturbance.

Eddie summed up the situation in a word.

"Stinky!"

Melissa shrugged.

"Well, that's an easy enough fix," she said. Entering the room, she kicked the door shut behind her and set Eddie down. The toddler had mastered the art of door opening, but it would slow him down if he tried to escape. "Stay here."

Changing Carley's diaper took longer than normal since Melissa had to keep an eye on Eddie, but as soon as she slipped the clean diaper into place, the wailing stopped. Peaceful silence prevailed, except for babblings from Eddie who systematically asked each of the stuffed animals their names. They visited regularly enough that Melissa had stocked the room with a variety of kid things.

"That's better. Sorry I made you wait, sweets. We had a

table-hitting incident, then I got distracted by the dog." Melissa wasn't sure why she felt compelled to explain this to the infant.

"Dinner's ready!" called Josie.

Melissa heard the faint cry through the door.

"Perfect timing," she commented, snapping the last button of Carley's onesie in place. Picking up the baby, Melissa turned to look at Eddie and considered the wisdom of picking him up as well.

How does Josie do this?

Before she could reach a decision, the door swung open.

"Did you hear me?" asked Josie.

"Yes. I was deciding how much pain I wanted in my back," Melissa said.

"Want to see how it's done?" Josie held out her arms for the baby. Once the baby was secure, Josie turned and knelt down. "Piggyback time, Eddie."

The words worked like magic, drawing Eddie over to his mother. He hopped onto her back, wrapping his arms around her neck and his legs around her waist. Josie held Carley away from her body until the boy was in place, then she adjusted the hold on her daughter and stood up.

"That's how it's done," she said.

"Impressive." Melissa truly meant it.

Dinner was a messy but delicious undertaking. Garlic bread, chicken parmesan, and spaghetti slathered in tomato sauce made up the bulk of the meal, but Josie had also prepared an impressive green salad to round it out. Carley spent the time sleeping in a baby carrier since it wasn't quite time for her next meal. Eddie picked at his food, getting more tomato sauce on his face than in his mouth.

"Thanks, Josie. That was great," said Melissa, once she'd eaten her fill. "I could definitely get used to this arrangement."

Home cooked meals weren't part of Melissa's vocabulary. Her job kept her too busy and too tired to deal with the thinking and planning necessary for home cooking. Bagged salads and frozen chicken provided the bulk of her sustenance, but she had no complaints. Still, it was nice to be spoiled once in a while.

Josie nodded in acknowledgment, but her attention stayed on cleaning the worst of the sauce from her son's face and hair.

"I don't think I'll ever get used to Josh's schedule," she commented. "The days off are great, but the days on are crazy and stressful."

Melissa understood what her best friend and sister-in-law meant. She had never understood Josh's fascination with a job that required 48-hour shifts. Medical school residency had been bad enough. She couldn't imagine purposefully spending one's career working such weird hours. His first year as a full-time firefighter, Melissa had wasted time worrying, but after that, she'd decided her worry had no bearing on her brother's safety.

The next two hours passed in a flurry of cleanup and wind down activities. Melissa tackled the mountain of dinner dishes while Josie scrubbed Eddie until he was sauce free. Then, Melissa read several stories to Eddie while Josie fed Carley and got her settled for the night. Finally, both children were slumbering, allowing the women to relax.

They sat at the kitchen table with large mugs of hot tea and generous portions of leftover birthday cake. And said nothing for several blissful minutes. Their friendship had lasted long enough to allow for comfortable silence. The cake slices disappeared and the tea cooled to a drinkable point. Melissa could tell the kids had run her friend ragged today. She offered a sympathetic smile but didn't have a lot of spare energy. Wondering where her energy went pulled her thoughts back to work. She loved her job, but seeing dozens of cancer patients every day was both physically and emotionally demanding.

"How are things on the man hunt front?" asked Josie.

Melissa snorted.

"What front? Most of the males I see in a day are under ten, over fifty, or taken. Sometimes I think the good guys are just gone."

"Don't discount the allure of an older man," Josie said in her sage voice. "Just think. If you married a well-established surgeon you wouldn't have to work."

"I don't think I could leave my job," said Melissa honestly. "And it's a moot point anyway since my prospects are non-existent."

A gleam entered Josie's eyes.

"We could fix that."

Melissa groaned. She'd seen that look in Josie's eyes before. She gripped her mug harder.

"Correction," said Josie. "We *will* fix it. Right now. Where's your laptop?"

"Why?" Melissa asked cautiously.

"You'll see." Josie's smile reminded Melissa of a cat left to guard baby birds.

Within five minutes, Josie began setting Melissa up with a Matchmaker Miracles profile. After arguing in vain against the idea, Melissa tried to see what her friend was typing, but Josie snapped the laptop shut before she made it out of her chair. She went for her purse to grab her credit card to pay for the three-month subscription to communicate with her matches, but Josie was faster with her credit card information.

"Think of it as an additional birthday gift," Josie said.

Melissa retreated to her chair and fiddled with her empty mug.

"You're making me nervous. Why can't I see what you're writing about me?"

"Go make us more tea," ordered Josie. "I should be done by the time it's ready. Then, you can see the grand results."

Not having a better idea, Melissa made a fresh round of green tea. She studied her friend while she waited. Josie had always been the bold, adventurous one. Her light brown hair matched her eye color perfectly. These days she often kept it restrained by a sloppy ponytail, but if left loose, the hair had a tendency to curl. Melissa knew her friend was self-conscious about her slightly hooked nose, but she thought it suited her.

The second round of tea was made and consumed before Josie finally finished with a flourish.

"There. If that doesn't entice the menfolk to come calling, we can conclude they're all dumber than posts," said Josie.

"Do I want to know?" Melissa wondered.

Josie made a face at her and bobbed her head from side to side, clearly pleased with herself.

"Girl, I made you look awesome."

"How many lies did you tell?"

"Not a one." Josie's wide brown eyes shone with pure innocence. "Come see if you don't believe me."

"Just read it to me," said Melissa, bracing for the revelations to come.

"I'll just give you the highlights." Josie closed the laptop, so she could get a better look at Melissa. "Aside from basic physical characteristics, I said you were a successful pediatrician who loves children, dogs, long walks, beaches, sunsets, good movies, and real connections."

"What's a 'real connection'?" asked Melissa.

"No idea," said Josie, "but it sure looked good on the profiles I skimmed before attempting yours."

Melissa stood up to put her mug in the sink.

"Where are you going?" Josie demanded. "We're getting to the good part." She opened the laptop again, then rubbed her palms together in anticipation. "Let's see your matches."

Chapter 6:
Choosing Victims

Ridley Creek State Park
Delaware County, Pennsylvania
Day 2: Morning.
These entries aren't really going to happen every day, but I don't want to put dates on them just in case the police get ahold of them. I shouldn't get caught, but no plan is perfect. I'm recording these thoughts so that if something goes wrong, somebody else can continue my great work.

I've set them to go live if I fall out of contact for a week or sometime in the middle of next year. By then, my work should be finished in this part of the world. If it works out, I'll move on to a new location and begin again. I know that's ambitious, but I never settle for half-effort. Much as staying here is tempting, I have determined that a year is about as long as one should stay in a single place while taking out human trash.

Guess that makes me a trash man.

With a clean record and enough cash, one can establish themselves in a matter of weeks and be back in business soon after.

I have chosen to move my plans forward quickly. It's only been a couple of days since my first real strike against the evils of this world, but I need to direct the police attention away from the body. I've taken some measly pot shots in the past, but this was the first move in the grand game. I should have let the dogs finish him off. The impression left on society was great, but I won't reveal too much right now. The media people have linked it to mischief night activities gone wrong. Fools. I have no regrets, but that is why I must do this second deed.

Not every kill has to be a step toward the ultimate goal. The path may have to be paved with some innocent blood, but I try to do my best to make sure those who fall deserve their fate. Humans make this too easy. Loose women lead men astray and give good women a bad reputation. People cheat on their taxes, beat their kids, and covet their neighbor's property.

They lie. They steal. They play emotional games. They kill each other in their minds.

Hypocrites. Cowards. Drunkards. Thieves.

Stop pretending to like each other.

Am I the only honest human being left?

No, psycho67 is honest too, but he's not good.

I know of only one truly good person. I wish she could know of my crusade, but she's too innocent to understand the darkness I face for her.

Victims must be chosen carefully.

There's a thrill to the hunt itself, which I will discuss later, but everything comes back to that first choice of whom to target. Prostitutes are especially vulnerable, but the smart ones travel in packs, at least to the street corners they work. Street kids too can be safely disappeared without family making a fuss. Gang members are trickier because the vicious little beasts travel in armed groups. I once had to shoot three of the blighters because they demanded a toll for driving through their hood.

I don't count putting down vermin as part of my quest, though it is tempting. I keep reminding myself it's not about the numbers, but it is in a way. I can't honestly count those gang kids because I didn't confirm the kills. It wouldn't be fair.

High end prostitutes—"escorts"—are protected more than most nighttime flesh traders. Still, they are convenient prey if you can spoof or steal a credit card number. There are hundreds of legal and illegal establishments in every corner of every nation. One need only find one with legal problems and choose from among their wares. Those businesses have a natural inclination to secrecy and discretion. They want to avoid police involvement almost as much as people in my profession.

I could have chosen a second male target, but I went with female this time for variety's sake. Men are more work. For one thing, their dead bodies are heavier. Most people expect killers to pick a type, meaning blonds or brunettes or cheerleader material or whatever. Maybe some do need to off a particular type of person to feel whole. I won't judge too harshly, though I will say, it's a tad foolish to give the police that sort of edge. The more variety one has in their victims, the less likely the police are to connect the cases.

That's the hope anyway. They may not link the new body to the other. Aside from choosing public lands in Pennsylvania for my dumping grounds, I have done things very differently this round. How much the woman suffers for the sins of the world depends on her luck. I don't know her real name, and this time, I don't care. There are times to dive deep into a person's life, and times it doesn't matter. This is a case of less knowledge being better.

The authorities can't say I have a type. They'll assume she's a target of opportunity.

Dumping sites should be varied, but hoarding bodies isn't recommended.

I may be overly cautious right now, but eventually, I'd like to try collecting more than one victim at a time. That will add a layer of complication to the kidnapping phase. I suppose I could mix in a few quick incidents, but the more one does, the more opportunities there are for random mistakes. Quick incidents are far less satisfying than letting the victim know why he or she has to die this way.

Maybe later, I'll record some thoughts about physical, mental, and other basic requirements for being a trash man. Not everybody can do it. In short, you need time, money, strength, will, and intelligence. The role is so misunderstood. I'm cleansing mankind. Society should thank me, but I have no expectations. It's a thankless role, and I accept that.

For now, I want to focus on choosing victims. I've covered the basic, easy-access types of people. Those who truly deserve to die are usually harder targets. They have families that will make a fuss if they're out of touch for too long. This is where one needs to be very selective, weighing the moral rightness of their removal vs. the increased risks of getting caught.

On the whole, women tend to be easier to control. They're more timid by nature. So in terms of a complete operation, they tend to be more convenient. By "compete operation," I mean kidnap, kill, and dump. There are always plenty of exceptions. People who give too much trouble tend to get themselves removed quicker.

Celebrities aren't worth the bother. Even minor ones have people who watch them constantly.

Rich people are harder because their families tend to have more connections, so the police often feel obligated to investigate harder.

Poor people tend to be more suspicious, but they have triggers they'll respond to.

Young people are more likely to respond to promises and simple schemes. They're so full of themselves that they can't imagine anyone plotting against them.

Middle class people make up the bulk of society. Here is where the most satisfying targets can be found. They're not rich enough to generate true public interest. A few family members will care, and ambitious news reporters will throw together a touching missing persons case, but that's about it. A week later—if they're lucky enough to stay news that long—something else will steal the attention. They're not even poor enough to upset the bleeding heart types.

Illegal immigrants are easy targets, but they tend to be small fish in the pond of people who need to go. As a group, they take care of their families. I respect that.

Race shouldn't matter, but it does. Economics and family dynamics just matter more. Broken families and single parent homes make it easier to find victims.

Old people that must be removed are best taken out wherever one finds them. They move slowly, and they have a hard time following directions because they can't hear you. That makes them unpredictable. Sometimes they're just too stubborn to take orders. Besides, if they made it that far in life, they're likely not long for the world. Nature is as likely to do the job as the trash man.

Children are tempting because they're easy to move. Unless they're neglected though, they are more difficult to isolate. In general, a trash man doesn't need to target children unless he wishes to divert attention from something else. They're also dangerous because society's wired to protect them. I don't know why. They're just as selfish and rotten inside as everybody else. The fact that their ways of acting out the evil in their minds is small shouldn't matter. In that case, a 24-hour kidnap-murder scenario is probably best. Straight murder won't drain police resources like a kidnap and murder.

Culling is a very important step. Some people help with this by going off to do some isolated activity far from civilization. Establishing control quickly becomes key in that case because, like it or not, you need the victim's cooperation if you want to stick to a plan that involves moving them.

Place of contact must also be considered. Public places are better for shock value, but the risk factors are incredibly high. It's difficult to control that many pairs of eyes. There will always be somebody who remembers something. Unless one can afford to change cars for every attack, public places should be avoided. If one is willing to take public transportation to a parking lot and hijack their victim, then a parking lot becomes a suitable location.

Office parking lots, especially parking garages, are ideal. These tend to have pathetic security cameras. A few of my own inventions could neutralize those measures, though it's usually not necessary. You'd be surprised by the number of security cameras that aren't actually hooked up to anything. The only reason they exist is to give people the illusion of safety.

Home invasions are an interesting but high-risk option that attracts amateurs and thrillseekers. Certain places have a higher percentage of the population who owns guns. When considering a home invasion, wear a vest, rent a uniform, bring a gun, and buy a fake law enforcement badge of some kind. Most people respond well to cops. I've never actually tried it, but I'm eager to test the theory. Rural homes are obviously more isolated, so there's less chance of being spotted coming or going. The most deserving targets own big beautiful houses in crowded neighborhoods. They own flashy cars too, for the express purpose of being envied.

It's better to break into a rich guy's garage and wait for him to show up than enter the house at night. The more you know about a person's movements and whereabouts, the easier it is to do your job. This would be my method of choice if I couldn't get a victim to come to me. So far though, both victims have been very accommodating.

Once a victim is selected, the fun part begins.

Devising a trap is one of the most satisfying aspects of the job. If a trash man uses the same method every time, he's begging to be caught. I know there's comfort in familiarity, but routines turn into patterns cops can recognize and predict. Besides, victims are unique entities. Like I said, sometimes, they have to be innocents to keep the police busy. Those unfortunates deserve the respect of a plan.

Getting the victim to do most of the work is satisfying and safest. Prostitutes and service workers are the most vulnerable to these simple plans. Essentially, you go to an empty house and hire the service worker to come do whatever they do. This even works for taxis and cars-for-hire. The house you choose to meet them at and the credit card you use should not be your own. These are rookie mistakes. I don't have to have tried this yet to see the wisdom in the plan.

This woman came from an establishment called Anything Goes, so my request to meet in a dark alley didn't faze her. She took one look at the wad of cash I'd brought along and hopped right into the back of the van. Always have a truck or a van if one wishes to do this kind of work. Cars just don't cut it for having the necessary space. I didn't think the woman would try to escape, but I've also taken simple precautions such as setting the child safety locks and installing a plastic shield between the back and the front of the van.

People say you have to depersonalize the victims to do the job. I've never found that as a must. Sometimes I need to know, sometimes I don't.

One last note: if you're going to snatch somebody from a public place, wear a few prosthetics. Witness memories are usually terrible anyway, but cameras don't lie unless I tell them to. Prosthetics are easier than manipulating electronics. I'm all for a high-tech plan, but when there's a low-tech solution to a problem, I go with it.

Chapter 7:
Winter Cash Windfall

Ridley Creek State Park
Delaware County, Pennsylvania

The woman had stopped screaming when her voice gave out. That had happened about an hour earlier. Andrew Novak had needed time to record his thoughts, complete the preparations, and perform the rituals. From time to time, the woman would moan into the gag, but the cold and exhaustion systematically sapped her strength.

He savored the last ritual.

The lottery ticket Andrew had brought with him was a new one. He'd bought a roll of the $2.00 tickets at a convenience store on the way to meet his date tonight. Since the very first ticket in a roll didn't often win, he'd chosen one at random. He wanted to give the woman a fair shot.

Plucking a quarter from the center cup holder in his Chevy cargo van, Andrew slowly rubbed it across the ticket's smooth surface. He traced each edge once just to get a feel for the ticket before actually moving to the winning symbols area. The goal of this game was to match the winning symbols to the play area symbols. One could also win instantly if they revealed a snowflake symbol. His winning symbols were a winter hat and a sleigh. Slowly, he scratched off the rest of the card's top row, revealing a wreath, a snowman, a pine tree, a candy cane, and a star.

Not looking good for her.

He started on the bottom row.

The quarter moved the opaque gray substance aside bit by bit, revealing a stocking, an ornament, a gingerbread man, a present, and finally, a snowflake. Excitement charged through him as he scratched off the area just below the winning symbol. It said: $10.00.

Lucky lady.

He was a little disappointed that he wouldn't get to use the hunting bow, but the ticket's win meant he ought to ease the woman to the hereafter as quickly as possible. Andrew leaned over and picked up the case he had stuffed on the passenger side floor space. Opening the snaps, he retrieved the handgun and inserted the magazine. Guns were less fun, but they got the job done.

Exiting his warm, toasty van, Andrew slowly approached the woman handcuffed to the tree. Remembering to put on his gloves, he stuffed the gun in his pocket temporarily and took out a new pair of baby blue gloves.

The van's headlights bathed the scene in a harsh glare. The cool night air smelled of clean pine. The woman leaned back against the tree, rhythmically tapping her head against the trunk. She started whimpering as he approached.

"I've got good news for you," he said.

She made a frustrated noise, which was muffled by the gag.

"You won," he informed her. Andrew drew the winning ticket from his pocket and showed it to the woman.

She blinked at it in confusion before searching Andrew's face for an explanation.

"You get to die quickly," he said, tucking the ticket away.

This news brought forth a surge of strength in the woman. She strained against the handcuffs and screamed into the gag until her voice failed. Tears flowed freely down her face until they disappeared into the bandana he'd pressed into service as a gag.

The woman sagged against the tree trunk and clenched her eyes shut. Her hair, makeup, and clothes had clearly seen better days. The pale skin of her legs shone through long rips in her pantyhose. Loose strands of bleached-blond hair whipped free of the updo she'd confined them to much earlier in the evening. Tears had conquered her mascara, ringing her eyes with black and leaving distinct trails down her face.

Andrew wanted to reach out and rub the tear marks away, but

he dared not touch her, even with gloved hands.

"Do you have any last words?" He surprised himself with the question. Lurch had confessed to a lot in his final hours. Andrew had no intention of giving the woman that long for her confession, but since her role here was that of decoy, he felt he owed her a small token in thanks.

Nodding eagerly, the woman stood a little taller. Her expression still spoke mainly of weariness, but her eyes flickered from fear to anger and back again several times.

"Since you won, I'm willing to do this quickly, but if you scream, I'll put the gag back on and take my time." Andrew kept his tone even. One didn't need to speak loudly to be heard in the still night air, even with the gentle rumbling from his van's engine. He waited until she nodded before slowly reaching for the gag. Finding that his fingers couldn't deal with the knot while the gloves were on, Andrew took out a pocket knife. "It's just to remove the gag," he explained as the woman flinched.

Trying not to scare her any more than he had to, Andrew slowly sliced the gag away. He could always stuff the whole bandana into her mouth if she gave him trouble, but he didn't need to keep her completely silent now. He wondered what questions she would ask. Would she beg for her life or spend her last few seconds on Earth cursing him?

"Please don't kill me," the woman whispered. "I have a family."

He cocked his head at her curiously.

"Why should that make a difference?"

The question pulled the woman up short, derailing her rehearsed speech. She paused to consider her answer before speaking.

"I don't know," she admitted at last.

"Everybody has a family," Andrew pointed out.

"I don't want to die," murmured the woman.

"Few people do. Life's very unfair on that score," Andrew commented. "Your will to live is good. It will make your sacrifice greater."

"Why are you doing this?" The question was a whisper.

Andrew nodded in satisfaction. He'd expected that question much sooner.

"I killed a man earlier this week, and I put his body—what was left of it anyway—in a public place. I need to keep the police busy. The more time they spend solving your murder, the less time they'll have for his."

Confusion crossed the woman's features. Her dark eyes widened as she recognized the story.

"That was you?"

"That was me," Andrew confirmed. "Cases like this are similar enough to get the police to talk to each other. As I said, I want them to link the cases, not concentrate on the first victim. I have a lot of work to do, and the more they chase their tails, the easier it will be to complete my work."

"What work?" inquired the woman. "More killing?"

"People are evil," said Andrew. He had the sudden urge to know this woman's name.

The statement drew an incredulous snort from the woman.

"Says the man about to murder me." Her voice started out weary but hardened as she moved into her next question. "How do you justify this?" She shrugged her shoulders but was limited by the handcuffs.

"I told you. Your death is a distraction, a necessary sacrifice," said Andrew. "I'm sorry things have to be this way, but I need to stay free long enough to punish the guilty."

"For what?" demanded the woman. Anger had moved her far past the fear. "You say people are evil, but so is murder. How is doing wrong to right wrong any help?" Her words came out faster and louder each moment. With great effort, she lowered her voice and changed her tone back to pleading. "Please. If you let me go, I won't tell anybody about you or your mission. I'll even tell them whatever you want me to. Just let me live."

"Sorry," Andrew repeated. He gently pressed the bandana to her lips and worked it into her mouth. "People lie. I can't trust you. I can't trust anybody." The last statement came out with a surprising amount of honest despair.

Fresh tears pooled in the woman's eyes. She understood the end was coming.

Stepping back, Andrew reached into his pocket to pull out the gun. Finding the winning ticket as well as the weapon, he experienced a flash of inspiration. The moment needed to be preserved. Reaching into a different pocket, he retrieved one of his disposable cell phones and pressed buttons until he reached the camera function. He had to tuck the gun into his waistband because he didn't have enough hands to maneuver the lottery ticket, the phone, and the gun.

The woman's shirt and flimsy jacket didn't offer much in the way of places to tuck the ticket where his camera would be able to capture a nice image. He supposed he could pin it to her with the knife, but he didn't want to hurt her like that. The answer came to him then. Tucking the phone back into his pocket, Andrew took out his knife again and sliced two vertical strips into the woman's jacket. He almost ended up cutting her anyway as her chest moved with her rapid breaths.

"Just relax. This won't hurt," he said softly.

The woman craned her neck back as far as it would go, trying to see what he was doing.

When the strips were long enough, Andrew tucked the lottery ticket into the space he'd created. He had to adjust it a few times and lengthen the left side to get the ticket to sit straight, but he managed to get it into a satisfactory position.

"Don't move. It's not very secure there," said Andrew.

Backing up three paces, he took out his phone again and typed in the unlock code. The camera app opened, ready to do his bidding. He lined up a few different shots to preserve the scene as a whole and to get a close look at the ticket. It looked perfect on the woman. He wanted to let her keep the ticket, but at the same time, he wanted the souvenir for himself. It wasn't a big win. He could afford to never turn it in.

A new impulse blindsided him. Before he could think too much, Andrew's right hand found the handgun while his left put the phone away. Slowly, he raised the weapon and viewed the woman through the gunsights. Seeing he was far too close, Andrew backed up several paces. He kept going until he was only a few feet from his van's front bumper. The headlights hit his body, casting a long shadow that nearly reached the woman.

When he peered through the gunsights, his gaze locked on the winning ticket. It had earned the woman this fate instead of the more painful one. His finger tightened on the trigger. He wanted to pull the trigger so badly his arms shook, but he didn't want to leave the ticket. Torn between the two impulses, he hesitated for a long moment before moving. Finally, he jogged forward, plucked the ticket out of the temporary straps and held it in his left palm.

"I will remember you," he said solemnly. He held the ticket to his heart before slipping it into a pocket.

The woman watched these proceedings with dazed eyes. The fear returned as Andrew locked eyes with her and stepped backwards.

When he was once again by the van's bumper, he lined up the shot and fired three times.

He didn't want her to suffer, and he didn't have time to dither. There was more work to do.

Chapter 8:
Innocent

Ridley Creek State Park
Delaware County, Pennsylvania

Pulling into the parking lot, Samuel Kerman felt his insides tighten. How many times would he be called out to a state park to check on a body? Parks were supposed to be fun, relaxing places where people could get closer to nature and explore the world. The fact that some creep decided to make these public lands his personal dumping grounds annoyed Sam. In a few months people would return again to enjoy the park's beauty, but Picnic Area #17 would never be the same again. Even if they could somehow keep the media people from finding out, the fact would remain that violence had consumed a human life here.

Stepping out of his Magnetic Gray Metallic Camry, Sam immediately spotted the focal point of the disturbance. A quick glance around the parking lot told him he'd beaten his sister and Dr. Mira Stratham to the scene. The accomplishment gave him a small sense of satisfaction, though he knew it wasn't exactly a fair contest given the longer distance they needed to travel.

A group of uniformed officials gathered around a tall tree. From this distance, Sam couldn't read the patches on their sleeves, but the variety of uniforms told him most of Delaware County law enforcement was well-represented. Double checking that he had both badge and gun, Sam made his way over to the crowd.

"Suit's coming," said one of the young officers near the back.

The comment opened the shell of people like a clam, revealing a woman kneeling before a body leaning against the tree. She must have sensed the change behind her, for she stood and turned, allowing Sam to catch sight of the badge. The woman placed both hands on her lower back and stretched, waiting for Sam to approach.

Slowing as he entered the semi-circle, Sam reached for his badge. Before he had it fully out, the woman spoke.

"You must be the FBI agent."

"Yes, ma'am. Agent Samuel Kerman. I was assigned to the John Doe found up in the State Game Lands north of here. I came to see if this case might be connected."

"I doubt it," the woman commented. She looked down at her gloved hands. "Forgive me for not shaking your hand. This is my only set of gloves. I'm Sheriff Mary Radley. This is my county, but as you can see, we're all just looking for answers for this woman." The sheriff gestured around at the gathered law enforcement people who nodded solemn agreement. As she mentioned the woman, the sheriff sidestepped to give Sam a better look at the body.

The dead woman slumped against the tree with her arms stretched out behind her. Sam didn't see the handcuffs until he moved closer and shifted left a few steps. Cause of death would have to be officially confirmed by the medical examiner, but it looked pretty clear to Sam. Death probably came from the three gunshot wounds, two high on the chest and a third in the center of the forehead.

When he finished with his initial assessment, quick introductions went around, but Sam wouldn't bet his life on remembering any of their first names. Thankfully, they each wore a nameplate to help him keep their last names straight. Slowly, the small gathering broke up with officers walking away in ones and twos to handle tasks that must have been assigned before Sam showed up.

"What makes you think this isn't related to the other park body?" Sam asked the sheriff, picking up an earlier conversation thread once they were alone.

Sheriff Radley shrugged.

"The news made a pretty big deal out of the staging in that scene. There's none of that here. No plastic bags nailed to trees or carved messages anyway. I had my people get copies of the files from the Bradford County office as soon as it looked like there could be a connection. Upon first glance, it's not impossible. It just doesn't seem likely."

"Would you mind if I had a forensic scientist who processed the other scene take a look at this one? She's on her way now." Asking was a formality. Sam's presence meant an official invitation for the FBI's help had already been extended, but he'd learned that phrasing things as questions made a much better impression on the locals than statements and demands.

"I'm not about to turn away help," said the sheriff. She looked at the body again and shook her head. "My ME's office is sending staff, but I told them they might have to wait a bit. This is a much bigger party than we're used to." She frowned over his shoulder. "Excuse me. I have to go coordinate my people. The vultures have arrived. We'll do our best to keep them back, but it's a big park." Handing him a card, she added, "Here's my number in case you need anything or need me to know anything."

Sam considered texting his sister to get their ETA, but knowing when they would arrive wouldn't actually help him. A time check told him he probably had about a half-hour to wait, less if his sister was driving. He spent the time searching the scene. A dozen people had been back and forth across the space around the tree, but he wanted to get a feel for the area anyway. He hoped they remembered to take pictures when the scene was relatively undisturbed. The cold night had preserved the body well.

Standing slightly behind the tree with the body, Sam peered back at the parking lot. He tried to imagine what the woman thought in her last moments. The state of her wrists told him she'd likely spent some time trussed to the tree. Although the murder might have happened swiftly, the ordeal had not been short. Closer examination of the woman's raw, bloody fingers supported the idea. His gaze immediately fell on the parking lot. There weren't any burn marks on the body, so the killer likely took his time lining up the shot from a reasonable distance.

Curious, Sam counted the steps between the tree and the parking lot. The trees here were less than fifty feet from the parking lot. Maybe the angle from the gunshots and the bullets themselves could give Sam some clues about the guy. The killer could be a woman, but Sam doubted it. Women who killed were usually far more straightforward, especially when offing another female. The incidents usually revolved around men and involved physical blows and very few questions about the perpetrator's identity. In contrast, this killer had watched his victim struggle against her bindings. He might have even watched her from his car, warm and comfortable while she suffered the frigid temperatures.

Despite the sheriff's observations about the obvious differences, Sam felt something familiar about the scene. He couldn't pin down the gut feeling's source. In Bradford County, the killer's statement came across as bold and arrogant. The medical examiner's report detailed numerous perimortem cuts that hadn't resulted in death. The killer had wanted that victim to suffer. Here, the killer had let the victim suffer, but it didn't seem as if that had been his intention. Aside from the bullet holes, she appeared in good condition.

"She probably never suspected a thing." The sound of Jenn's voice pulled Sam out of his thoughts. She walked up beside him. "I don't think I could ever do a job like that."

"Like what?" Sam asked, piercing his sister with a questioning look.

Jenn eyed him critically.

"How long have you been standing there lost in thought?"

His glare told her to get to the point.

In answer, Jenn motioned back toward the body where Dr. Mira Stratham stood taking about a thousand pictures on her digital camera.

"Doc S. says the woman's probably a hooker or an escort," said Jenn.

"How can you tell?" Sam asked. He swept his gaze over the body again from head to toe and back.

Most of the body was hidden in the confines of a long, thin black coat. She didn't have much in the way of jewelry. Her hair appeared disheveled but healthy and well-maintained. Her nails were chipped from her struggles. Nothing specifically jumped out at him to back up the claim.

"The shoes," answered the scientist. "Nobody comes to a park in the middle of the night wearing flimsy footwear like that."

Sam studied the thin straps of the black shoes and silently

agreed. Taking out his notepad, he started creating a new to-do list.

To Do:
Look up escort services.

"How did she get out here?" Jenn wondered, not speaking to anyone in particular.

"The killer must have brought her in a vehicle of some sort," said Sam. "Did she struggle?" He addressed the question to Dr. Stratham.

"On first glance, no, but the medical examiner will be able to tell you for sure. I'm not seeing any signs of stun gun damage or injection sites, but there's a lot we're not going to see until the autopsy."

Sam added a mental note to talk to the vice people. He hadn't given prostitutes much thought, but he had assumed they stayed near populated areas so they could make the most money possible in an evening. Maybe the vice guys would be able to tell him if their victim was known in their circles.

"Is there anything useful in her pockets?" Sam asked. "Like a license," he added wistfully. Murder victims found in the woods rarely came with identification. Sam had meant to check on that sooner, but since he didn't have gloves, he left that to the experts.

Dr. Stratham carefully reached in and turned the victim's coat pockets inside out. The right pocket turned up empty, but the left held a crumpled notecard. After taking several pictures, the scientist maneuvered the card into a large plastic bag before trying to smooth it out enough to read. The big block letters spelled out one word.

INNOCENT

"Guess that answers the question of a link," said Sam.

The women nodded agreement.

"I could have told you that before," Dr. Stratham noted. She bent down, picked up a small plastic evidence bag, and waved it under Sam's nose.

"What is it?" he asked, not in the mood to squint.

"More gray dust-like particles," said Jenn.

"Where did you find it?" Sam demanded.

"Right here." Dr. Stratham reached over to the body and gingerly tugged at a piece of fabric until Sam saw the slit cut in the coat. "There's another thin strip like this over there." She pointed to a section several inches over from the one she was tugging on.

"What do you think it means?" Jenn wondered.

"Not sure yet," replied the scientist. "Maybe it held something. I'm guessing whatever that something is, it must be the source for that gray substance we found at both scenes. I've never seen anything like it."

I hope we never see it again.

Sam wasn't fully committed to the thought. He wanted to catch the bad guy, but he knew that the odds of that happening without more bodies along the way were slim to none. The sight of his sister leaning over the body to listen to something Dr. Stratham said filled Sam with a sense of urgency. No matter what this woman did for a living, she was somebody's daughter and friend and perhaps somebody else's wife or mother. People would miss her. In the killer's mind, she'd been innocent, so why was she dead?

Chapter 9:
Matchmakers

Samuel Kerman's Apartment
Narberth, Pennsylvania

Unlocking the door to his apartment, Sam Kerman tried to organize his thoughts into an adequate excuse for the mess. Two seconds later, he gave up, sighed, swung the door open to let his sister enter ahead of him, and braced for her reaction.

Jenn halted one step in when she tripped over a running shoe he forgot to warn her about. The lights came on, illuminating her disapproving frown. Kicking the large shoe out of the way, Jenn turned in a slow circle.

Sam took in the same living room scene. It actually wasn't too bad today. He had remembered to take the pizza box down to the garbage room and even emptied the recycling. Three half-finished water bottles occupied coasters at various points around the room. Work files covered every inch of the coffee table and most of the couch cushions. The mate to the shoe Jenn had kicked poked its head out from under the coffee table, flanked by an air freshener. Sports magazines overflowed from the corner. The controller to one of his game consoles lay upside down on the couch where he'd tossed it a few days ago. The remote lay facedown like a dead rodent halfway between the coffee table and the table holding the television. The room's sole armchair sported his disassembled go-bag.

"This place is … an absolute wreck." The slight pause Jenn put between the first and second halves of the statement reiterated her disgust just in case he'd missed it in her expression.

"Can I get you a bottle of water?" Sam didn't expect her to take him up on the offer.

"No, thanks, I can't eat or drink anything until tomorrow, or I'll pop," Jenn replied. "That buffet was amazing by the way. Thanks again for the treat."

"Sure. Everybody should experience cheap, quality Chinese food when they visit Philly," said Sam. "Make yourself comfortable."

"Where?" Jenn asked pointedly.

After kicking off his shoes by the door, Sam closed and locked the apartment door and plotted a safe path to the couch. Gathering up the files from the nearest couch cushion, Sam created a stack and placed it on the coffee table. He did the same for the files on the other two cushions.

"Ta-da!" he announced, waving to the freshly cleared space.

Jenn chewed on her bottom lip.

"This is worse than I'd feared," she muttered. She perched primly on the couch cushion nearest the door and fished her phone from the cavernous depths of her purse.

Sam didn't mind. He figured the phone would keep her entertained for the next few minutes.

Like a baby with a pacifier.

The thought amused him as he headed for the bedroom to grab some extra sheets and blankets. Since he only owned two sets of sheets and one of them was already on his bed, Jenn would have to deal with the couch tonight. It made no sense to send her home to their parents' place or to her college apartment. She would need to return to Ridley Creek State Park for at least the next two days, possibly more.

She'd better not nag the whole time, or I'm kicking her out.

Sam knew the thought had no teeth. Thirty-two or not, his parents would kill him if he tossed his baby sister out on her ear. Resigned to this fact, Sam stripped the dirty pillowcase off of the spare pillow and applied a fresh case he had just found. Balancing two blankets and a set of sheets atop the pillow, Sam returned to the main room. His sister looked up at him with an evil grin.

"Do I want to know what that look means?" he asked cautiously.

"Yes, and I'll need your credit card," said Jenn.

"What? Why? What have you done?" The three questions nearly piled up on one another. Sam wanted to rush over, seize his sister's shoulders, and shake the story out of her, but he knew that wouldn't be necessary. She wanted to tell him, but she was delaying to make him suffer. His grip on the bedding tightened.

"Credit card," Jenn repeated slowly. Her left hand rose, fingers wiggling to receive the card while her right hand tapped furiously at the phone keys.

"Not until you tell me what I'm buying," Sam said. He circled around the coffee table to dump the sheets and blankets on the far end of the couch then plopped down beside his sister. Leaning over, he squinted down at the small text. He couldn't see much, but the words "Matchmaker Miracles" told him enough. He groaned. "Not this again. Remember what happened last time I let you talk me into a stupid dating site?"

"This is different," Jenn declared. She let her hand drop since she wasn't getting the card until she convinced him. "That was a blind dating site, mostly for fun. You could use more fun around here." She eyed the bare walls of his living room before returning her critical gaze to Sam. "This is serious. I made you a profile on Matchmaker Miracles. It's a relatively new site, but it's got great ratings and cool success stories."

"Wonder who they paid off to get the ratings," Sam muttered.

"Oh, don't be a big baby," Jenn scolded. "This will be good for you."

"That's what nurses say when they come at you with a needle," Sam complained.

Jenn must have sensed the kill, for her hand popped up again and waved for the credit card.

Knowing he wasn't going to have any peace until he caved, Sam reached for his wallet and fished out a card. As it brushed her fingertips, Sam pulled back an inch and issued one more warning.

"If I find weird charges on my credit card statement, I'm coming after you."

Jenn's eyes widened.

"'Statement,' as in paper statement?" Her voice sailed higher with incredulity. Looking pained, she shook her head. "Sam, you are such a dinosaur." The look turned pitying as she heaved a sigh.

"Let's deal with this. Then, I'll fix your banking situation."

Snatching the card, Jenn started entering the appropriate information into the boxes to finish the profile.

"What's wrong with my banking situation?" Sam wondered.

"There's this little thing that's been around for a few decades called 'online banking.' It's very handy and easy to use, even for dinosaurs."

"Don't get sassy with me, you young whipper snapper," said Sam, affecting his "old man" voice.

Jenn tried to keep a straight face, but failed and ended up laughing.

"You're so weird." Bringing her phone closer, Jenn squinted down at what she'd entered, presumably scanning for mistakes.

Sam stayed quiet. He didn't want to mess with her concentration while she held his credit card in her hands. When she sat back with a self-satisfied smile, he repossessed his precious card.

"You're welcome," said Jenn.

"I'm not thanking you yet," Sam said, trying hard for a gruff tone.

"You will," Jenn assured Sam with a knowing smile. A few seconds later, she got serious again. "Now, let's see about bringing you out of the banking stone age. Which bank holds your accounts?"

"I'm an FBI guy. We're supposed to keep a low electronic profile," Sam said.

"Low does not mean nonexistent," Jenn insisted.

"You're so annoying." Sam recognized the statement as an unconscious surrender. He could face down bank robbers and murderers, but dealing with his sister always seemed to take more work. She'd always known how to get her way when it came to Sam or their father. Mom was the only one who stood a marginal chance of resisting Hurricane Jenn when she rolled full-force. Granted, many of the improvements she sought were beneficial in the long run, but she could be a pushy little thing.

***

The Killer's Lair
Undisclosed Location
Was the notecard too much?

The thought bothered Andrew Novak. He wanted the murders linked, but he didn't want to make things too easy for law enforcement. If he gave too many hints even the dullest pencils in the box would pick up on the fact that they're being baited.

A pair of pleasant pings announced that a few of his programs had found something interesting. He always had about a half-dozen programs running in the background. Some searched for potential victims while others kept track of the names he gathered from various news sources. A third set of programs kept track of his siblings' online activities. The internet had long been his strongest connection to the world. Information was one of the pillars of life. It made everything he did possible and supplied the bulk of his legitimate income.

The notification was a hyperlinked name: Samuel Kerman.

Curious, Andrew clicked the link and waited while several windows populated his desktop in a cascade fashion. The first box contained an old article about the first body dumped on Pennsylvania public lands. He had of course already read this article, but he skimmed it again anyway to discover what the program found intriguing. A tiny footnote in the last paragraph said the FBI had assigned Agent Samuel Kerman to the case. The next three boxes contained similar articles, but the fifth browser proved very different. A slow smile spread over Andrew's face as he read the bright, cheerful words splashed across the top in peaceful shades of pink and blue: Matchmaker Miracles.

He had set up the site on a whim to gather information on people. The site's popularity meant that it generated a tidy sum each month too, but he didn't expect to keep it running much more than a year. The beginning history and testimonials were complete lies, but the match program Andrew had written actually worked well enough to generate real success stories within a few weeks. The site would celebrate its six month anniversary in a few days.

As a newcomer, it's number of customers was paltry compared to some of the online dating giants, but Matchmaker Miracles was accomplishing what it needed to for Andrew. Because he had designed much of the site himself from scratch, he had backdoor entrances to every profile. Since his last visit to the website, seven new profiles had been created. The latest of these had caused two separate search programs to ping. Apparently, FBI Special Agent Samuel Kerman, poster boy for the feds on this case, was a 92% match for Andrew's sister, Dr. Melissa Novak.

Mixed feelings rose in Andrew. The temptation to delete the agent's profile or tweak the settings to hide the match battled the urge to see where things led. Melissa's profile had generated a few dozen matches in the days since being formed, but she had only logged in once to check them and shown little interest so far in the men on display.

Andrew sat at his desk and pondered the situation. He could bury the agent's profile or highlight it for his sister. Part of him didn't want to involve her. They were at the very beginning of this game, but the man was still the enemy. If he veered too close to the actual truth, he'd have to go. That might end up hurting Mel, and Andrew really wished to avoid such an outcome. Still, having them go on a few casual dates could give Andrew an edge in terms of keeping track of the agent. Also, the gambler in him couldn't resist upping the stakes. Life wasn't worth living if it didn't involve manipulating others.

Working behind the scenes like this could be a heady experience, like entering god-mode on a video game. People were endlessly fascinating. For the most part, they kept to predictable patterns, but a few managed to break the molds along the way.

A surprisingly strong protective instinct made Andrew stop and re-read the agent's profile a few times. He didn't want to set his sister up with a psychopath after all. Common sense told him law enforcement jobs attracted those sorts from time to time.

Name: Samuel H. Kerman
Has kids: 0
Wants kids: maybe someday
Smoker level: never
Drinker level: occasional/social
Education: Master's degree
Occupation: federal employee
Short description: I'm a fun-loving, easy-going guy with a good sense of humor, a strong work ethic, and a solid sense of myself. (Full disclosure: My apartment's a mess, and I'm a lousy cook unless we're talking pizza or pies. I enjoy working out. I don't have pets, but I'm open to the idea of them.)

What I'm looking for: A woman with a beautiful soul who can be my lifelong partner. I want her to share my hopes and dreams, to challenge me, and to grow closer to me every day.

Andrew doubted the agent had written the profile himself. A lot of people needed friends or family members to kick them down the online dating road. He didn't hold that against them. Over time, those persuaded to commit to the cause shaped their profiles with accurate representations of themselves. He wondered what the H. stood for. It shouldn't be too difficult to find out. If Kerman had left so much as a baby-sized digital footprint, Andrew would find it.

All right, Agent Kerman, I'll help you out, but the choice still belongs to Mel. How will you measure up? If you hurt her, there will be severe consequences.

Chapter 10:
First Date

Prime Time Bar & Grill
Princeton, New Jersey

Sam couldn't believe how quickly two and a half weeks had flown by. Thankfully, no more bodies had been dumped in public lands, giving him a chance to organize his thoughts about the case. The forensics machine was cranking away at the mountain of evidence gathered, but as Jenn frequently reminded him, it would take some time for everything to be processed properly.

Both bodies had been autopsied, but had revealed little new information. Despite the number of packages holding pieces of the first victim, his fingers, toes, and right arm were either missing or damaged beyond repair. That meant getting fingerprints would be difficult. New techniques in gathering latent fingerprints from skin gave them some hope, but Sam wasn't going to hold his breath for results. He'd have to work some other angles on identifying the victim. The Bradford County ME had complained about having to piece the guy together like a gruesome jigsaw puzzle.

Some parts of the skull had been smashed to little bits, but once it was restored, Sam could get a 3D scan and an approximate image of the man's face. This would allow him to compare it to missing persons files. If he was lucky, the man disappeared from a state that kept archived electronic copies of their missing persons files. Despite leaps and bounds in technology and communication, most law enforcement communities still functioned like islands with a network of rickety bridges connecting them. If he was really lucky, the man would be a local, which would make questioning his next of kin that much easier. He hated that part of his job, but it was a necessary evil.

The interview with the second victim's family had been tough, especially after he learned Haley Doherty had left a young daughter behind. Sam pondered how ordinary the second victim's life had seemed on the surface. By day, Haley worked as a clerk in a local hardware store. By night, she supplemented the meager income by freelancing for a new kind of high-tech prostitution. The vice crew had scored big time for Sam, connecting Haley to Anything Goes, Inc. within five days of him giving them the scant information he had. It helped that Haley's parents had filed a missing persons report promptly when she failed to pick up her daughter the day after the murder.

A gentle, tentative knock on Sam's car window startled him, but he confined his reaction to a muscle twitch in his shoulders. His head flew left, and he found himself staring up at his date. He had to quell the urge to leap out of the car lest he knock her over in the process. That would be an unfortunate beginning. Smiling, he turned off his car and got out, pausing long enough to let her step out of the way as the door swung open.

"Sam?" asked the woman. Her tone was confident, yet soft and controlled, yet questioning. She turned his name into a warm invitation.

He liked her voice. Every line he'd rehearsed mysteriously vanished, so he dragged out the process of closing his car door. Heat rose up his neck toward his ears, but hopefully, a combination of cold winter air and enough shadows hid most of the reaction. He feared he would simply stare at her tongue-tied.

Say something!

"Hi, you must be Melissa." Sam winced. His voice had as much character as a block of concrete. His right hand flexed as he resisted the impulse to offer her a handshake. "I'm Sam."

Real smooth. The thought sounded suspiciously like Jenn in his head.

An eternal second of awkward silence stretched between them.

They stared at each other.

"Can you tell I'm out of practice?" Sam asked.

The question broke the awkwardness before it could flip to tension. Light laughter from Melissa finished it off.

"You and me both," she admitted.

"I'm not sure I should shake your hand or try for a hug." The statement escaped Sam. He shoved his hands deep into his pockets so he wouldn't be tempted to try either.

Melissa's laughter bubbled brighter. Leaning forward, she wrapped him in a brief embrace and kissed him on the cheek.

"Hugs are okay where I come from," said Melissa. "They sort of come with my job."

Sam's unease began melting. He saw her shiver.

"I'd love to hear all about that, but we should probably head inside. Shall we continue the getting-to-know-you thing over some hot drinks? I'm told they serve an amazing hot chocolate." Turning so they stood side-by-side, Sam offered his arm to escort her.

Once inside, the hostess quickly settled them into a quiet booth near the back. Soon, they had tall glasses of ice water to tide them over until they decided what they really wanted.

"I'm glad you could make it on such short notice," said Sam. He leaned forward, eager to learn everything he could about this woman.

They'd been exchanging emails and phone calls for several weeks, but this was the first face-to-face meeting. Melissa Novak was much prettier than her profile photos. The still images couldn't convey her sense of presence or the kindness in her blue eyes. Her hair hung loose, brushing the tops of her shoulders. It too seemed to have more body
and life outside the confines of a picture.

"You too. I'm glad I could steal you away from murder and mayhem for a while. How's that going anyway?"

During their first phone conversation, Sam had elaborated on his occupation. Jenn's innocuous "federal employee" answer had been designed to not scare potential dates off, but Sam wanted to be as honest as possible. He didn't want to waste his time with anybody who couldn't deal with his job. He couldn't legally discuss details of the open investigation, but he did mention his current case was a murder. It didn't take her long to figure out which one. As part of being the FBI's public face on this investigation, Sam had had to endure several news interviews.

Sam shrugged.

"It's hard to tell. We're doing everything we can, but the truth of the matter is that often times we're just waiting for the perp to make a mistake." He toyed with his water glass, running his finger down the condensation on the side and absently making a smiley face. The case threatened to hijack his mind again, so Sam shook his shoulders to help him focus. "I'm sorry. I'll try not to be lousy company."

"No apology necessary," Melissa replied. "It's my fault for bringing it up. Let's talk about something more pleasant. Shall we avoid work talk altogether?"

"Not necessarily. I'm sure you have a lot of interesting work-related tales to tell."

A far-off look swept over Melissa's face.

"The kids I work with are the strongest, bravest people I've ever met, but most of their cases are complicated and heartbreaking."

"You don't have to talk about it if you don't want to, but you're welcome to," said Sam.

Time passed quickly as Melissa regaled Sam with quotes and anecdotes about some of her favorite patients over the years. The waiter came and took their order. Sam asked for a medium-rare prime rib, and Melissa requested the parmesan crusted chicken breast. Sam would have settled for water to accompany the meal, but since Melissa ordered an iced tea, he got a soda. The interruption allowed them to ease into a new phase in their conversation.

Thanks to Matchmaker Miracles, they already knew they both enjoyed working out, watching movies, and walking. They learned that his idea of a workout mostly involved weights and treadmills at a gym while her idea encompassed running along open roads or park trails. Sam's movie preferences ran heavily toward the action, adventure, and thriller categories, while Melissa's likes entailed way more Disney titles, romantic comedies, and the occasional suspense story. Strangely, they both enjoyed science fiction and fantasy stories. They agreed that the best kind of walk was late at night with a clear open sky filled with stars.

When their food arrived, Sam paused to appreciate the nice presentation the chef had arranged. As he worked his way through the steak, Sam peppered Melissa with more specific questions about her job, hobbies, and family. He fielded just as many or more questions from her, especially when it came to family. Being a trained investigator, he honed in on the topic. He didn't want to make her uncomfortable, but he was curious as to why she volunteered relatively few tidbits of information. Finally, his gentle interrogation yielded results.

"My dad passed away when I was a teenager. Mom got cancer soon after, so it fell to me to keep things normal for my brothers. We're not blood related since I'm adopted and they were surprises for my folks, but they're still my brothers. They're twins, but about as different as night and day. I keep in pretty close contact with Josh, but Andrew moved to California for college and fell off the map." Melissa's one-shoulder shrug tried to tell Sam the loss of contact didn't bother her.

It didn't work. Sam had spent enough time around Jenn to pick up on Melissa's disappointment.

"Do you have any contact with him?" Sam inquired. He flagged down the waiter and ordered two hot chocolates since Melissa didn't seem interested in a more official dessert.

"He sends me flowers on my birthday every year. It's a nice gesture, but I'd rather see him, you know?" A pensive expression took over. When she spoke again, her voice was slightly haunted. "I try to reach out, but it's like he's actively blocking me. He always was better with computers than people, but I'd chalked that up to a teenage phase. He should be more ... social. I feel like I failed him in some way."

"Because you're older than him?" asked Sam, understanding the sentiment. Jenn made his job of keeping in contact ridiculously easy, but as the older sibling, he understood the instinct to protect and pave the way for a younger loved one.

She confirmed his guess with a nod, then forced a smile.

"Sorry. I'm usually not quite so prone to doom and gloom. I must be tired."

"It's no problem. I enjoy getting to know you better." Sam sensed it was a good time to press his luck. "I know the night's not over yet, but would you like to go on a second date someday?" He gulped down some of the scalding hot chocolate that had arrived to keep from staring while she composed an answer.

"I'd like that," said Melissa. This smile had a bit more life to it than the last one.

"Great. Now the hard part: what would you like to do?" Sam sipped at his ice water to counteract the near boiling hot chocolate he'd just poured down his throat.

"I'm sure we'll figure out something. The truly hard part will be wrangling another time when we're both free. The physical distance thing could be difficult."

"I have off most weekends," said Sam.

If there are no new bodies.

"I'm on call some weekends, and the ones I'm not on call, I'm busy painting or spackling or doing some other home repair project."

A lightbulb blazed over Sam's head.

"Why don't I help? I can paint." He realized he probably sounded too eager. Another thought struck him. "I hope it doesn't sound like I'm trying to invite myself over. I'd like to help if I can."

Melissa shook her head.

"We just met. That wouldn't be fair."

"If it needs doing, then we'll get it done. We can have a nice dinner after if we've still got the energy for it."

The waiter came by and dropped the bill on their table. Melissa reached for it, but Sam was faster.

"Mine!" he crowed triumphantly.

At first, Melissa looked stunned, but the expression soon turned amused.

"You know I don't expect you to pay just because you're a man, right?" she asked tentatively.

"I know, but you came a long way to meet me on a work night. This is just a small way to thank you for the effort."

She eyed him suspiciously.

"If we … continue dating, will you ever let me pay for things?"

"Of course," Sam said cheerfully. He left enough cash for the meal plus a generous tip then rose and crossed to help her into her coat. "You come skydiving with me, and I'll let you pay." He was joking. They had both admitted to a healthy fear of heights.

To his surprise, she said, "Deal."

Chapter 11:
Tech Savvy Perp

FBI Field Office
Philadelphia, Pennsylvania
Samuel Kerman tried to concentrate on the report summarizing the gas chromatograph readouts from samples collected on or near the second victim. He especially wanted to know the identity of the gray dust found on both bodies, but his mind kept wandering away from the technical reports and back to Melissa. What would her hair feel like? He loved her laugh and the way she spoke about the children she worked with. The element names and percentages in the reports meant nothing to Sam, so he skimmed past the details to the conclusion.

Chemical identity: unknown.

Well, that's a lot of help.

Instinct told Sam he ought to care about this mystery substance, but his gut was fuzzier on explaining why. In the grand scheme of evidence, it probably wouldn't amount to much without some suspects to link it to. The first body, John Doe, couldn't give Sam many leads since he was still in too many pieces. The second body, Haley Doherty, gave him plenty of people to question and leads to follow. While enlightening, most of the information gathered was useless.

Anything Goes, Inc.—Haley's nocturnal employer—simply had too many safeguards in place to protect the identity of their shady clients. People either paid a premium for paying in cash when they met their date or paid through a third party website called shadowsales.com. For a small fee, this company would store people's credit card information in one server and assign a unique client number. They would use their own credit to cover the client's expenses. For 24 hours, the client information could be linked to the item or service purchased, but after that point, both got scrubbed. Scrubbing involved scrambling. After 24 hours, the clients could only be linked to a category of product, not an actual purchase.

Sam didn't know too much about high-tech matters, but he was fairly certain a system like that could be beaten, dismantled, or at least peeked into long enough to gain answers. On the other hand, he could not predict whether a judge would sign off on the time and effort needed to pursue a long shot person of interest in this case.

What should we do?

The question initially concerned the murder cases, but Sam's mind offered up several pleasant date options instead of new investigative angles. Finding a movie they both enjoyed might be tricky, but it was worth considering. When the weather turned nicer, they could check out some of the hiking trails in the Adirondacks or a state park somewhere. He'd probably suggest a park in New Jersey, seeing as Pennsylvania parks had been catching more than their fair share of bodies recently.

Unfortunately, much of what needed to be done concerning the case either lay outside his control—like the speed with which forensics tests could be accomplished—or had been done already. Being caught up had allowed him to go on a date with Melissa last night, but he didn't like waiting for the bad guy to make a move.

Leaning back in his chair, Sam toyed with a pencil, stared up at the ceiling, and let the case details run through his head. Two bodies had shown up in separate parks or public lands in Pennsylvania within a week of each other. That told him the perpetrator was likely familiar with the tristate area, but didn't want to lead investigators to his doorstep. The forethought meant the guy probably had a grand game plan. Sam could almost hear the professional development lecturer drone about political correctness and its role in the workplace, but in the privacy of his own head, he'd go with "guy" until proven wrong.

The first victim had been male and practically shredded. The medical examiner had said large animals, likely dogs, had eaten some of the body. That spoke of some serious animosity. Sam's stomach did a flip within him at the memory. The killer had declared the first victim guilty of something, so identifying him needed to be a priority. Still, without easy access to fingers, fingerprints were difficult. The lab people would work up a DNA profile to glean some information, but as yet, there was no missing persons DNA databank to throw it in for a match.

The second victim had been female, declared innocent, and shot. She had been easily identified, and obviously, stalked through her job.

Why a second victim?

If the killer had nothing specific against the second victim, why bother? The move gave investigators more to work with. The gray dust, similar dump sites, and messages about guilt or innocence were a pretty solid signature combination. That meant he probably wanted investigators to appreciate his handiwork.

Sam's computer pinged like it wanted to update or had a special alert for him. He ignored it.

The plastic bags holding victim one's body came up with little usable trace evidence. Sam would have donated a lung for a nice fingerprint on one of the plastic bags, but the killer must have worn gloves.

Heavy footsteps rushed by his office first one way and then the other. Sam glanced up, but then buried his head in his notes again.

Both victims were white, so it followed that the killer was likely white. Statistically, serial killers tended toward white and male anyway. Sam tried to keep an open mind, picturing the killer as a large black woman wielding a knife. The image didn't work for him, and it shattered a moment later when Agent Newhouse poked his head into Sam's cubicle.

"Hatcher says to unplug your computer, shut down your laptop, and turn off your phone," Newhouse announced. "There's a meeting in Conference Room B in five minutes. Be there." The man's tone zipped with a buzz of agitated excitement.

Before Sam could ask any questions, the agent had moved on to the next cubicle and was giving Adana Okiro the same speech. After following the instructions, Sam exited his office and followed the crowd to the meeting. He would have had a hard time getting in the door, except that it soon became clear SAC Louis Hatcher wanted him front and center. Agents and support personnel alike shuffled out of the way, moving Sam along like a leaf on an angry river.

Hatcher and Jordan Berkowitz stood up front near a chair which held a laptop. It had been rigged to a projector so that the laptop's screen filled the wall behind them. They made quite a contrasting pair with Hatcher in a dark suit and Berkowitz sporting a blue FBI T-shirt and wrinkled khaki pants. The SAC's bald spot gleamed under the overhead lights, while Jordan's shaggy dark hair hung low over his forehead, almost covering his eyes.

The room rumbled with speculative conversations, which Sam ignored. As soon as he reached the front, Hatcher waved him forward impatiently.

"We've been hacked," said Jordan Berkowitz. The young man's eyes were bright with excitement. "I think I caught it in time, but it was brilliant. He must have—"

"Show him," Hatcher growled.

Jordan knelt by the chair, moved the cursor over the update box in the corner, and looked up at the large screen. Dozens of textboxes popped up then blinked out. Jordan typed something into the keyboard and one of the textboxes enlarged to fill the screen. Large, bold letters glared out from a white background.

Sam now understood why he'd been plucked from the pack of agents filling the room.

To Special Agent Samuel Henry Kerman:

Back off. I will destroy the unworthy. In ones, twos, and threes, they will die because you fail. You can't stop me, but you will fear me.

Let the games begin.

Hand of God

Hatcher quelled a surge of murmurs by raising his hands for silence.

"The tech people will be inspecting every device in the building. In the meantime, don't open or update anything on either your work or home devices. That goes for cell phones and electronic notebooks too. If it's been linked to our servers, it needs to be looked at."

Several cries of dismay filled the room.

"How long will that take?" a male voice demanded.

Sam couldn't see the speaker.

"As long as it takes."

Groans met Hatcher's answer.

"What happened?" asked Agent Okiro. The dark-skinned woman stood half a head taller than the four people standing near her.

Hatcher waved for Jordan to answer the question.

"The hacker inserted a program within a code that made it look like a routine update. When I clicked on it, the virus replicated itself as fast as it could and tried to send copies to other devices through the Wi-Fi. I think I caught it, but my team will need to check your devices to be sure. Don't want to let this thing loose."

"Why?" asked Sam. "What makes it dangerous?"

"Normally, it'd just be a nuisance," said Jordan. "It's an infinity virus with a simple message that replicates and deletes the versions of itself that are three to four generations old. That's why the boxes appear and disappear. Confined to one device, I could isolate and kill it, but this baby's been modified so it can hop to different devices through the internet. It's really a beautiful program."

Hatcher's glare wiped the smile off of Jordan's face. He straightened and excused himself to organize the sweep to clean any infected devices.

Sam added "tech savvy" and "arrogant" to his paltry profile for the killer. He supposed the killer could have hired someone to create and release the virus, but to even make such a purchase, he would have to be able to navigate the Dark Web. A friend working vice had once tried to tell Sam how to access the series of forums and websites that offered everything from information on bomb making to a marketplace for illicit drugs. Sam's conversation takeaway had been that it took some hacking skills to access the Dark Web.

"Kerman, I want to see you in my office in ten minutes." Eye contact added gravity to Hatcher's statement. "We need to discuss this."

Sam wanted to protest. He felt like a kid being unjustly hauled into the principal's office. His mind churned with possible defenses he could raise to whatever Hatcher said. This was the biggest case of Sam's career. He didn't want to get pulled off it because the killer had called him out by name. The message moved the contest to a far more personal plane.

I accept the challenge. Sam thought at the killer. *You slip up once and you're mine.*

Chapter 12:
Media Primer

FBI Field Office
Philadelphia, Pennsylvania

Roughly ten minutes later, Dawn Hopper told Sam he could enter the inner sanctum. The meeting's uncharacteristic promptness reinforced the urgency Sam had seen in his boss's eyes. He closed the door as he entered, assuming this would be a private meeting. Two steps into the room, he realized they weren't alone.

Adana Okiro rose gracefully as Sam approached. They exchanged cordial nods. For the first time, Sam noticed the woman might be an inch taller than him. He wasn't used to looking up to meet people's eyes, especially women. Despite being cubicle neighbors, he hardly knew her, though he vaguely recalled she worked with people. He couldn't remember in what capacity.

"I trust you two know each other," said Special Agent in Charge Louis Hatcher. He waved them into seats then settled onto his office chair again. "But you may not know why I've summoned you."

Sam and Adana nodded agreement with this assessment.

Their boss leveled a gaze first at Adana, then at Sam, before splitting a second stare evenly between them.

"Kerman has point on the park killer, and Okiro's here to give you a media primer. You can use the conference room next to my office, but I want this done right now. As soon as the media gets wind we've been hacked, they're going to swarm. I want a formal statement prepped by then, and you'd better both be ready to field questions in a press conference."

Sam nearly sagged in relief. He wouldn't need to fight to stay on the case.

As if sensing his newfound comfort, Hatcher's eyes fixed on Sam like heat-seeking missiles.

"Pay attention to what she has to say, Kerman. I can't stress enough the importance of getting the PR part of this right. You say the wrong thing and lawyers will be lining up to file suits against the Bureau. If that happens, I will not be happy." The last statement came out slower than the rest, and Hatcher's eyes narrowed to slits. He looked like a reptile ready to swallow a squirming lunch.

"Yes, sir," said Sam, working hard to keep the relief from bleeding onto his face. "I will."

Hatcher sighed, sat back, and allowed his eyes to return to normal. His expression turned imploring.

"Kerman, I don't have to read minds to know what you're feeling. I was you some time ago: young, undefeated, confident. But this isn't the movies. Not every killer gets caught. So far, the reports I have on you are decent. I'm told you have a level head, but at the end of the day, you need to remember this is a job, not the sum total of your life." Thus far, Hatcher's tone had been decidedly sympathetic, but it hardened as he uttered one more warning. "Do not under any circumstances let this guy inside your head."

Sam acknowledged the warning solemnly. To do anything more or less would simply invite a longer lecture.

After a final, brief staring contest, Hatcher released Sam and Adana to the small conference room budding off of this one.

"I leave him in your hands, Agent Okiro," said Hatcher, as they each stood.

Since she was already closer to the side office, Adana entered first. Although much smaller than Hatcher's main office, this room contained a large office chair, a full-sized desk, and two interview chairs.

"Please have a seat," Adana said. She sat on the left guest chair and nodded for Sam to take the other one.

He did so, feeling her dark, hawk-like eyes follow his every move.

"Relax your shoulders, but sit up straighter," Adana

instructed.

Sam tried to follow the directions by pulling his shoulders back, but he figured something was wrong when she shook her head. Standing, Adana came over and gently pressed down on his shoulders, lowering them just a hair.

"First lesson: body language speaks volumes," said Adana. As she spoke, the woman straightened her shoulders and gestured with both hands in a rolling motion to emphasize her last words. Her chin rose slightly but her lips remained close together. After maintaining the pose for a few seconds, she smiled. Her eyes roamed his face freely, cool and professional. She nodded as if coming to a conclusion. "I can work with this."

The comment brought an amused grin to Sam's face.

"Good. Don't underestimate the power of a smile, but keep it small and pleasant. Too much and they'll sense you're trying too hard." Adana reached out and adjusted Sam's tie. "Keep the tie perfectly centered, but if it shifts, let it. Adjusting it during an interview is bad form and a sign of insecurity."

"What should I do with my hands?" Sam wondered. His had started to sweat thanks to the intensity of Adana's scrutiny.

"Keep them open and rest them in your lap if you're not using them, but feel free to enhance your statements with gestures as necessary," she answered. Returning to her seat, Adana sat and studied Sam's current posture. "Lean forward when delivering an important statement. It indicates interest and emphasis."

Sam did his best to obey the directions.

Adana made a few minor adjustments then nodded satisfaction that his body language would convey the right messages in an interview.

"Second lesson: avoid issuing or answering challenges. You can promise the Bureau will do its utmost to apprehend the perpetrator, but keep ego and bravado out of it."

Sam bobbed his head. Hatcher's words from before still rang in his ears.

"Besides the legal reasons the SAC mentioned, there are personal risks to issuing or answering challenges. He briefly discussed this."

"What happened to him?" Sam asked the question softly, aware of how much he didn't know about his boss.

"I don't know every detail, but I gather he didn't take the advice he gave to you," Adana said. "It's easy to make high profile cases personal crusades, but they're not solved overnight. Be prepared to follow every lead wherever it goes, but don't be too disappointed if the trail runs cold. These things happen."

Sam disagreed and shook his head vigorously to show it.

"I know this guy's been quiet for a while, but he's not going to wait too much longer," Sam insisted. "He's addicted."

Adana weighed the statement before reluctantly nodding agreement.

"Keep that opinion to yourself if anybody asks," she advised. "We don't want to spark wrongful death suits if there are future victims. You may think the statement harmless, but we're dealing with a twisted mind. It could be enough to be taken as a challenge. That brings me to lesson three: be brief. The less you say, the less they'll try to hang you with later."

Adana's media lessons continued over the next half-hour. Then, she handed Sam a list of questions he could expect reporters to raise and left him alone to study. She stayed in the room, working on her press release, scribbling several pages worth of notes out by hand since they weren't allowed to touch computers yet.

An hour before the actual press conference, Adana made Sam take a break and go grab lunch. He ordered two deli sandwiches for them from a local place that delivered since Adana didn't want him leaving the building for fear the reporters might hunt him down. The turkey, cheese, and avocado sandwich with spicy mustard went a long way in cheering Sam. After scarfing down the sandwich, he resumed his question studies and read through some answers he had written on the cards.

At last, the pair headed back to Conference Room B where the press conference would be held. Adana took one last opportunity to give him a pep talk.

"Maintain eye contact when you answer questions and be clear about who you're calling on when you select reporters. Keep a good mix of men and women. They should have logos on their microphones to indicate which company they work for. If you remember my notes, you can almost predict which questions each will raise. Good luck."

Lengthening her stride, Adana swept in front of Sam as they

approached the correct conference room. Nerves prevented Sam from hearing most of her press release, but she made a point of calling him forward to answer questions once her piece was done.

Sam sailed through the first three questions because Adana's power of prediction was uncanny. Has the hacker claimed to be the park killer? Was anything else compromised? What is the FBI's next step? In short, his answers were "no," "not to my knowledge," and "we will continue our efforts to apprehend the criminal or criminals." The fourth question was also predicted, but when faced with it for real, Sam's crafted answer eluded him.

The woman from the Philadelphia Inquirer looked straight in his eyes as she spoke.

"Agent Kerman, the hacker singled you out, presumably on behalf of the park killer. Are you afraid for your life?"

Sam could feel tension spike in Adana, who stood two feet behind and to his left.

His insides coiled like a snake ready to strike down a threat. Since his mind went blank, he had a chance to evaluate both options afresh.

Yes.

An admission of fear would come across as honest and realistic, but it could also be interpreted as weakness. The FBI could not appear weak.

No.

A denial would smack of bravado and challenge. It could be taken as strength, but he had no way to keep it from spiraling out and becoming more.

Turning so his shoulders squared with the woman who had asked the question, Sam leaned forward and gripped the podium lightly.

"Yes and no, ma'am. In a job like this there's always the possibility of a dangerous turn, but that goes with the territory. The fear that exists is no more or less than that faced by my colleagues every day. Working for the FBI is a privilege many strive for. We have a motto to rally behind: honesty, bravery, fidelity. They're small words with big impact. The best we can do is to do our best every time we wake up to face a new day."

Sam held the lady's eyes for a two-count before calling on the next reporter. His brain switched over to a kind of autopilot.

Despite the length of the fourth answer, Sam generally kept the rest of his answers short and sweet as instructed. As the press conference wound down, the three television reporters stiffened almost as one. They kicked their camera men into gear and pressed forward, converging on the podium Sam stood behind.

The man from NBC News arrived first.

"I'm told the killer has one more question for you," the man announced. He thrust a cell phone at Sam and hit a button.

Uneasy silence fell as everybody strained to hear.

A deep, mechanical voice filled the air.

"Agent Kerman, how much do you value your sister's life?"

Sam's hands clenched the sides of the podium. He wanted to seize the phone and hurl it across the room. Before he could find any words, the phone call ended, but the reporters still looked at him expectantly. The large, looming camera eyes stayed with him, recording his reaction.

"What's your sister's name, agent?" asked a woman.

"The killer just threatened your sister during a live press conference, how does that make you feel?" asked another woman.

"What will you do now?" asked the NBC guy.

The three questions hit Sam simultaneously.

"Excuse me," said Sam. "I have work to do."

He backed away from the podium and left the room quickly.

Chapter 13:
Would You Like to Play a Game?

The Killer's Lair
Undisclosed Location
Crouching outside the bars of Cell 3, Andrew Novak watched the woman inside sleep. He had never been much of a pet person, but quiet moments like this, showed him some of the appeal. This was a first in many ways. Before the South Street Lady, Lurch had been his longest lasting prisoner, occupying Cell 1 for a full two days. This woman possessed an incredible lucky streak. Each morning, he'd wake her up and let her choose one of the lottery tickets in his extensive collection. If she chose a winner, he posed a question: do you want to live? So far, she'd always said yes, and her winning streak was approaching eight days now.

Why do you want to live?

After a rocky start, they had settled into a comfortable rhythm. Several times a day, Andrew would bring her a meal, sometimes he would include a sedative and sometimes he would leave the food alone. Cell 3's accommodations included a commode hidden in the far left corner behind a truncated shower curtain to afford some privacy. When it looked like she would last more than a day, Andrew brought her a bunch of blankets to soften the single bench bolted to the back wall. She had put them to good use, fashioning a bed, a pillow, and even something that passed for a chair.

A hint of sadness touched Andrew as he realized his prison

was probably more stable than the woman's usual housing situation. What kind of society allowed women like this to freeze on cold winter nights? He called her the South Street Lady because that's where he'd found her sitting on a flattened cardboard box with a plastic cup of coins clutched in her hands. A thin, filthy blanket provided minimal protection against the cold rain that night. Andrew had prepared an elaborate story, but he didn't need it. All he had to do was open the back of the van and offer her a thermos of warm soup.

Once she was unconscious, he had stripped off her clothes and wrapped her in a warm blanket. Afraid of what might be traveling on the disgusting rags, Andrew had stuffed everything including the cup of coins and a sad, torn dollar bill into a large trash bag and thrown it in a dumpster behind a busy restaurant. Only after thoroughly washing her whole body, did he wrestle her into a pair of sweatpants and an oversized T-shirt. He never shopped at consignment stores for himself these days, but he remembered the activity well enough to do it for his collection. Over a period of six months, he'd gathered enough clothes to supply several prisoners for years.

In sleep, the woman's face lost some of the worry lines. Even the deep bags under her eyes smoothed out. Her long, stringy white hair had resisted his cleansing efforts, so he'd shaved much of it off the first night. The haircut, clean clothes, and thorough washing had taken years off of her appearance. He'd allowed her to choose her own outfit after the first night. That had been an interesting excursion. Even with handcuffs on and a grim fate hanging over her head, the woman couldn't contain her wonder and delight while walking down the long aisles of clothes laid out on tables.

He wished he could let her live. Driving her to a new city would have been easy. It would make him feel great to help her get a new start in life, but psycho67 had balked at the idea. He was the only one Andrew could trust if he wanted a second opinion on an idea. They weren't exactly friends, but over the years, a mutual respect had grown between them.

Psycho67 reminded Andrew that promises were useless and people lied. If Andrew let the woman live, she would talk. She likely didn't know enough about his operation to endanger it, but she knew his face. He couldn't risk it. Still, nothing said he needed to act this second, so he waited and watched.

The blankets the woman had wrapped tight around her body like a cocoon rose and fell in concert with her slow, even breaths.

When his legs started to burn, Andrew stood and unlocked the cell door. He wanted to deliver the morning meal before she woke up. He wasn't afraid of her, but he preferred to be cautious rather than risk unnecessary confrontations. Despite his wishes, the woman snapped awake and sat up as he approached. As she struggled to free her arms from the blankets, she stared at him with a mixture of wariness, fear, and loathing.

She said nothing. He liked that about her. The woman didn't bombard him with a million pleas and questions. Instead, she studied him almost as intently as he watched her.

Slowly setting the tray on the ground, Andrew backed out of the cell and locked it again. The lady's eyes flitted from the tray back to Andrew then again to the tray. Once convinced he wouldn't return, she fought the rest of the way free and lowered her body to the ground next to the food. Today's breakfast included a bagel with some strawberry jelly and a paper cup of water.

"Thank you."

The words were so soft, Andrew almost missed them. Even after he heard them, he didn't know what to do with them. He grunted acknowledgment and patiently waited for the lady to finish her meal. Accustomed to his expectations, the woman consumed the entire bagel and drank the water. Next, she crushed the paper cup flat, piled everything onto the tray, and slid it under the two-inch gap at the bottom of the bars making up the cell door. Returning to the bench that doubled for her bed, the woman sat down and looked at Andrew, waiting for him to report the latest lottery verdict.

"You won." He didn't tell her that the first ticket she'd chosen for today had lost, as did the six subsequent ones. He could barely explain it to himself.

The woman shrugged.

"Doesn't matter. You're going to kill me today."

The lack of emotion surprised and intrigued Andrew.

"How do you know that?" he wondered.

"Your hands are dirty," the woman pointed out.

How could dirty hands betray his intentions? He stared down at the blackened fingertips.

Andrew had scratched off almost ninety tickets this morning. Of those, nine had been winners. Upon realizing he needed to deal with the woman soon, Andrew changed the details of the running bet. One ticket a day was failing to satisfy him. So, instead of days, he made them worth hours. Nine winning tickets meant nine hours. Checking his watch, Andrew decided to start counting from now. Real time read 8:11 a.m., so he would kill her late this afternoon.

"How do you want to die?" he asked, surprising them both.

"In my sleep," she answered.

Andrew shook his head.

"That's not an option." An idea struck him, causing him to stiffen. "But I suppose it could be. Would you like to play a game?"

The woman's stare turned curious.

"Wait here." Andrew rushed off before the ridiculousness of that statement could set in. Racing from the cell block, he made it to the side room off the operating room where Lurch had died. Finding a long roll of lottery tickets, he snatched up the whole thing then considered he didn't need quite so many. After tearing off a few dozen tickets, he double checked that he had two coins in his pockets. Spotting a stack of notecards and a black marker, Andrew picked up these items as well.

Returning to Cell 3, Andrew tossed the marker and three notecards into the cell along with a dime and half the lottery tickets.

"Write the ways you want to die on the notecards, one per card," he instructed.

"Why?"

"Why not?" Andrew returned. For some reason, he felt compelled to explain. "I'm a student of death and life. I want to see and experience as many forms of death as I can. So far, I've only killed with a knife and a gun, but you can still choose those ways to die if you wish."

A sense of triumph went through him when the woman retrieved the marker and the cards from the hard ground.

"I'm not interested in the weird or painful methods. I want to know the best way to kill somebody. You help me with my research, and I promise to ultimately choose a relatively painless death for you."

"What are the rules?" asked the woman.

"You won nine times in the tickets I used this morning, so we could potentially go nine rounds. I don't think we'll need that many. First, we create a list of how to kill people on the notecards. Then, you choose a ticket and scratch it off, and I will do the same. If we both lose, nothing happens. If you win, you can eliminate one of the methods I've written down. If I win, I can eliminate one of the methods you've written down. We'll go back and forth until there's only one method left."

Within a minute, the woman generated a list of three preferred methods to die. She wrote these on individual notecards: overdose of sleeping pills, gun, and blunt force object. When he had her answers, Andrew created more cards for some methods he'd considered: strangulation, drowning, burning, falling, animal attack, poison, electrocution, broken neck. He wasn't sure he could carry out each type of murder, but the game would be a good brainstorming activity.

They both lost on the first two tickets they selected. Andrew won on round three. He removed burning from the list of possibilities because he didn't think it right for her. The lady won round four and took animal attack out of play. Round five was a tie because they both won $2.00 on their chosen tickets. Andrew decided that meant they should choose two methods to give immunity to for two rounds. He protected strangulation and she protected sleeping pills. The game continued back and forth, slowly knocking out poison, electrocution, drowning, and blunt force object. They went well over nine rounds, but Andrew was enjoying the game too much to stop. Finally, only sleeping pills and strangulation remained.

They were down to three tickets. He had one and she had two. Andrew's ticket won and the lady's lost. She ran fingers nervously through her remaining hair and cradled her head with dismay. Feeling generous, he let her try again with the final ticket, but that too lost. Although tempted to grant her wish to die by sleeping pills, he suddenly wanted to feel the pulse of life in her.

"How will you do it?" The woman's question came out soft and resigned.

"I'll wear gloves," Andrew whispered. He didn't want to meet her eyes, so he looked at his blackened fingers.

"Don't," said the woman. She swallowed hard. Tears pooled in her eyes and her jaw clenched with bitterness and anger. She leaned forward. "You do this yourself. No wire, no weapons." Some of the tears slipped out. "You earn this with your bare hands."

As he watched her quietly weep, Andrew thought he'd never seen anything more beautiful. This woman didn't deserve to die, but Fate had dictated otherwise. He would honor this last request. Maybe stealing her life could lend more meaning to his quest. It would be hard work. It would be a sacrifice in the name of knowledge. Society had thrown this woman away, but in death, she would gain new life. He would immortalize her in his accounts. Once released, her soul could join his and lend him the strength to carry out his mission.

Chapter 14:
Pulse of Life

The Killer's Lair
Undisclosed Location
Day 3: Early evening.
I killed a woman today, and I think I regret it. These sacrifice kills are harder on the mind than you can imagine, but I must learn. Psycho67 says it's good that this still hurts. It proves my humanity's intact. To accept the mandate to stomp out evil, one must understand life. Today, I felt the pulse of life beat strongly against my fingers, and felt nails scratch the flesh on my forearms as I worked.

I gave the police a whole body this time. It's risky, but worthwhile. Her fingers had a part of me in them, so I had to be careful with the cleanup. It was a good fight. Strangling somebody is hard work. They don't go quietly into the night. Smothering might be easier, but that would also be less satisfying.

Eyes hold the window into the soul. There's a brief moment the second before death when the eyes light up with realization. It's as if universal truths flood the mind in that instant. I wish I could experience that and come back to record my observations, but it's too risky.

Nothing about this kill is as I originally planned. I took her in a day early because the opportunity presented itself. I kept her alive longer than expected because she was lucky in every drawing for more than a week. My original choice of death for her was burning, but we ended up playing a game that eliminated that as an option. I won the game, but in the end only strangulation and sleeping pills remained. I knew what I had to choose.

Had she won, it would have been sleeping pills, a highly unsatisfactory manner of murder. It's like feeding a rat poison. There's no honor, no struggle, and no hardship involved. The victim doesn't even know why they must die. I may never test this method unless I must perform another merciful killing.

My next major kill must be a righteous one. I've done some research and found some fools who might fit the bill. They're college students accused of attacking a woman in a drunken rage, but they were never charged because she refused to pursue the matter. I believe some threats from one of the young men's fathers might have something to do with the woman's sudden change of heart. I can pursue the father or the young men, but probably not both. Since the father has younger sons to care for, I will let him have a second chance at turning out useful members of society. I prefer to take action against the most guilty anyway.

I'm still working through details, but I believe I have a plan. It might have to wait for fairer weather though. I'm told that's normal. Killing people is harder in the dead of winter. To keep my skills sharp, I may find some smaller targets, but the next big statement will come in spring if I go with the method of killing I want to. For now, I'm keeping that secret to myself, but it will be spectacular if it works as I imagine it should.

I don't always claim the little kills. Let the cops believe a couple of gang kids took each other out. Those kinds of people don't even deserve the recognition of a major statement.

Drawing out three victims will take a lot of coordination and planning. I will need to subdue them quickly as I cannot risk involving another person. I asked psycho67 if he would join me, but he says his personal plans are consuming much of his concentration. He sent a gift in his stead.

Supplies will have to be ordered well in advance. I believe shadowsales.com has a program tracking certain kinds of sales. They may even sell this information to the authorities or other interested parties. I like the site, but if they cause me trouble, I'll have to take action. I can write a program to counter their tracker, but I'm not convinced the effort is necessary. As long as I'm cautious and don't order everything online, it should be fine.

I should return to my account of today. My initial plan for the South Street Lady was to leave her body in Nockamixon State Park, but she deserved better than that, so I took her home to Philadelphia.

A city never truly sleeps, but in the wee hours of the morning, roughly between three and four, one can usually work in peace. I found a nice bench on the University of Pennsylvania's campus near South Street. I moved her to the van soon after the kill so that if she stiffened, I could at least place her on a bench. I think she would like that. A bright blue and red scarf and matching knit hat completed the image. A thick winter coat will protect her on this last night in the City of Brotherly Love.

I thanked her for helping me get better and placed a notecard with her. This one said: Discarded by Society. Maybe that will give them something to think about. I helped her. I ended her suffering, which is more than I can say for the hundreds of people who walked by her every day. When guilt would reach an unbearable height, they'd give her a dollar to appease their consciences then slip into a coffee shop and drop eight more on a donut and a hot beverage.

It's sickening.

Maybe the whole city should go.

No, that can't be right. I'm not above using innocents to advance my cause, but surely, an entire city holds people worth preserving for the future. Bombs are too random. They lack control and precision.

Psycho67 won't be happy when he hears I left the South Street Lady at home in the city instead of the intended park. He's always talking against taking unnecessary risks, but it's my risk to take. He can't speak until he carries out his own plans. He keeps saying grand plans take time, but I'm starting to think he's all talk and no action. That would be disappointing. If true, I might have to end our relationship. I enjoy talking to him. He's so much like me. It's like he believes in me more than I do sometimes.

Some risks are worth taking to honor the fallen.

I laid the woman out on the bench as best I could. She looked peaceful. No more worries. No more strife or hunger or discomfort, only rest. Although I feel more drawn to punish evildoers, there's a sense of accomplishment in helping someone find peace. It feels right.

It won't take long for them to find her. This time of year in a state park, it could take days to find a body, unless I'd placed her in the middle of a cross-country skiing trail or by one of the Ranger stations. Here, she will be taken care of quickly. I should have left a camera nearby to watch over her, but I'll have to remember that for the future. The campus is pretty well wired. I could tap into their system if necessary, but I'll give it a few hours more before I take that step. They had a malfunction this morning, but it only lasted as long as I needed it to.

Three and a half minutes. That's how long it took to properly strangle the South Street Lady. I'm glad I wore gloves because I had to do it twice. I'd always thought that such a thing took seconds. I was mistaken. My first attempt was a simple approach from the front. That's how I got the scratches, and when I watched the light of life fade away. But as I went to prepare the body, I felt her pulse. I'd only knocked her out. My second attempt was far more intimate. I looped my left arm around her neck and drew her back into my chest, curling my right arm up as a brace to increase the pressure.

She woke up briefly, but her clawing hands could find little purchase on my pants. The lack of oxygen made her lethargic. Then, she stopped moving. I held the embrace for an extra minute beyond the point where she ceased struggling. To pass the time, I counted. I sensed the moment her soul left her body. It was a beautiful moment, like setting a captive creature free. The mortal matter she left behind required some cleanup, but that's to be expected.

I couldn't decide what to do with the fingers. It seemed wrong to cut them off and let the dogs have them. I ended up clipping the nails short and scraping underneath the area I couldn't clip. Then, I soaked her hands in bleach just in case I missed something. Those nails may never have received such care in life. That's sad.

I did not find any shoes that adequately fit her, so I put her in a few pairs of warm wool socks. I should have fled as soon as I left her body, but I had too much raw energy coursing through me, so I spent some time driving through the city streets. There are enough night deliveries to make a white van disappear into the background, even late at night. I took the precaution of obscuring part of the license plate with mud.

On my travels, I drove past the FBI building on Arch Street. It made me think of the agent, which made me think of Mel. I haven't kept up with either of them in a few weeks. I should check in with them. Calling the agent during that interview had been foolish. I'd done my homework on him, so I knew he had a sister. In fact, I think she might be involved in the investigation somehow. One of my facial recognition programs believes it saw her at one of the state parks. I can't be sure. The program's got some flaws and the picture resolution was terrible. I'd posted a bounty on a Dark Web site dedicated to candid pictures of crime scenes, but the few who answered the call were amateurs.

It doesn't matter. I'm not considering making good on the threat. That was just to rattle the agent. The news coverage indicates that was accomplished, but those people do a lot in the editing room. I can't trust them as a source. On the other hand, I look forward to seeing what they do with my South Street Lady. Had she died in her natural habitat, city workers would have collected her like another piece of trash. The police would have written a standard report, and the city would churn to life around her unhindered. Hopefully, I've made her more than a footnote.

I wish I could do more, but I need to stay out of Philadelphia for a few weeks. It's not safe to be predictable.

I need to do something radical.

Chapter 15:
A Regular Sight

University of Pennsylvania
Philadelphia, Pennsylvania

Curious college students held up cell phones, trying to snap pictures of the crime scene. A line of policemen attempted to hold them back. The students' presence bothered Sam, but he tried not to show it. This was probably the most excitement experienced on the campus this decade. He knew if the roles were reversed, he'd be doing much the same, but even in the years since his college days, the cell phones had taken over the world.

How many of these photos will end up on social media sites?

At the request of law enforcement, the major social media players were attempting to take down the pictures already hitting the internet, but it was a tough task. The kid who reported the body had only done so after posting it to every site he could think of. He was no doubt trying to cash in on the momentary fame.

Sam's blood pressure spiked as he remembered the selfie picture the idiot had taken with the card he'd found on the body. If Sam had his way, the fool would spend half the day in the police station waiting for someone to take his statement. That would serve him right for tampering with evidence. Nevertheless, the notecard was the reason Sam had been diverted here before he could step foot in his office today.

He spotted a young man climbing a nearby tree to get a better vantage point.

"Sergeant!" Sam called.

A short, dark-haired woman appeared at Sam's side almost instantly.

"Yes, Agent Kerman?"

"Get these people out of here," Sam ordered.

Sergeant Kristal Bannister quirked a neat eyebrow at him and frowned.

"That's not going to be easy, sir."

"Do the best you can. Do any of your people have a roll of caution tape? The whole area should be cordoned off if possible. I want to give the forensics people some room to work when they get here."

"I'll see what I can do." The woman nodded in lieu of saluting and hurried away to bolster the crowd control efforts.

"Thank you," Sam murmured, even though the woman was already ten paces away. He caught the tree climber's eye and shook his head. The kid got the point and slunk away, looking dejected.

After pulling on gloves, Sam went to the body and picked up the notecard which had fallen to the ground. He slipped it into a plastic bag to preserve anything that the selfie fool hadn't destroyed already.

A long, soft curse sounded from behind him.

Turning, Sam watched a tall African American officer approach.

"Do you know her?" Sam inquired. Something in the man's tone told him he did.

"Name's Martha," drawled the man. "She a regular sight in these parts. Homeless last few years. Tried to help her a few times, but she wouldn't accept much aside from a spare sandwich or loose change now an' then. Kept to herself. Moved on when told. Taught some of the younger ones which corners were good for panhandling. She gonna be missed. Guess that explains her absence these last few weeks. I was beginning to wonder."

"How come nobody reported her missing?" Sam felt foolish raising the question because he suspected he knew the answer.

"Homeless folks don't keep to normal schedules," replied the man. His nameplate read T. Johnson. "Ain't nobody keepin' track of 'em. They move on to warmer street corners an' alleys in the winter months. Lucky ones find a bed in a shelter from time to time." The officer removed his hat a moment out of respect for the dead woman. "Is there anything I can do to help?"

Sam started to shake his head and thought better of it.

"See if you can find some of the local homeless people. Ask them when they last saw Martha. Maybe we can work up a timeline with their help." Handing over a business card, Sam added, "Maybe somebody even saw something that will help us catch this guy."

"I hope so," said Officer Johnson. He took the card and settled his cap back onto his head. "I'll get on that right now."

As he watched Officer Johnson leave, Sam knew it would be a late night. Pulling out his cell phone, he sent a quick text message to Mel telling her he might not make it for their dinner date. This was the fourth canceled dinner date, though one of the cancellations had been due to her job rather than his. Still, he wondered how long this could go on. They enjoyed regular phone conversations and exchanged lengthy emails, but eventually, they'd have to meet in person if their relationship was to have any chance of moving forward. Calling her would have been preferable, but he remembered she had wall-to-wall appointments scheduled today.

Pulling out his work phone, Sam updated his boss and told him how he would be spending the morning. Hatcher informed him that he was calling a press conference for 3 o'clock this afternoon to announce the official formation of a task force to investigate these murders. Sam started to protest until assured he would have a prominent role on that task force. The media had taken to calling the slayings works of the Parkside Killer, but Sam knew that was a misnomer. The bodies might show up in parks, but they weren't killed there In fact, a good chance existed that at least two of the murders had taken place at the same location. He would have to discuss the possibility with Dr. Stratham and Jenn when they arrived.

Sam wasn't sure how he felt about Jenn being seen around this third body dump, but he couldn't bar her from helping her new boss. The college internship had ended around the New Year, but Dr. Stratham had extended an invitation to continue on for a small stipend. It meant at least another six months of sleeping on his couch, but Sam didn't mind. That switch had happened a week into her stay. He could sleep anywhere. Besides, he liked being able to keep an eye on her. The killer's question during that press conference a few weeks back still made him queasy.

He frowned up at the sky and hoped Jenn and Dr. Stratham arrived soon. The weather reports were predicting snow showers on and off throughout the day. So far, the skies had been content to look gray and menacing, but Sam wanted the evidence collected and the body secured before Mother Nature could interfere.

"Hey, Space Cadet," Jenn greeted softly. It was her standard greeting when she found Sam lost in thought. The traces of amusement dropped out of her tone as she absorbed the sight of a middle-aged woman curled up on a park bench. "Is it him?"

"Probably, but I haven't seen any gray dust on her clothes," Sam admitted.

"Her hands are unusually clean," said Dr. Mira Stratham, already leaning over the body. "There's a lingering scent of bleach too."

"What happened?" asked Jenn. "She looks perfect from here."

"Strangulation," Sam said. "You can see some of the bruising on her neck if you look close enough. I'm
betting there's more under the scarf."

Dr. Stratham nodded confirmation and continued her examination. Camera in hand, she documented every inch of the body.

"I want to bag the scarf and the hat," said Dr. Stratham. "The killer likely handled them last."

Jenn dug around in the giant satchel she'd taken to hauling about with her. Coming up with two brown paper bags, she held them open while Dr. Stratham gingerly dropped first the hat and then the scarf into the bags. The scientist's camera clicked a few more times.

Sam watched her work without comment until he noticed her entire body freeze.

"What are you seeing?" he demanded, noting that the scientist was fiddling with the focus on her camera.

"Jenn, I need tweezers and a small plastic bag," said Dr. Stratham.

Two seconds later, Jenn handed over the requested items. Working swiftly and surely, Dr. Stratham maneuvered the tweezers in between the stubby remains of the dead woman's white hair.

"Looks like he gave her a haircut," Jenn commented, "and a

bad one at that. I wonder why."

Sam waved her to silence, and she rolled her eyes at him. Together, they watched Dr. Stratham work. Soon, the scientist zipped the plastic bag closed and held it up so they could see.

"It's definitely him," she said.

Tiny, clumpy gray specks clung to the plastic.

"What is that?" called an excited female voice. "Is it important?"

"Hide that," Sam ordered. He shifted to place his body between Dr. Stratham and the reporter.

"Agent Kerman! Is this the work of the Parkside Killer?" shouted the woman.

Sergeant Bannister went to quiet the reporter and move her back from the police line.

Although he really wanted to ignore the reporter, Sam understood a day might come when he needed to be on the media's good side.

Turning to shield his lips from prying cameras, Sam said, "I'll handle the media. Keep the gray dust thing under wraps. We may want to release the information someday, but I'm not convinced he's leaving it on purpose. If we tip our hand, he could stop, and we'll have a harder time linking future cases to him."

Jenn and Dr. Stratham agreed. The key evidence disappeared into the depths of Jenn's satchel.

Wandering over to the largest gathering of media people, Sam politely informed them he had no comment yet and invited them to the press conference at the federal building at 3 o'clock. When he disentangled himself from the media hounds, Sam checked in with Officer Johnson. The man managed to get a local soup kitchen to allow him to run interviews with people on behalf of Martha.

The rest of the morning passed in a blur of interviews. The nearly endless stream of homeless people regaled Sam and Officer Johnson with tales of Martha's kindness. Most of them didn't know her last name, but one old woman said she thought it might be Reed. Around 12:30 the soup kitchen's director, Mrs. Bailey, insisted they take a short break for lunch. Sam felt guilty for taking food that could go to homeless people, but a warning look from Officer Johnson convinced him to accept the offer.

Martha Reed's life story slowly unfolded like a puzzle whose pieces first needed to be gathered through a scavenger hunt. Nobody knew where she came from. She just showed up on a bus one day. After about a year of moving from one dumpy, overpriced apartment to the next, she moved to the streets. The remaining details covered how she treated others, which was generally well, and which street corners she frequented at various points of the year. Sam's mind had started to get mushy with information overload, but he refocused himself when a nervous, mousy teenage girl plunked down in the chair opposite him.

"I think I saw him take her."

Sam sat up like a dog on alert.

"What did you see, when did you see it, and where did you see it? Do you remember the day?"

The girl shrugged.

"A guy and a van. I can't remember where exactly, but I think it was near Walnut Street over by U Penn. A week ago, maybe two. I can't remember, but it was a Thursday or a Friday. I remember because I'd scored a bed at a shelter and came to see if Martha wanted to share. She'd done me a few good turns in the past, and I wanted to return the favor. But when I was still a block away, a van pulled up, and Martha got in. At least I think it was her. It looked like her."

"Tall guy, short guy, fat, thin, muscular?" Sam fired the descriptors in rapid succession. He nearly groaned when the only answer he got was an additional shrug. "How did you see him anyway? Did he get out of the van?"

"What color was the van?" asked Officer Johnson.

The girl's eyes brightened.

"I remember that!" she exclaimed. "White. It was white."

Dutifully, Sam made a note about the van's color. The chances of it being useful in the long run were slim. Sam had seen at least four white vans this morning and he hadn't even been looking for them. He imagined that in a city this size, there would be thousands of white vans moving through.

"Did you notice anything about the van?" Sam wondered. "Were there any dents? Did you see the license plate?"

"The plate was covered in mud. Sorry."

Sam nodded and thanked the girl for her time. Any

information was good information at this point. This was the first time they knew of a definite hunting ground. Sam mentally adjusted his map of the killer's activity, adding a pin for the city of Philadelphia. He'd have to ask Officer Johnson to pull the cameras from the area for Wednesday through Friday, just to be safe.

Is this guy from Philly or was he passing through?

Chapter 16:
Deadly Disenchantment

The Killer's Lair
Undisclosed Location
Andrew Novak frowned at the wall of six large monitors. Each screen showed part of the same image. A peaceful little village sprang up in rolling green hills with fenced in sections for sheep, cows, and goats. The sheep pen was empty except for two lonely, bleating sheep. In the center, a popup box informed him that his city had been breached and his sheep had been carried off. Anger flared up in him, but he pushed it back so he could think. He knew who the culprit was without reading to the end of the message.

KingCool45. Couldn't take a hint, could ya?

He did it every day. Andrew could deal with him. When a nice "please stop plundering my sheep herds" message failed to get the desired response, he'd looked into the matter more closely. Turns out KingCool45 played every day at the same time from the same IP address, which traced back to Belcose Technical Charter School in Lansing, Michigan. That explained why Andrew's sheep herds did fine on weekends and holidays. This was probably the only game a novice hacker could slip past his school's ridiculously random filters. *Empire of Destiny* contained no blood or gore, but it did allow players to attack each other for the resources needed to strengthen their fledgling empires.

Switching over to a new computer, Andrew signed in under the false account he'd created. According to the game rules, this was considered cheating, but he didn't sweat the details. Hacking the system to create a character that had made it to the Space Expansion Age would probably put the game makers in more of a dither. It took some finagling, but Andrew managed to get the system to place his new character in the same neighborhood as his virtual bully. A few more strings of code conjured an army of clones with plasma weapons, which he promptly turned loose on the neighbors. The AI was so bad that even with grossly overpowered soldiers, he managed to lose a few battles, but Andrew made certain to handle the KingCool45 smackdown personally.

Once the king's knights had officially surrendered, Andrew plundered the gold mine. He wanted to steal back the sheep, but that would have tipped the kid off. He could use the gold to trade for sheep anyway. At least his honor had been defended. The plundering problem was a nuisance to blame on the game designers. Whose brilliant idea allowed players more than three ages apart to dwell in the same neighborhood anyway? It was a bully breeding ground. It made more sense to keep the competition close so the rewards would be useful. Somebody in the Colonial Expansion Age had relatively few uses for sheep.

Having nothing better to do on this snowy winter morning, Andrew decided to flex his hacking muscles. One needed to practice to keep skills sharp. A few quick, legal searches led him to the website for Wild Imagination Games. Andrew had heard of most of their games, but he'd only tried a few. *Empire of Destiny* was the only one that appealed to him. *Princesses and Ponies* obviously had a different target audience than him. *Pirates vs. Zombies* had been interesting for a day before boring him due to lousy graphics.

A banner along the top announced that a new game, *Cops vs. Killers*, would launch next week. After reading the description, Andrew wasn't sure what to think. The rated R game had "viewer discretion" warnings everywhere. It promised a unique experience for gamers. As the title suggested, players could create characters that were cops or killers. As a cop, they needed to gather evidence to lock up the killer, but as the killer, they could design ways to kill people. Cops earned medals and money for captures, while killers earned trophies and medals for successful kills. To be considered a "success," the killer needed to fool three cops into falsely accusing other characters of their kills.

Since the launch date loomed close, Andrew knew the game had been finished. He found the beta version and broke into the code to see how the game ticked. Killers chose the weapon, the time, the place, the victim, and the tools of the trade. Tools included everything from shovels to plastic garbage bags to gloves to duct tape. More tools meant a greater chance of getting away with the murder, but tools cost money. Rudimentary graphics would act out the kill before a text box would describe what evidence would be left behind. Then, the killer needed to wait up to three days or three accusations until they could move on to a new kill. If three people were falsely accused, the killer reaped the money and medal rewards along with a trophy for their private collection. Certain targets had greater value and risk factors.

Andrew's anger flared. The game made a mockery of murder. It cheapened the time, effort, and real-life risks he was taking to right the world. He took a break to eat a frozen lasagna. Never work angry. It was one of psycho67's rules. Andrew didn't hold to every one of his friend's rules, but that one struck him as wise.

When he returned a half-hour later, Andrew had formulated a plan. The game had to go, and the game maker had to go too. Dismantling the whole company would take more effort than Andrew wanted to expend, but if he put his mind to it, he could remove the company's founder and most of the game files. He'd kept a few toys in his virtual chest for such an occasion.

Putting off the decision on which program to unleash, Andrew spent a couple of hours researching his target: Anton Polzin. The founder and CEO of Wild Imagination Games was a Russian expatriate residing in California. Since Andrew didn't fancy a cross-country trip to exact his brand of justice, he considered other ways to hurt the man. A guy like that, whose whole life revolved around computers, would be relatively easy to reach.

After setting some of his more invasive programs to work, Andrew checked on his sister through the hospital's cameras. Mel sat alone in the cafeteria eating a sandwich. The number of times she checked her watch told Andrew it must be one of her busier days. The angle of her head suggested she was reading something. Since he didn't see a paper or a book, Andrew assumed it must be her phone. Cell phones were getting harder to hack, but the backup files kept by the phone companies were still guarded by Swiss cheese security.

Pulling up her text message log, Andrew read the agent's message about canceling their date and Mel's reply about suggesting they could work out a late night coffee instead of dinner. That message had been sent an hour ago and the agent hadn't answered yet. Mel wore her worried frown. Part of Andrew wanted to kick the agent into sending Mel a reply, but the other part of him admitted the delay was probably his fault. They should have found the South Street Lady's body by now.

A few pings told him the information mining programs were starting to bear fruit, so he closed the connections to the security cameras at Mel's hospital. The initial results were better than he'd hoped. Mr. Anton Polzin had an impressive online presence. He also had a habit of leaving his laptop on and connected to the same network as his work computers. For somebody who relied so heavily upon technology for their bread and butter, Anton was pretty lax about security. The company's cyber security impressed Andrew, but the program was crippled by incompetent application. It was the home security equivalent of locking everything down tight except the garage windows.

In a few more minutes, Anton's computer spilled its secrets. The fool had a file labeled "passwords" with most of his safe words tucked inside. It had been locked, but the password for that was a combination of his anniversary and his wife's name. His desktop background was a picture of the wedding complete with convenient time and date stamp in the upper right hand corner.

Mr. Polzin also happened to be fond of parties. His Facebook page had hundreds of pictures of Anton with various attractive women—not always his wife—at different parties. Andrew guessed that if he dug deep enough, he could find some compromising photos or videos to email Mrs. Polzin, but he didn't bother. A quick check into her showed much the same quality of a photo collection. Apparently, they enjoyed an "open" relationship. Andrew didn't understand the appeal, but he also didn't care enough to waste disapproval.

Wiping the images from his mind, Andrew got down to the business at hand. First, he found Mr. Polzin's online banking information. Next, he authorized several large scale purchases of bitcoins, traveler's checks, and gift cards. The transactions should trip the security enough to get them to freeze Mr. Polzin's accounts until they could sort the matter. It would be a nuisance to fix. He considered sending a threat to shut down the *Cops vs. Killers* game, but he doubted such a thing would be taken seriously.

How could he hurt somebody solely through the internet?

If Andrew destroyed the man's computers, he'd simply buy new ones. Anton's credit already stood on shaky ground. There wasn't much Andrew could do to make it worse. The open relationship ruled out making the wife jealous.

The answer came to him in a flash of inspiration. At first he'd lacked the funds, but after controlling Lurch's accounts he'd only lacked the inclination to hire a hitman. Spending his own money for such a thing seemed wrong, but with the codes to Anton Polzin's personal accounts, Andrew could pay for the kill with the man's own money.

Quickly accessing the bank accounts, Andrew canceled each of the transactions he'd set up. The bank's system might notice the anomaly, but their investigation would take hours to even start. Nobody would care since the problem seemed to have righted itself in a matter of minutes.

Pulling up yet another computer, Andrew accessed the Dark Web. He never used one of his usual computers for this sort of activity. After this one task, he'd scrap the laptop. He'd built it from spare parts anyway, so it wasn't much of a loss.

Anything Goes, Inc. had a sister company called Everything Dies. Their website consisted of a simple forum where one could post jobs, offer services, or bid on existing jobs. Even here, nobody ever spoke plainly. They hinted and teased and danced around the truth. That bothered Andrew, but he swallowed his distaste.

Andrew found the West Coast job opportunities and skimmed one at random to make sure he was in the right place. A woman had a tipsy, troublesome bear that kept invading her house and hurting her precious flowers. She was headed to Washington State to visit with family for the weekend, and if somebody took care of the bear before she returned, she would reward them greatly. Interested parties should click on the attachment for more details. Translation: the woman's husband beat her and her daughters when he got drunk, and she wanted somebody to off him before they returned from their vacation.

Wording the job listing took Andrew twenty minutes, but since the proposed payment was so high, he immediately received a lot of interest. He didn't recognize the names, but he thought he'd read a Dark Web article on Stinger44. The unknown hitman always stuck with "stinger" but he changed the number as jobs were completed.

The conversation quickly moved to a private area of the forum where they hashed out the details. Stinger44 promised to complete the job within 48 hours. He even agreed to no money down, which is unheard of, in exchange for some screen shots of what he would be receiving in full later. Andrew took the liberty of opening an untraceable account for Stinger44 in the Cayman Islands using a bogus credit card. They wouldn't fuss as long as real money entered the account before Monday afternoon. Andrew needed to walk the hitman through the process of claiming his payment three times, but he'd hired the man for his nerves and his gun not his computer skills.

When they concluded the business, Andrew arranged for an email to be sent automatically from a new account he created for just that purpose. The email would contain the final passwords and a reiteration of the instructions for retrieving the money. It was to be sent only if three national news outlets ran simultaneous articles reporting Anton Polzin's death. If that happened erroneously, then the man's accounts would be cleared out anyway. Andrew supposed that in itself would be a kind of justice.

With that matter accounted for, Andrew turned his talents to dealing with the offending game. Much thought led him to conclude the best course of action would be to seed the program with replicating bugs. Essentially, the game would have so many problems the makers would have to pull it to sort the mess or risk customer backlash.

If only real world problems went away as easily as virtual ones. Ruining lives from the safe anonymity of his bunker was less satisfying than hands-on murder, but it would occupy him for now. Come spring, he could get back to his personal version of cops vs. killers.

Chapter 17:
A Late Second Date

Melissa Novak's Private Residence
Hillsborough, New Jersey
I should have called.

The thought looped through Sam Kerman's head incessantly as he pulled up in front of the single family Colonial style home. Mel had shown him pictures of her place, but he'd never actually been there. Climbing out of his car, Sam ducked into the backseat to grab the supplies he'd brought. With a bag in each hand, he stared at the red door within its white frame. A lamp near the door gave off a bright, welcoming glow. The distance from the curb where Sam had parked to the door wasn't long, but it felt like miles.

Walk up to the door and knock. She'll be glad to see you.

The pep talk helped, but Sam worried about the late hour. He was taking a huge risk, and the long day plus the hour-and-a-half drive had numbed his brain. According to the GPS the ride should have taken an hour and twelve minutes, but he'd detoured to make some purchases at a grocery store.

Time's still ticking.

The reminder failed to unstick his feet from the pavement.

The distinctive sounds of a lock disengaging hit his ears a moment before the door cracked open. A dog bolted out and started barking its head off. The white streak charged at Sam who could only lift the bags high to keep them out of the dog's reach.

"Sal! Get back here!" called Melissa's exasperated voice.

Upon reaching Sam, the dog stopped abruptly and sniffed deeply. Smelling the food, the dog plopped its butt down right in Sam's path and looked up at him expectantly.

"Whatcha got there, Sal?" asked another woman's voice.

The dog got up, whined, danced around Sam, yipped, and sniffed the air from multiple angles.

Two figures appeared in the doorway. Sam squinted but couldn't tell which figure belonged to Mel. He suddenly felt ridiculous with his arms raised out to his sides like a giant scarecrow.

A brilliant flashlight beam struck Sam full in the face.

"Ouch!" he cried. Instinctively, he brought the grocery bags in front of his face to shield it.

"Stay back! We have a gun!" yelled the strange woman.

"Give me that," said Mel. The flashlight beam stopped blinding Sam, but it stayed trained on him. "Sam? Is that you?"

Sam slowly lowered the bags and blinked furiously.

"It's me," he admitted. "Sorry about the hour. I should have called, but I wanted to surprise you."

Mel laughed.

"Mission accomplished. Come on in. Don't worry about Sal, just step over him if he gets in your way."

"Sam? As in, 'The Sam'?" hissed the other woman.

"Let him in and I'll introduce you," said Mel. The words carried the essence of an eye roll.

"I'm sorry." Sam uttered the second apology as he crossed the threshold into the house, trying not to trip over Sal. "I wouldn't have come if I knew you already had company over."

"It's not a problem," Mel assured him, leading the way into the kitchen. She took the bags from him and laid them on the table before attempting introductions. "Sam, this is my friend and sister-in-law, Josie."

"Best friend," Josie corrected. She thrust a hand out to shake Sam's hand now that it was free from the groceries. "It's so nice to meet you. Mel's not gushed about a guy like this since—well, I don't think she's ever gushed about a guy like this."

Sam's face reddened.

"I do not gush," Mel protested, though her cheeks flushed as red as Sam's. She launched into the rest of the introduction. "Josie, this is Special Agent Samuel Kerman with the FBI. He's—"

"Gorgeous," interrupted Josie, thoroughly enjoying herself. She snatched back her hand which had gripped Sam's longer than necessary and headed for the bags. "Ooo, what's in here?"

Mel slipped over to Sam and greeted him with a quick kiss on the cheek.

"Sorry. This is 'sleep-deprived Josie.' She's a lot like 'raving lunatic Josie,'" Mel whispered. "She and the kids stay here when my brother pulls extra-long shifts."

"He's a firefighter, right?" Sam asked, hoping he got that fact correct.

"You want to make s'mores and hot chocolate!" Josie cried. "That is so romantic." She clutched the bag of large marshmallows to her chest and looked to Mel. "If you let him go, I'll never forgive you."

"Mellos!" cried a young voice from behind Sam.

He whirled in time to see a tiny figure stagger into the room.

Sal barked a greeting.

"Eddie! How did you get out?" Josie dropped the marshmallows onto the table and scooped up the blinking child. After planting a kiss on his ear, she added, "You little escape artist."

"Mellos!" Eddie shouted. He pointed insistently.

"We see them, Eddie," said Mel. She went to soothe the agitated dog, then looked ruefully at Sam. "I'm guessing this wasn't what you had in mind for tonight, but do you mind?" Her eyes begged Sam for understanding.

"If Agent Sam's all right with it, Eddie and I will steal a few mini-marshmallows and be on our way," said Josie. "I think I hear some bedtime stories calling our names."

Suddenly, every eye was upon Sam.

"Please," said Eddie, expertly working the toddler charm.

"I'm okay with that," Sam assured. He suppressed the urge to extend an invitation for them to join in the s'mores making. Nevertheless, he felt compelled to add, "It's Mel's house. It should be her decision."

Eddie's heart-melting gaze slid over to Mel. Sal added a whining plea on Eddie's behalf.

"You can make s'mores and hot chocolate if you want," said Mel. She glanced at the clock. "It's only eleven. Call it a precursor to breakfast, but Sam and I are going to be in whatever room you're not." This last, slow comment was directed at Josie.

"Roger that," Josie said, unable to keep from grinning. "Lemme at that chocolate, and me and my little man here will be on our way."

"First, put Sal down the basement," said Mel. "He won't like it, but I don't want him getting ahold of marshmallows then barfing them up again."

Josie made a face.

"You make a compelling argument, my friend." Josie took hold of Sal's collar. "Come on, boy, it's the basement for you."

Sal looked at Josie with sad eyes until Eddie came over and gave him a big hug.

"Bye bye," said Eddie.

The love seemed to mollify the dog.

Within ten minutes, the semi-neat kitchen looked like a tornado had blown through.

Two tornadoes, Sam mused, watching Josie and Eddie gleefully squish miniature marshmallows onto each other's noses. Eddie had enjoyed his marshmallow toasting duties too much to stop at two s'mores, so Josie reluctantly agreed to eat one. Before they knew it, six large s'mores lined the counter.

"What will we do with them all?" Mel asked, looking overwhelmed. The effort to brush a strand of dark brown hair off of her forehead only succeeded in placing a smudge of chocolate there.

Sam squared his shoulders.

"We'll just have to suffer and eat two each," he said bravely. He smiled and tapped his forehead, making eye contact with Mel.

"I have chocolate on my face, don't I?" she asked.

"Sure do," said Josie. Without warning, she attacked Mel with a warm washcloth until the bit of chocolate was removed.

Eddie yawned mightily, so Josie scooped him up.

"Guess we'll have to take a raincheck on that hot chocolate," she said. "That mess making done wore me out."

"I'll make you one anyway," said Mel. "You'll want it after you get him down to sleep."

"You know me so well," agreed Josie. She rocked her son as she spoke.

Eddie tried to rally but only managed to reposition his head and bring his sticky thumb up to his mouth.

Once the major distractions had exited, Sam helped Mel restore order to her kitchen. Together, they wiped counters, salvaged the marshmallows that could be saved, and put the excess graham crackers in plastic containers to keep them fresh. The additional, fully functional s'mores were also bagged, though Sam doubted they'd be any good by tomorrow. By the time cleanup duties ended, the milk was suitably warm to make hot chocolate with the instant packs. Weary, Sam sank onto one of the kitchen chairs and studied the giant s'more resting in front of him. Two large marshmallows had been melted over an entire chocolate bar and sandwiched between toasted graham cracker shells.

"I'm full just looking at it," he said.

"You can do it. I believe in you," said Mel. Her eyes twinkled at him as she bit into her dessert. The top cracker broke, flipped up, and hit her in the nose, which made them both chuckle. "There is no polite way to eat this."

Sam shrugged and took a huge bite of his s'more with much the same results as Mel, except that his just fell apart. They enjoyed the treat in relative silence for a while. The crunch of graham crackers seemed loud in the newfound quiet.

"Thank you for coming," said Mel, pulling Sam's thoughts out of neutral where they'd gone in the quiet moment. "This was a nice surprise."

"I wish I could have gotten here earlier. I really wanted to take you out to dinner like we'd planned, but ...." Sam let the sentence trail away. He didn't want to ruin the moment with talk of murder.

"I saw it on the news," Mel finished softly. "I caught part of the press conference between appointments." She shook her head. "That poor woman. Who would do such a thing?"

"We'll catch him," Sam promised. He was comfortable enough with Mel to let his concern show up in his features. "I just don't know how long it will take."

"Hey, why so gloomy in here?" asked Josie. "Aren't you two supposed to be tucked in a quiet corner exchanging sweet nothings by now?"

"We were discussing the murder case Sam's investigating," said Mel.

The announcement brought Josie up short.

"Ah ha. Well, quit that," she ordered, splitting a gaze evenly between the pair. "Ya can't solve it at midnight tonight anyway, so you might as well enjoy the time you have together." Spotting the third hot chocolate, Josie swept it up and breezed out of the room.

"She's right," Mel admitted. "Let's talk about something happier."

"You know about my week, so tell me about your week." Sam sat up straighter to let her know he was listening.

Mel took a long sip of hot chocolate before answering.

"Let's see. I worked, then I painted, then I worked, then I removed the paint and repainted, and that about brings us to now." She gave him a crooked smile to let him know her week had been fine.

"I forgot you were still painting. I meant to help with that," said Sam. "Do you still have more to do? I can come back next Saturday."

"With an offer like that, I'll make sure to save you some painting," Mel commented.

"Great." Sam caught sight of the clock and drank about half his hot chocolate in a few quick gulps. "I should get going. There's a small chance I might end up in the office tomorrow."

Mel hesitated a fraction of a second as she too absorbed the time.

"You can stay if you want," she offered. "The couch is suitable for sleeping as long as you clear it of toys first."

Sam wanted to accept the offer, but his sister would freak out if he failed to return to the apartment tonight.

"I'd like that, but unfortunately, my kid sister's crashing at my apartment these days. If I skip curfew she'll sic the national guard on my tail." Sam rose and took his half empty mug over to the sink. He poured the excess down the drain and rinsed out the mug.

"Don't worry about cleanup," said Mel. She stood, clutching her mug.

Closing the space between them, Sam took her mug and placed it on the counter to his right. Then, he used his hold on her arm to draw her into a hug. She smelled like shampoo and chocolate. Sam enjoyed the odd mixture.

Mel shifted, and Sam let her break the light hold he had on

her. He wanted to hang on and kiss her, but he didn't want to scare her off by moving too quickly. As he fought his instincts, Mel leaned up and planted a light kiss on his lips.

"Thanks again for coming," she whispered.

Sam's heart soared and his thoughts dwelt on Mel the entire drive home, but somehow, he made it back to his apartment in one piece.

Chapter 18:
Tools of the Trade

The Killer's Lair
Undisclosed Location
Day 4: Mid-morning.
It's lonely without the South Street Lady. I've never held a captive that long. She was with me well over a week. I never thought myself desperate for human contact. I'm usually comfortable with the company I keep online. Keeping captives is more work and far more dangerous than killing strangers from afar or swooping down on the unworthy like a bird of prey, only to leave their corpses behind.

The game maker is dead. Stinger44 was as good as his reputation. Guess he'll be stinger45 or greater the next time I contract him. There will be a next time. Murder from afar is less satisfying than carrying out the sentence oneself, but it's also more convenient. It opens a world of possibilities too. I am only one man. I cannot be in every state or country. This could extend my mission beyond the confines of this physical location. With enough planning, I could even extend the mission years into the future. It would only take enough bank accounts and people willing to work as stinger44 did. The situation's somewhat unique in that the man who needed killing had enough money to tempt a professional. Unfortunately, not everybody who needs to die has that kind of money to redirect.

I may need to post these sooner than expected. Always thought blogs were for teenagers and losers, but they do allow information to be shared quickly. The world needs to have my knowledge, though in all fairness I cannot claim to be the source of everything. Much of what I know, I owe to my good friend, psycho67. I'm not sure if he studied criminal justice, watches too many movies, or has tried these things himself, but the lessons I have tested are sound.

Killing is hard work, and it takes a lot of forethought to do it right. I broke the rule about not killing someone I know with Lurch, but I should be sufficiently removed from him to get away with it. One should never enter the prospect of killing lightly. Those who do it on a whim are the fools lining the prison cells.

Killing is also expensive. I've built up enough legitimate income to sustain myself while I work, but I can see why many choose to tolerate the slights of the unworthy. I've been fortunate enough to have skills that can earn money without the need for an office job.

Killing also takes a lot of stuff. My stockpiles will need to be extended should I wish to keep people alive longer. People are a lot of work. Keeping them fed, sheltered, watered, and cleansed is an endless, thankless task. I've built up a solid collection of canned goods over time. I never went to the same grocery store twice on that errand. Army surplus stores are great for MREs. Meals-ready-to-eat may not be the best food in the world, but they probably last the longest. I recommend them for long campaigns. There's no point to keeping people alive for long, unless you want something from somebody else or need to be around people.

Ransom's always a tricky business. Don't even try it if your goal is to ease the innocent to the afterlife or take out the trash.

I got lucky with the South Street Lady in that she was content to not make much noise or conversation. From what I read on the Kill Street Info forum, this is not always the case. A lot of guys have the misfortune of picking up screamers and whiners. I don't understand them, the guys who choose to keep people like that alive as long as they do.

What are the tools of the trade? To answer that question well, one must understand the needs of a killer.

Restraints: Duct tape is strong, but the sticky nature of it easily takes pieces of anything that touches it. This makes them evidence gold mines. Zip ties are easier to break out of, but there's less risk of leaving part of oneself behind after handling them. They can also be used easily with gloves, not so with duct tape. I'm glad I tested this theory before trying it in the field. Handcuffs work better than zip ties if one can remember to wipe them down. The surface picks up fingerprints easily. Rope has gone out of style, but it's easier than zip ties or handcuffs for restraining feet. Tape's probably stronger, but rope is slightly less likely to preserve DNA for investigators.

Means of control: My knowledge here is fairly rudimentary. Drugs such as ketamine and GHB have their uses, but they're not much good to me in a capture. I tend to use them to control captives already obtained. To use them during a capture requires far too much public exposure. Stun guns are better for actually subduing someone, but they require a lot more privacy. Lies and stories are actually the best means of control. Innocent and unworthy alike tend to want to help a stranger in need. This method's becoming harder to accomplish because self-absorption seems on the rise, but it still works.

Obtaining prescription and illicit drugs must be done slowly. Never be stupid enough to have it mailed directly to your base of operations. Post office boxes were made for this sort of thing. In fact, the amount of packages delivered directly should be limited. Delivery people keep busy, but they also have eyes and ears and mouths to spill what they've seen and heard.

Isolation's the key. Somehow, the target must be lured to a place they can be controlled.

Psycho67 says threats are useful, especially when dealing with small groups. Nobody wants to be responsible for harm befalling a friend or family member. That's ingrained in us.

Weapons: I've not gotten to test everything yet. That's my major project for this year, but I'm taking a short break to let things settle and to gather my resources for the spring and summer pushes. Knives are messier than they're worth. They're very personal and pretty satisfying, but they're not my first choice. Handguns are cold and impersonal. They get high marks for efficiency, medium for being personal, and low for satisfaction. Hands are very personal, but killing with one's hands is too risky. You have to be far stronger than the target, and the cops are getting better at capturing fingerprints. Blunt objects are effective but less personal than knives. To be most effective, they require an ambush. Sniper rifles require a lot of skill. Hunting rifles require a moderate amount of skill, but are very impersonal. Ideally, kills should be personal, efficient, and satisfying.

Cleaning supplies: Death is a messy and smelly business. Plastic sheets, garbage bags, paper towels, fresh wipes, and bleach ought to be staples on one's supply list. If buying an excessive amount of these items, consider frequenting several stores and spreading out types of items purchased. Never use a rewards card for a specific store as these are used to track your buying habits.

Clothes: Where possible, long sleeves and sturdy pants like jeans are preferable. People fight back. Normal fingernails become weapons when people are desperate. Carry spare clothes and blankets.

Vehicles: I use a white van, but vehicle choice is a highly personal thing. Vans are good because they give one room to work. The back can be kept relatively clean and covered in plastic. If one sticks a paint can or two in the back, the plastic can even look legitimate. There's a forum topic devoted to personal vehicles. I don't remember every response, but most of us have large vehicles. That's just a matter of practicality.

Dedication: Understand this will be a physically demanding job. One must be physically fit and relatively agile. There's a lot of lifting and fighting involved.

Anchor: Have a reason for what you do. Psycho67 calls the motive an anchor. A healthy mind is important when entering such weighty work. From time to time, one needs to remind themselves what they're fighting for. There's good in the world, very little of it but it's there. That's worth fighting for. An anchor can be an object or an idea, but mine is a person. I imagine it's harder to have an anchor that's a person because it means she can't appreciate the work being done for her. If my anchor were an idea, I would be the only one who has to know.

Speaking of my anchor, she continues to correspond with the FBI agent. I'm no longer certain this is a good thing. His investigation has been spinning wheels to nowhere thus far, but they recently formed a task force. That means more agents, which increases their chances of succeeding. I won't let that happen, even if it means hurting my anchor.

Only cause an excess of pain when they deserve it. There are times you'll need to attack an innocent person either to confuse the police or because they unwittingly become collateral. If it becomes about the pain, you've lost your focus.

Killing is lonely but honest work. We are called to a higher purpose than the masses. The general population will look down their long noses and condemn the work as evil. They will continue to lie, cheat, and steal in legal ways while they murder each other in their hearts.

Don't be like them.

Chapter 19:
A Mountain of Evidence

FBI Laboratory
Marine Corps Base Quantico
Quantico, Virginia

Sam let his eyes sweep the massive building that had just swallowed him. It felt great to be back on the base, but he'd never had cause to wander the FBI Laboratory before. His first stint here had been as a Marine sniper in another lifetime. His second major visit had been roughly four years earlier to attend the FBI Training Academy. This time, he was a suited guest, which made him feel old. Before he could get too depressed, a young man with short, dark hair waved at him.

Striding over briskly, the man thrust his right hand forward for Sam to shake. The white lab coat bore a nameplate that read Nikhil Kumar.

"Welcome, Agent Kerman," said the scientist. His slight Indian accent gave the words a sense of urgency. "I am glad to meet you. Jennifer has told me much about you. I am Dr. Nikhil Kumar, a criminalist here at the lab. I am to give you a brief tour of the facilities and an overview of the evidence for your report."

Sam confirmed his identity with a nod and concentrated on not crushing the man's hand. The warmth in the man's voice when he spoke of Jenn made Sam look at him in a different light. He knew Jenn had visited the lab several times during the course of her work for Dr. Stratham, but she'd never mentioned anybody in particular.

Dr. Kumar led Sam on a swift trek through half a dozen long corridors. As they passed labs with specific specialties, the scientist gave Sam a brief overview of the kind of work that went on there. Some spaces looked more like a mechanical garage, while others resembled kitchens or a tinker's workshop. Still other rooms possessed the stereotypical feel of chemistry or biology labs. Their ultimate destination, the lab Dr. Kumar worked from, was one of the smaller labs that gave off a definite chemistry vibe. The sharp odor of disinfectant tainted the cool air.

"Where is everybody?" Sam wondered, surprised to find the lab empty.

"Many people are at lunch right now, but I arranged for the space to be clear for your visit," Dr. Kumar explained. "I wanted to lay everything out and didn't want to have chain of custody problems."

"Good thinking," Sam complimented. It couldn't hurt to be on the man's good side, seeing as his case would have a large forensic component to it. "Show me what you've got."

"My colleagues and I started with the John Doe case. We labeled each bag and took swab samples of the organic matter found inside," explained the scientist. He gestured to a lab table holding the plastic bags that had once held pieces of the Bradford County John Doe. "We have a solid DNA profile for your victim, but that won't help you unless you can find samples linking to a missing person."

"Did you find any hair or fibers that don't belong with the body?" Sam asked, drawing heavily from his limited knowledge of forensic lingo.

"A few," confirmed Dr. Kumar. He picked up a tiny vial containing some hairs. "There was not enough skin to get any DNA, but microscope analysis tells us it is canine."

"Does that help?" Sam inquired. His hopes had risen with the news that there were other hairs and fallen when told the hairs came from a dog. They already knew dogs—or some other large animal—were involved from the bite marks and missing pieces of their victim.

"One never knows what will help until the case is solved," replied the scientist with a philosophical shrug. "That is why we study everything." Dr. Kumar picked up a plastic bag containing one of the bags found in the park. "The killer is not as clever as he thinks. He wore gloves much of the time when handling these, but this one contains a partial print."

"Did you run it through AFIS?" Sam tried to keep his hopes from rising this time. The Automated Fingerprint Identification System stored a vast number of full and partial fingerprints both from known offenders and unsolved crimes.

"Yes, Dr. Stratham insisted we follow every lead possible," assured Dr. Kumar. "But the only match we got was from a gun used to kill two gang members in Trenton about a year ago."

The news surprised Sam.

"Our killer offed some gang members?" Sam didn't really expect an answer. He was simply airing thoughts. "That doesn't fit with the rest of this." He waved at the room as a whole.

"I can only speak for what the evidence tells me," said the scientist. "The nails used to fix the bags to the trees were standard 2-inch round head nails."

Sam winced.

"Probably bought and sold in every hardware store in the country," he muttered.

"Yes, but they may still bring down your killer."

"How so?"

"He held some of them between his teeth," reported Dr. Kumar, looking very pleased.

The emotional roller coaster brought Sam up to a peak. He silently pleaded with the scientist to tell him they had the killer's DNA.

"We have his DNA."

Sam let the air whoosh out of his lungs.

"But you still need to give us a suspect to compare it to," the scientist cautioned.

"I will," Sam vowed. For the first time in months, he felt a genuine ray of hope warm his chest. "What else can you tell me about him?"

The next item Dr. Kumar picked up was a large, glossy photograph in a protective plastic sheet. Sam recognized the image immediately. It showed the crudely carved letters declaring that the victim had deserved his fate.

"The angle of the carvings suggests that the person who left the message was right-handed."

Sam grunted acknowledgment of the news. Ninety percent of the world's population fell into that category. He needed something better than that. DNA was great but useless until he found a suspect.

"Did you find the same DNA on the other two bodies?" he asked.

"No. The killer was more careful with those, but they are definitely linked," said Dr. Kumar. He put the photograph down and selected a large plastic bag that held three tiny plastic bags containing dark specks. "This gray substance is the same."

Each of the smaller bags had neat labels indicating where it came from. The scientist returned the bag to the lab bench and picked up a manila folder. Holding it out for Sam he explained.

"This contains a chemical analysis of the gray substance obtained at each site."

Sam opened the folder and saw a graph with squiggly lines that meant little to him. It looked like a terribly erratic heartbeat monitor readout. Sifting through the multiple graphs, he noted that the strange pattern was repeated in each sample. The pattern itself meant nothing to him, but he understood the significance of it being the same.

"What is it?" he wondered.

"I don't know yet," admitted Dr. Kumar. "I can tell you what it contains, but it does not match any known substance we've tested before."

Another dead end.

Suppressing a sigh, Sam handed the file folder back. Having solid evidence to tie the three cases together was good, but the unknown nature of that substance limited its usefulness. He felt like he hadn't accomplished anything in the six months since bodies started showing up in Pennsylvania state parks.

The killer had gone quiet again. The first two bodies dropped in relatively quick succession. A couple of quiet months followed until the woman was found on the University of Pennsylvania campus. Now another couple of quiet months had passed. The busy lab had even caught up to the copious amounts of evidence left at each scene.

"Do you have any guesses for what it might be?" asked Sam, trying to mask his desperation.

"I do not like to guess at things like this, but I will think on the matter," said the scientist.

"Call me right away if anything occurs to you." Sam pulled out one of his cards, scribbled his cell phone number on the back, and gave it to the scientist. "Is there a number I can reach you at?"

"I will give you a card before you leave," promised the scientist.

They moved down to the next lab bench and examined the evidence array for the second victim.

Haley Doherty.

The woman's name echoed in Sam's head. He made it a point to keep the victim's identities fresh in his mind. He wanted to remember they were once people with hopes, dreams, and families who mourned their loss.

"Did the bullets tell you anything useful?" Sam's cynical side doubted it, but he had to ask.

Dr. Kumar shook his head.

"They were too damaged for most types of analysis, and they yielded no fingerprints. However, the weight and size suggests they are 9mm bullets."

I hate this guy.

"Common nails, common bullets," Sam muttered.

Couldn't he have the decency to use custom made, one-of-a-kind bullets with his name etched on the side?

The thought prompted another question from Sam.

"What about the card he left with the second victim?"

"It again tells us he is right-handed, but there was not enough written down to generate a profile."

This time Sam didn't quite manage to hold the sigh in.

The reaction prompted a sympathetic smile from the scientist.

"The third victim was unique in several ways," said Dr. Kumar. "For one thing, she had traces of the gray substance embedded in her hair."

"What does that mean?"

"I'm not sure, but whatever it is, it transfers very easily. The distribution pattern suggests she had it on her hands, but the killer cleaned those pretty thoroughly." The scientist hesitated.

"Go on," Sam prompted.

"I am merely speculating," he said, clearly uncomfortable

with doing so. "The attention the killer gave to her hands suggests she may have wounded him, probably by scratching. We scraped under her nails anyway, but the results were inconclusive."

A mental image of the strangled homeless woman came to Sam. He hoped her scratches had left scars he could find. It gave him a small sense of satisfaction to suspect the woman named Martha had fought back.

Dr. Kumar walked Sam through the rest of the evidence, but nothing new and exciting popped out. When the presentation ended, the scientist retrieved one of his cards for Sam and escorted him back to his car. They shook hands again, and Sam got on the road back to Philly. He wasn't looking forward to the three hour drive, but at least it would give him time to digest everything he had learned at the lab.

His suspect profile was still ridiculously vague. They were looking for a right-handed man who was reasonably fit. Sam assumed that much from the amount of lifting required. Martha had not been a small woman, and the ME had clearly concluded she was long dead before being moved to that bench. The threat delivered to the FBI office told him the man knew his way around computers or at least worked very closely with somebody who did.

We have your DNA.

Sam wasn't naïve enough to believe that would solve everything, but he knew it could go a long way in getting a conviction once they caught the monster.

Chapter 20:
Complicated Capture

Ricketts Glen State Park
Columbia County, Pennsylvania

Irritation filled Andrew Novak from the bottom of his hiking boots to the tips of his ears. The instructions had been crystal clear: private party at a cabin in the woods, come thirsty and come alone, just the three of you. Half the irritation was aimed inward. He should have known the frat boys would bring an army of sycophants with them. Rules didn't apply to them. Now, instead of three targets, he had twenty or more.

The spiked keg of beer he'd left wouldn't go far among so many. The GHB dose spread so thin would probably just make them dizzy. He hadn't put a lot in to begin with because of the dangerous potential of the combination. His plans would be ruined if the boys slipped into a coma and died in their sleep. That would be too nice. They deserved much worse.

Flipping to another of the five cameras he'd installed in the cabin, Andrew noticed the college crowd had come with a full arsenal of booze. The situation could be salvaged. He just needed to wait. Many of them would drink themselves into a stupor long before morning.

Noticing Matthew Nelson and Jacob Tieber huddled in a quiet corner, Andrew found the camera nearest them and restored the sound. To minimize confusion, he had kept all cameras defaulted to mute, but he wanted to hear what they had to say since they were two of the primary targets.

"When's your buddy gonna show up?" Matt Nelson asked.

"I don't know. I've never met him," replied Jake.

"You've never met him?" Matt echoed, looking shocked.

"I met him online playing *Hordes and Heroes*," Jake explained. "We got to talking, and he said the cabin was free this weekend if I wanted to meet up. Said if I brought a friend or two to a private party I wouldn't regret it. What's the big deal?"

Matt shrugged, but he didn't look happy.

"It's just strange he wasn't here to meet us."

"Relax, man. Go get a drink. Grab a girl. Have some fun," said Jake. "The blond that came with Tammie has been eyeing you."

Andrew muted the sound. He didn't want to listen to stupid boys give each other posturing pep talks. Besides, he needed to think. The kit he kept in the van had a decent stash of drugs these children might find fun. They probably knew how much their bodies could take, but it might knock out a few of them. How would he get the drugs to the kids? Which would be better, rohypnol or ketamine? He wanted whichever one would be less dangerous if mixed with GHB. Accidental overdoses would detract from his message.

Pondering the delivery question, Andrew tucked the iPad into the backpack at his feet and trotted through the woods to his van. If the party got too loud, the neighbors might complain. Although he doubted the rangers would care enough to investigate a noise complaint, the sooner things got settled, the better. They might not even have somebody in the office this time of night. Nevertheless, Andrew was glad he had chosen to conduct this operation in winter as the clothes provided better cover.

When he saw the stash in person, Andrew chose the ketamine pills. Special K would appeal to them. He also donned a ski mask and scribbled a short message on a notecard explaining the gift. Sneaking close to the cabin wouldn't be a problem, but he hoped none of the partygoers decided on some fresh air at the wrong time. Before he could shut the door, the stun gun and Taser caught his eye. He pocketed both, grateful to be wearing cargo pants.

As he reached to shut the door, another container caught his attention. The small canister was marked "helium" but in reality, it contained fentanyl gas. He'd bought it on a whim from a buddy on the Dark Web. It had been an impulse buy and possible gift for psycho67. At the time, Andrew had thought of it as a very expensive gag gift, since psycho67 often complained about needing a captive audience to be taken seriously.

Hauling the canister to the cabin would be a lot of work, but it would take care of his people problem. His research on the stuff said it could kill but he only needed them out for a few minutes while he moved the guilty to a secondary location. Then, he'd open the window and doors and dispatch help for the innocent. If a few of them died, they would be considered acceptable losses and sacrifices for the cause.

Liking this new plan, Andrew unloaded the hand cart from the back and strapped the canister in place. Next, he exchanged the ski mask for a gas mask. Finally, he worked his way around to one of the back rooms. Loud music pounded through the cabin, but Andrew didn't mind at the moment. The noise gave him enough cover to wrestle the canister in through a back window. After jamming the door shut, he looped the hose down under the door and unscrewed the valve to create a slow exit for the gas. It hissed, but he knew nobody would hear. Climbing back out the window he had entered, he looped around to the main door and waited. He wished he'd brought the police baton with him, but a sturdy branch would do. He waited, holding a large stick like a samurai sword, ready to clobber the next person through that door.

Nobody came.

A few thuds and cries of dismay emanated through the door. Muffled curses and moans somehow made it to his ears on a wave of tuneless music. He counted to sixty then opened the front door. Even with the door wide open, Andrew hesitated. The branch would be useless in close quarters, so he dropped it by the door and cautiously entered the cabin. An iPhone sat on a little pedestal attached to some portable speakers and continued filling the air with poisonous noise. Andrew's head started to hurt now that the door didn't shield him. Drawing his gun, he shot the phone. The screen shattered into dozens of satisfying shards, and the kinetic force knocked it back several feet before it hit a wall and dropped like a stone.

Blessed silence fell.

Andrew gazed around at his handiwork.

"Hey! What's happening?" asked a girl. Her head flopped right and she fell asleep before Andrew needed to consider a response.

A few people stirred, but most were out cold. Spotting his quarry, Andrew quickly zip tied Matt, Jake, and Todd Clements and moved them one-by-one out the door. The fresh air would hopefully revive them soon. He hadn't left them in the gas long. The boy nearest the door stirred, so Andrew kicked him over onto his stomach and secured his hands behind his back. Putting them in a recovery position would increase the chances of survival, but Andrew figured nature would decide who lived and who died at this point. He helped by opening each window then returning to the back room to shut off the gas. Since he didn't feel like lugging it back, Andrew decided to give the law enforcement people a break and leave the canister. He knew enough to wipe down the handle and sides. He couldn't make things too easy on them.

By the time he finished wiping the container free of fingerprints, Andrew expected his three main captives would be ready to move. To his dismay, they were still unconscious. One boy, Todd, hardly seemed to seemed to have a pulse. The van might have a shot of adrenaline that could help—or give them heart attacks, but Andrew didn't want to leave them. He glanced nervously at the cabin. What if one of the other college kids woke up before Andrew could move his captives? Putting a bullet into each of them would be the safest course of action, but he refused to give up on his main plan so easily.

Lightly slapping their cheeks, sprinkling water on their faces, and rubbing their bound hands got no response.

Footsteps approached.

Andrew drew his gun and ducked into the shadows created by the light spilling from the doorway. He didn't want to take out the elderly ranger, but he couldn't get caught either. Spotting the branch lying next to his captives, Andrew holstered the gun and dove for the branch.

"What the—" was as far as the ranger got before Andrew's stick slammed into his head. The man collapsed like a sack of thrown laundry, but he was still conscious and grabbed his bleeding head. The next blow caught him across the shoulders, finishing the job of flattening him. He lay still.

Time seemed to speed up. Andrew would have to move quickly. Racing to his van, he leapt inside and maneuvered the vehicle as close to the cabin as possible. Then, he rolled his targets down to the van as swiftly as possible. The zip ties kept limbs from flopping about, but hauling the three college boys still gave Andrew a great workout. He left the ranger where he'd fallen. The man was too bulky to move. As long as he stayed unconscious while Andrew worked, no reason existed to kill him.

After slamming the van door shut on his cargo, Andrew retrieved his backpack and used the ranger's cell phone to dial 911. When that failed, he took the phone with him. He'd call from the road. He needed a new park anyway. This one would have cops crawling everywhere in a few hours, and Andrew's remaining plan could not be rushed. Due to unforeseen circumstances, he might even have to wait a day to deliver justice. Broad daylight heightened the excitement and danger.

A brief stop at the secondary site allowed Andrew to pick up the supplies he had brought to finish the job. Perhaps he didn't need another park. Pennsylvania was a very large state with a lot of open land. Really, the only requirements Andrew had in a new location were privacy and space. The idea of a mountain seized his mind and wouldn't let go.

Pulling over, Andrew checked on his prisoners. Since he would need to go to Benton for a decent Wi-Fi connection, he added more zip ties to the captives' wrists, bound their feet with ropes, stuck gags in their mouths, and threw thin, opaque black hoods over their heads. The harsh treatment plus the earlier chemical assault might kill one of them, but Andrew played the odds that at least one would survive to help him make his next statement. For good measure, he handcuffed their bound wrists to the rings he'd had installed at various points around the van. Finally, he tucked his gas mask and other tools of the trade into the chest making up the long bench seat behind the driver's seat. A heavy duty lock would keep the goods locked inside. He doubted the boys would have the energy to make mischief, but his kit had too many secret weapons to take chances.

As he climbed back into the driver's seat, Andrew planned the rest of his day. He would track down breakfast first. Not many places would be open for a few hours, but if he parked in a diner lot, he'd probably find working Wi-Fi he could commandeer. He would spend the morning checking on various internet business, such as finding a great location to off the trio. In the afternoon he would find a quiet place to feed and care for his cargo. At night, they would all attend to the main event.

Chapter 21:
Explosive Statement

Red Rock Mountain
Luzerne County, Pennsylvania

The sun set shortly after 7 o'clock, but Andrew waited until after midnight to begin his final preparations. The day hadn't gone exactly as planned, but he enjoyed it. Supply stores were plentiful, so he bought a new jacket, camouflage pants, three new backpacks, a couple of flashlights, a popup tent, and a better hunting knife. He also stocked up on water and food suitable for taking on a trail. The grizzled old man who had sold him the supplies asked how long he intended to be hiking, but he didn't press when Andrew gave a vague reply.

The surviving boys had protested and complained until trained properly to behave better. After seeing Jake, the alpha dog, zapped a few times with the stun gun, the other young man became a model prisoner. Unfortunately, Todd never woke up. Andrew would need to think of a special place to display him. In a way, Todd deserved to die slightly less than the other two, so Andrew wasn't too upset about the easier end he'd received.

Although it slowed their progress, Andrew forced the boys to carry the supplies with the backpacks strapped to their chests so he had a clear shot at them with the Taser at all times. They only passed one couple along the hiking trail, but Andrew spotted them with enough time to warn his charges. If they tried anything more than friendly nods, they would die along with the others. Upon instruction, the boys set down the packs and sat down to eat some energy bars. Andrew spent the brief break sipping from a water bottle and keeping one hand on his gun. For that minute, the boys held the power of life and death in their hands. One plea for help, and the other hikers' fates would be sealed.

They spent the latter half of the day hiking up Red Rock Mountain, then sat on a flat area to enjoy the view. The sunset had been spectacular. In truth, any one part of the land could look bleak if one looked close enough. Distance gave the view a magical makeover. One no longer saw individual trees but a patchy blanket of brown and green.

Leaving the boys unbound for the ascent had been a calculated risk, but Andrew kept the Taser and handgun close. Both young men wore only the thin, long-sleeved T-shirts they'd sported at the cabin party the previous night. The thin material would be useless against the Taser's sharp prongs. The mountain air chilled them, but once they were moving, the exercise warmed them up.

Worn out, the boys threw down the packs at the first opportunity. After a quick meal of tuna fish packets and crackers, Andrew told the boys to get some sleep. He helped them with that by slipping some GBH into their water bottles. By the time they woke up and shook off the drug's effect, Andrew had applied new gags and bound their hands and feet again. He'd arranged a blanket around them in case somebody joined them on the mountain tonight. Most people had sense enough to get off the mountain before nightfall, but Andrew tried to anticipate and head off possible complications.

Throughout the day, the young men had fired questions, most of which Andrew ignored. As his preparations neared completion, he decided to enlighten them. He moved them inside the popup tent and woke them by smashing the police baton into their shins. They thrashed and screamed into the gags, but quickly ceased when they realized the hopelessness of their situation.

"Please pay attention," said Andrew. He propped one of the flashlights on a backpack containing food so that it shone like a spotlight on the two prisoners. "If you want answers to your earlier questions, I'll need a promise that you won't scream for help when I remove the gag. You're going to die tonight. How long the process lasts is up to you. Nod if you understand."

Despite receiving two nods, the anger in Jake's eyes told Andrew he'd be trouble. Taking out the stun gun, Andrew reached for Jake's gag and prepared for anything. When the boy tried to head-butt Andrew, he simply moved the stun gun into position and let the kid bash his head on the metal piece. The urge to flip the switch and put a few million volts through the boy nearly overwhelmed Andrew, but he resisted the temptation. He left Jake to moan and looked hard at Matt.

"Do you want to have a civilized conversation?" he asked the young man.

Matt's nod was cautious, and he kept his head very still as Andrew removed the gag.

"Good. What would you like to know first?"

"Why?" the kid croaked.

Andrew held an untainted water bottle to Matt's lips and checked the time. His watch read 1:34. This would have to be a very quick conversation. There was still much to do.

"Maria Becerra," Andrew answered.

The kid's eyes widened.

"We were never convicted," he protested.

"Are you guilty?" The question was conversational.

"It wasn't my idea, man," Matt said. "I tried to stop them."

"Did you attack that girl?"

"No! We barely touched her." Matt swallowed hard, as his confidence melted under Andrew's stare. "Okay, Jake might have stolen a kiss and tried to feel her up, but she liked it. We were all drunk, even her. You can't blame us for that. She was hot."

"She was sixteen," said Andrew.

"We didn't know that!" Matt shouted. Frustration made him bold. "It's not like we check chicks' licenses when they want to party with us. She looked twenty-something."

"What happened next?" Andrew knew the answer, but he still wanted to know what Matt would say about it.

"I left to get another drink," Matt said sullenly. "When I returned, she was screaming her head off and clutching her shirt closed. Jake was trying to calm her down. I figured they were having a spat, so I gave them some privacy."

"You left the girl alone with him." Andrew's flat tone made his disapproval clear.

"He's my friend. What was I supposed to do?"

"Help her."

"You weren't there, man," Matt snapped. "So don't lecture me on right and wrong. How about you? Kidnapping's gotta be ten times worse than anything we did." When Andrew failed to respond, the kid continued in a firm tone. "I didn't touch her. I don't deserve this. If you have a problem with Jake, take it up with him. Leave me out of it."

Andrew gave the young man a hard stare, then put the gag back into place.

"I believe you," he said.

Drawing his gun, he smashed it into Matt's head, knocking the kid over. Next, Andrew grabbed the blanket and threw it over him. Finally, he stood, wrapped the gun in a towel, and shot the boy three times through the blanket. Even with the makeshift silencer, the gunshots sounded loud in his ears. Jake started screaming obscenities into the gag, but Andrew ignored him. Even if people heard the shots, nobody would do anything yet. When Jake started to stand, Andrew picked up the baton and gave his shins another solid smack. Tears of pain fell down Jake's face.
His features looked ghostly in the flashlight beam.

"Your time will come," Andrew promised, "but you don't get to exit so easily." He cast a glance over to the backpack holding the fireworks he'd brought for the occasion. "Shall I start with the Black Cats or the Roman Candles?"

Jake's eyes bulged.

"Would you like to say any last words?" Andrew wasn't sure why he was giving the kid one more chance to talk civilly.

The boy nodded like a bobble head.

"Too bad," said Andrew. "But I have something to do first. Enjoy your last few minutes of life."

Remembering his ritual, Andrew settled on the ground and scratched off the three lottery tickets he'd brought with him. He'd pulled them from his stash earlier in the week. Even if he won, he probably couldn't turn them in as it had been over a year since they were issued, but they fit the occasion. The Four Star Fifties ticket had been a July 4th special from a few years ago.

The rules were simple. In Game One, if the player's area had four star symbols, the player won $50 automatically. In Game Two, the player needed to match an amount three times to win that prize. A star there would mean an automatic win for the amount shown, a double-star symbol would mean double the prize, a three-star symbol translated to triple winnings, and a four-star symbol resulted in quadrupled prize winnings.

"If you win, I set off the entire stash at once and you go up in a glorious blaze that will likely kill you quickly," Andrew explained. "If I lose, I divide them differently to drag the process out."

Jake's breaths huffed out in labored gasps.

"I'm rooting for a win," said Andrew. "You have three chances, one for each of the tickets. Since your friends are dead, I figured you deserve the three chances. I'll even do you one better. If we win on two tickets, I give you more GHB before we begin. You might not feel a thing."

Sweat broke out on Jake's brow.

As he started scratching the Game One player's area, Andrew stopped and tilted his head.

"Would you like to watch?" he asked Jake.

The boy shrugged like he didn't care, but his eyes were desperate for information.

In another moment, Andrew sat next to Jake and angled the ticket so he could watch as the player's area was slowly revealed.

They lost in Game One.

They lost in Game Two.

"That happens," Andrew commented. "Can't win them all, but you still have two more chances."

Both games on the second ticket lost too.

Jake started mumbling against the gag.

"Do you want to go through with the last one?" Andrew inquired.

Jake's muffled affirmative answer didn't take much interpretation.

Andrew drew the dime down the Game One area in a cross pattern, dragging out the process. Then, he stopped and switched over to Game Two. Slowly, he drew the dime over the scratch off area. The first amount revealed was $2.00. The second amount revealed was $20.00. Andrew paused. That wasn't a good sign for Jake. The lottery game makers liked to give prizes that sort of looked like each other on losing tickets. Wanting the sense of anticipation to last longer, he switched back to Game One. The first two symbols were a firework and a star. The next two were also fireworks. Game over. They'd never get four star symbols on Game One now. Andrew dutifully scratched off the other two symbols, revealing stars.

So close, but still a loss.

Jake groaned.

Returning to Game Two, Andrew swiftly swiped his dime over the next two money amounts, revealing $10.00 and $100.00. He stopped and stared, feeling in his gut this ticket would win. Eager to find out, he furiously removed the last of the stuff hiding the numbers.

Both amounts said $2.00.

Andrew met Jake's eyes.

"This is going to be awesome," he promised.

Without further ado, Andrew dug into the backpack until he pulled out ten Roman Candles and five strings of 100 firecrackers. Casting his eyes upon Jake, Andrew tried to think which would be better: setting the firecrackers off with the Roman Candles or vice versa. Coming to a decision, he propped Jake up with the backpack containing the empty fireworks containers.

Donning surgical gloves and a ski mask, Andrew draped a string of firecrackers across Jake's lap, over each shoulder, and down each leg. He used zip ties to hold the strings in place as much as possible. Not quite satisfied with the handiwork, Andrew fixed some of the Roman Candles so they pointed into the boy's center mass.

The flashlight was moved to Matt's body so Andrew could put the food backpack outside. He had seven Roman Candles left. Taking out a small vial of hand sanitizer, Andrew emptied the contents onto Jake's head.

Knowing this part would be dangerous, he pulled on thick work gloves and arranged the long, easy-strike match box on the ground next to him. Striking a match, Andrew watched the flame a moment, mesmerized by the fire's beauty. He held the flame up in a pseudo-salute and farewell to Jake. Then, he lit the first Roman Candle in his hand and took aim.

Chapter 22:
Ten Bucks and a Dream

Melissa Novak's Private Residence
Hillsborough, New Jersey

Sam arrived at Mel's place around ten in the morning. Since he wouldn't make it to a gym today, he'd settled for a quick two-mile run on the city streets of Philadelphia. The March weather so far followed logic nobody else could understand, but today had dawned 65°F and looked like it might break 70°F before noon. The previous week had featured a mixture of rain, ice, and snow. If the weather stayed nice today, maybe he could convince Mel to take him on a running tour through her neighborhood later. Thoughts of the possibility occupied him while he waited for her to answer the doorbell.

"You look chipper," Mel noted as she swung the door open for him. She frowned at his nice jeans and preppy polo shirt. "I thought we were painting today." It had become a tradition for them as often as they could arrange mutual time off, which admittedly was quite rare.

"We are," Sam assured her. He gave an exaggerated sigh that drew both shoulders up in a semi-helpless gesture. "But my sister is still staying with me, and I was informed that I can't go meet a lady wearing painting crap." Sam let his shoulders drop to a normal level and held up the gym bag he'd dropped to the ground while he rang the doorbell. "I have everything needed in here, and a spare suit in a different bag in case I can steal you away for a nice dinner this evening."

Mel's laughter lifted Sam's mood to the clouds.

"I've got to meet your sister," she said, stepping back and waving him inside. "I like her already."

"You can keep her," Sam offered helpfully. "You said you wanted a sister."

"I wanted one when I was nine, so I could braid her hair," Mel explained. She gave him a quick hug as he swept in. "I'm guessing she's a little old for that."

"She still sleeps in Hello Kitty pajamas, so you never know," Sam said. He headed for the bathroom to change but stopped a step into the kitchen when a tiny figure dressed as Spiderman materialized before him.

"Who are you?" demanded the miniature Spiderman. Hands on hips, chest puffed out, and head held high, Spiderman regarded Sam with wide eyes.

"Eddie, mind your manners," said a woman's voice from the direction of the refrigerator. "Sorry, Sam," called the voice. Josie appeared behind Spiderman and nudged the boy aside. "You can ignore us. This isn't a weekend we were scheduled to be here, but Josh wanted to fish with some buddies. Can I offer you some of Mel's eggs or blueberry pancakes?"

The wonderful smell of coffee wrapped around Sam.

"Do you have some extra coffee?" he asked.

"Of course," Josie confirmed. "How do you take it?"

"Who are—" Eddie's question cut off abruptly as his mother's hand clamped over his mouth.

"Any way it comes," Sam answered honestly. "Between the Marines and the FBI, I'm pretty sure I can drink anything called coffee."

"I'll take one too if you're making it," said Mel. "You know how I like my coffee, and somehow you always make it better than I do."

"Yes, I can press that Keurig button so much better than you can," said Josie. "Here, while I make your wimpy coffee—extra cream and a pound of sugar—you're on Spiderman duty." She picked Eddie up from behind and plopped him in her friend's arms.

"I'm Spiderman!" Eddie declared.

Sam felt there was no other sane answer except to agree, so

he nodded.

"You're a mess," said Mel. She carried Eddie over to the sink and picked up a damp washcloth. "Sam, you can go change if you want. As soon as I get this near him, he's going to scream bloody murder." Her eyes twinkled at him. "Run while you can."

"Good idea." Taking the out, Sam fled to the bathroom.

Eddie's screams could be heard through the thin walls, but it was nice not to have to face the toddler's wrath in person. In less than a minute, Sam changed into painting-appropriate clothes. The faded, hole-filled gym shorts had followed him since freshman year of college, and the T-shirt had been a fair freebie from back when time actually allowed him to take in such things. The bright yellow shirt bore two dots for eyes, a squiggle for a nose, and a slash for a mouth. According to Jenn, it made him look like a grumpy version of the sun. Other paint jobs had given the face some added character. He idly wondered what color would decorate it today.

After running a comb through his short hair, Sam ran his hands under cold water and rinsed his face. The face staring back at him looked ridiculously happy for someone who'd given up half their weekend to paint walls. It would be great. Mel's attire and haphazard hair bun declared she would be right beside him. If the day proceeded as planned, this would be the most consecutive time ever spent in each other's presence as the previous two painting dates had ended about midday.

By the time Sam returned to the kitchen for his coffee, the cleansing ordeal had passed, and Eddie sat in the family room in front of the TV.

"I'm going to take him for a walk soon, but Sal deserves his own walk first," explained Josie, handing Sam a cup of coffee. "I put a little sugar and milk in it, but you can always add more." She waved to the table where a container of milk and another of sugar waited to be useful.

Sam's brows jumped slightly.

Noticing the reaction, Mel picked up and expanded on the explanation.

"Since the start of the renovations—"

"Otherwise known as forever," Josie interjected.

Mel shot her friend a dirty look but shrugged agreement.

"It's been a while," she admitted. "Poor Sal's been

experiencing more of the basement and backyard exiles than he's used to. Josie wants to walk him alone for once." Peeking into the family room to check on Spiderman, Mel added, "The show should keep his attention while we work. Carley had a long night and should sleep a while yet. We'll just have to break often to make sure Spiderman doesn't find trouble."

"He's very good at that," said Josie.

The morning painting session went well, despite the distraction of Eddie-watching duty. Mel's prediction of the show holding the boy's attention turned out to be false. As soon as he realized what they were doing, Eddie wanted to help paint. Mel dug up some clothes Eddie had sort of outgrown and changed him into them before consenting to let him near the walls. Sam knew they'd probably have to redo any section Eddie touched, but the sight of the boy's delight made the extra work a small price to pay.

Eddie never got his morning walk, but he had a blast "helping" with the painting. He almost got Sal into the game, but Mel intercepted him as he approached the dog with paint-covered hands. The calming green color looked great on the walls, but Sam doubted the dog would appreciate a new color. Josie and Sal retreated to the family room to stay out of the way.

Lunch consisted of homemade pizza. Everybody had a fine time making a mess.

Afterwards, Eddie and Sal were gated into the family room while Josie cleaned up and Mel and Sam got back to work.

"We're going to the park," Josie announced, upon finishing the cleanup chore. "Just me, the boys, and my baby. Be very jealous. You two will be here completely alone. Can you handle that?"

"Yes, Josie. We're big kids now," Mel replied with a half-smile.

"You sure you don't need a chaperone?" Josie wondered. She looked to Sam. "That face is dangerous."

Predictably, he felt hot blood rush to his face.

"Go away," Mel ordered her friend. She tried to avoid looking at Sam, but couldn't help it.

They both sighed when silence stole over the house.

"Does she ... always have that much energy?" Sam asked carefully. He dipped his paint roller into the pan to begin covering the tiny Eddie handprints dominating the lower quarter of the wall they were working on.

"Just about," said Mel. "I think this might be a medium energy day. Full energy and she'd be vacuuming, dusting, or spraying every visible surface with disinfectant. I try to snag her on full-energy days. Saves me the trouble of hiring a maid." Mel grinned to let him know she was kidding.

"How did you two meet?" Sam inquired.

"She grew up three houses down from us," said Mel. She paused her painting to deliver the rest of the story. "Her parents divorced around the time a heart attack took my father, so we sort of clung to each other for support. She's three years younger than me and two years older than my brothers, so she fit right in."

"Thanks for sharing." Sam's phone emitted an old-fashioned ring before he could say more. Frowning, he made sure his right hand was currently paint-free before checking the caller's identity. The phone read: Hatcher. Sam involuntarily straightened his shoulders and quickly stooped to put the paint roller down.

"What's wrong?" Mel asked.

Sam shrugged to indicate that he didn't know yet. He hesitated only a second more, knowing the call would change his afternoon plans drastically.

He had a job to do. Accepting that fact, Sam took the call.

"Agent Kerman," he said crisply.

"Drop whatever you're doing and get on the road," Hatcher ordered, not bothering with pleasantries. "We've got three bodies at two drop sites today. Dr. Stratham and Jennifer will head to Red Rock Mountain to inspect that scene. I need you to meet the secondary team at World's End State Park. I'll text you the address."

"Yes, sir." Sam wasn't sure his boss heard the acknowledgment before the call disconnected.

"There's another body," Mel stated. Paint from her neglected roller started to drip onto her left hand. Dropping the roller into the pan, she hastily wiped her hands on her shirt.

"More than one," Sam said, still trying to absorb the fact.

Mel tried to mask her disappointment, but Sam could see it in her lovely blue eyes.

"Guess you're leaving then," she said. "Better go change into that suit you brought. I'll fix you a coffee for the road."

Finding no fault with the plan, Sam dashed out to his Camry

and grabbed his other bag. Since this one always held a suit and rarely left his car, it wouldn't be the freshest thing he ever wore, but it would be more appropriate than his painting gear. He changed quickly. As he knotted the tie, a gentle knock sounded on the bathroom door.

"Come in," he called.

Mel entered and slipped something into his right jacket pocket.

"Thanks for coming by today. This is just a small thank you. I've been meaning to give it to you for a while but kept forgetting."

Their eyes met in the mirror.

"My father used to say you can do anything with ten bucks and a dream. He used to give us lottery tickets for special occasions. Guess it sort of rubbed off on me." Mel encircled Sam's waist with her arms and rested her head on his back for a moment. "Be safe out there, agent. I'm just getting used to having you around."

Sam turned and gave her a quick kiss. The soft words sank into his soul and infused him with a new protective instinct. He needed to catch the bad guy because people like Mel shouldn't have to share the free world with murdering wackos.

"I'll be careful," he promised. "And I'll try to call later."

Chapter 23:
High Dump

World's End State Park
Sullivan County, Pennsylvania
Roughly three and a half hours after leaving Mel's place, Sam stood under one of several thousand trees in World's End State Park staring up at a body. This one was male, and he didn't look light. Sam wondered if that meant the killer had the upper body strength of a bear or if he was smart enough to haul some sort of winch about with him.

"Didn't think I'd get so lucky," muttered Ranger Douglas Palmer. He kept his eyes trained on the body hanging twenty feet above them from the lowest branch of a red maple tree. "You want me to get him down now?"

"How are you going to do that?" Sam asked.

"Got some gear in my truck that will help me climb the tree," explained the ranger. "When I get up there, guess I'll just cut him loose."

"You can't do that," said Sam, not having much of a better plan in mind. Besides sounding disrespectful to the dead guy, his boss would not be happy about letting a body freefall to the ground. Dr. Stratham and the Sullivan County medical examiner would yell too. "Do you have a ladder that will reach that high?"

"Nope."

"How about a really long rope?"

"What for?" asked the ranger.

"He got up there somehow," said Sam. "We need to get him down in a similar way. I need to try and preserve the evidence."

Ranger Palmer grunted and trudged away, presumably headed to the parking lot for the rope Sam requested. While he waited, Sam focused his attention on the ground. Jenn would scold for not doing that sooner. Taking out his work phone, Sam snapped several pictures of the tree and the surrounding ground.

Although no expert on reading the ground, Sam could tell someone had hauled a hand truck through the area. The warm weather and some rain this week had softened the ground, leaving muddy gashes where the wheels had gouged the earth. Several shoeprints could be seen, but none of them looked useful. Mud must have caked the bottom of the shoes—or boots. About the only thing Sam could guess was that they belonged to a man due to the size.

Why did the killer move the body this far in?

The distance to the parking lot probably amounted to only a few hundred feet, but most of the other body dumps in state parks had been much closer to the parking areas. This park had thicker forests than some of the others. The killer had spent a lot of effort to make sure the casual observer wouldn't discover the body. One needed to have started the Double Run Nature Trail, and even then, they would need to look left and up at just the right moment. Hearing the ranger's return footsteps, Sam decided to pose the question to him.

"How did you find the body?"

"Anonymous tip," answered Ranger Palmer.

"What did it say?" Sam pressed. He was pleased to see the ranger returning with a large coil of rope draped over his shoulder like a bandolier.

"Gave the coordinates and told us to take a look," replied the ranger. He wore a climbing harness and carried a serious-looking grappling hook. "I was on patrol, so I accepted the task." He stopped at the bottom of the tree and pulled on climbing gloves. "We find all kinds of stuff from tips like that, but mostly, it's guilty tourists telling us where their trash can be found."

"Can I help?" Sam asked.

"Not right now, but I'll need you later," said the ranger. He looped the end of the skinny rope through the hole on the end of the grappling hook and tied it off.

Sam stepped back as the ranger swung the rope around in tight circles. It took him three tries, but finally, the grappling hook looped a few times around the branch and held fast to the rope. The ranger climbed the tree and scooted out to where the body hung.

"I'm going to tie him to the new line then cut the old one," said Ranger Palmer. "When he gets close enough, I need you to grab his legs and lay him out flat."

In fits and spurts, the body descended from on high. As instructed, Sam reached up and grabbed the stiff legs, easing the body down as gently as possible. His stomach started roiling as he looked into the unnaturally glassy eyes. He had to curl his gloved hands into fists to avoid tampering with the body by closing its eyes. Trying not to look, Sam snapped a few pictures in case he had to answer questions later about the body's condition. The ranger joined him a moment later.

"You need to do anything before I take it to the coroner's office?" Ranger Palmer had thrown the grappling hook down once it was no longer needed. Stooping, he gathered it up and started coiling the rope again.

"Won't the sheriff want to send an investigator?" Sam wondered.

"Doc Graham already has the autopsy set up for tomorrow. She extends a cordial invitation for you to attend, and I think one of the sheriff's deputies will be there too."

"Do you know the coroner?" Sam wondered, picking up on the familiarity and casual shift in the man's word choice.

The ranger's head dipped to confirm the connection.

"Doc Graham's not the coroner. She's a semi-retired ME from New York City. County's got a case-by-case contract with her for doing autopsies." The ranger finished coiling the rope, looped it over his shoulders again, and stood. "She's also my mother-in-law."

"Ah, that explains the move to Pennsylvania," said Sam.

"Wendy—that's my wife—is one of the coroner's assistants. The coroner is my cousin, Joe Fisher. If you hadn't guessed, the entire county's sort of a sprawling small town. I drew body transport duty because I'm an authorized assistant too. Besides, most of the rest of the crew's over in Luzerne helping the Ricketts Glen people."

"I see. I'll be over there later today," Sam remarked. The talk of small towns prompted another question. "Do you recognize him?"

Up close, Sam could tell he'd been young and made dead fairly recently. Aside from the trauma caused by the ropes, the body hardly bore any marks. He supposed the kid could have suffocated from hanging by the neck, but the bruising there didn't look bad enough. The neck seemed too well-attached to be broken.

"No. He's not from around here," said the ranger. Without belaboring the point, the ranger strode off. "I'll go grab a tarp so we can move the body."

Sam wanted to rip the gloves off his hands, but he kept them on longer to check the man's pockets for identification. He found nothing, which meant that the killer had probably emptied the pockets first. Maybe Jenn and her magic people could conjure prints from the inside pockets. Sam could use a break like that.

He didn't like this turn of events. As he drove here, Hatcher kept Sam updated on the team's progress since cell service in the middle of state parks could be spotty. He'd sent T.J. Newhouse to Red Rock Mountain and Adana Okiro to a cabin with fifteen possible witnesses at nearby Ricketts Glen State Park. Sam was under orders to join Adana when he finished here, but Hatcher told him to check in first. Depending on how quickly he could get done, Adana might not be at the cabin. She would follow the victims to Bloomsburg Hospital, a forty-minute drive south of the park. Sam was eager to read their reports.

Something told him, this ambitious move on the killer's part marked a turning point. Real answers were close at hand. He could almost taste them burning in the back of his throat. This latest murder spree was gutsy in the extreme. With fifteen possible witnesses, there had to be someone who remembered something useful about the killer.

How did he control them?

Before he could ponder the question, Ranger Palmer arrived with a blue tarp. As reverently as possible, Sam and Palmer transferred the body to the tarp. Sam felt weird about being a temporary pall bearer, but he carried his end of the body with as much dignity as he could muster.

We'll find you answers, kid.

Looking at the young man's face made Sam sad. He appeared to be a year or two younger than Jenn. The shine had long since worn off the murder case. Now, Sam just wanted it over. The longer it dragged on, the higher the body count soared. The man had doubled the bodies in one night. That spoke of planned acceleration or the workings of an unraveling mind. Sam wasn't sure which would be worse.

Chapter 24:
Changing Luck

Geisinger Bloomsburg Hospital
Bloomsburg, Pennsylvania

The dashboard clock read 8:08 as Sam Kerman pulled into the parking lot at Bloomsburg Hospital. A frustrated groan escaped him upon spotting the media vans camped outside the doors. Before exiting his car, he drank half the coffee he'd bought to see him through the night. It was part of the reason for his tardiness. The drive from Mel's to the hanging body rolled him right through the lunch hours, and he'd needed to eat and call her before heading to the hospital. He couldn't say much about the case, but hearing Mel's voice had done him good.

A second coffee for Agent Okiro waited patiently in the other cup holder. She would have to settle for cold coffee later when he managed to smuggle it in. He couldn't bring it in now because it would send entirely the wrong message to the public if the media people caught him strolling in late with coffee.

Deciding she might have some good ideas for getting him into the building unseen, Sam called Adana. She directed him around back to an employee entrance where a kindly nurse waited to let him in. The woman looked delighted to be part of the subterfuge. For a moment, Sam found her cheery attitude odd, but then, he figured one would have to wear good cheer like armor at a place like this. After quick introductions, the woman updated Sam as she led him through the brightly lit corridors.

"Agent Okiro is currently meeting with the victims' families. She's promised to hold a press conference after that, which is why most of the reporters have stuck around."

Sam felt sorely out of the loop. The three-minute conversation with T.J. Newhouse had left him with more questions than answers. Two bodies had been found in a popup tent atop Red Rock Mountain. One was shot three times in roughly the same pattern as the killer's second official victim. The other had been systematically blown apart with fireworks. Sam had considered the strangulation of the homeless woman heartless. He couldn't quite define what he should call this latest brutal attack. Adana had been too busy to answer his call, so he was walking into this meeting blind.

"Will I get a chance to talk to Agent Okiro before the press conference?" Sam wondered.

"I don't know, sir," replied the nurse. She halted so suddenly Sam nearly stepped into her. A hand flew to her forehead. "Oh, dear me, I almost forgot!" Her hands frantically searched the pockets of her scrubs until she came up with a neatly folded piece of paper. "Here, she wanted you to have this."

Sam thanked her and wasted no time opening the paper. It held a series of notes in Adana's neat, spare script.

Quick Update:
- Unknown gas used on 23 victims, age range 17-23.
- Results: All lost consciousness. 4 died. 5 in intensive care. 3 missing, presumed dead.
- Missing 3 = key (Matthew Nelson, Jacob Tieber, Todd Clements); background checks and interviews ordered
- Ranger Scott Harvey knocked out at the scene – interview completed
- Interviews with surviving victims under way
- Parkside Killer? – unknown link, but likely same perp

Feeling slightly less lost, Sam tucked the note away and waved for the nurse to lead on. Wishing him luck, she left him outside a door marked Executive Conference Room C. Slipping inside took a second, and orienting himself took several more seconds.

Adana sat at the far end of the table with a notebook and a pen in front of her. Every seat around the table was occupied by upset people. Additional people huddled in tight groups around each chair, giving Sam an idea as to who belonged to which family. Expressions ranged from vacant to angry, but the raw wound in every eye was consistent throughout the crowd. Conversation had ceased when Sam entered, but then several people spoke at once. Adana stood and waved to capture most of the crowd's attention.

"This is Special Agent Kerman," Adana introduced. "He's part of the task force that will investigate last night's incident."

"What are you doing here?" demanded a man. Murmurs of assent rose around him, so he raised his voice accordingly. "You should be out there finding out who killed my boy!"

"Jeff, please! We don't know he's dead," said the woman seated in front of the belligerent man.

"I know this is hard for you, for everyone." Adana paused to sweep a compassionate gaze over everyone in the room. Her voice had a gentle, irresistible quality to it. "But the more information you can give us, the sooner we can figure out why your loved ones were targeted. That in turn will tell us more about the person or persons responsible and lead to an arrest."

"Shouldn't bother arresting the—" began the man called Jeff.

"What's being done to catch this guy?" interrupted a different man. This one stood next to Adana, looming over her seated form.

Adana and Sam exchanged a quick look. He quietly signaled for her to continue. They couldn't legally tell the victims' family much, but the interviews would go much smoother if they could gain some trust.

"Our first task is to conduct interviews with each victim and relevant family members," Adana explained. "It would help if you all gave some thought as to a possible motive here. Also, we'll need as much information as you can give about where and when you last spoke with your loved one."

"Can we see them?" asked a woman.

The desperation in her voice told Sam she was likely mother to one of the kids in intensive care.

"That's not my call, ma'am," Adana said gently, "but we will coordinate with the hospital staff to get you information as soon as it's available."

"What should we do?" inquired the woman sitting in front of Jeff. She sounded lost. "Our son is still missing."

"Agent Newhouse will be scheduling interviews," Adana informed the people. "I suggest you sign up for a timeslot and then go to a waiting area or the cafeteria and try to rest for a while. Priority will be given to families with missing children so we can locate the individuals as soon as possible. Mrs. Tieber, you can begin. Speak with Agent Newhouse when we conclude here."

Sam knew Adana was aware of the three additional bodies, but she obviously wanted to break that news in private, so he let her handle the parents as she wished. A wave of pity washed over him as he saw the sparks of hope fighting for life behind Mrs. Tieber's eyes. Nobody he knew actually liked next-of-kin notifications, but cases like this could shake even the most stoic veterans. Telling anybody of a loved one's passing would be hard, he supposed, but this was infinitely worse because the deaths were sudden, violent, and involved young adult children.

The press conference sounded much the same as the debriefing with the parents, and Sam fulfilled much the same role. He stood back and lent quiet support as Adana fielded questions. When subtly directed, he stepped forward and delivered a few sound bites assuring the public that the FBI would put their full effort behind bringing the killer to justice.

The two hours following the press conference were earmarked for family interviews. Sam and Adana handled the Tieber interview together. The kindly nurse who had met Sam at the door, Patricia Anderson, waited outside the door to take a cheek swab from both Mr. and Mrs. Tieber. Before she came in, Adana explained the necessity.

"I have bad news, and there's no way to ease into it," she began. "Three bodies were found at locations near the cabin where the attack took place last night."

"Why weren't we told this before?" Mr. Tieber asked.

"Because this needed to be a private conversation," Adana said, unfazed by the man's cold tone. "I'd like Nurse Anderson to take a cheek swab for DNA comparison."

The small bit of color in Mrs. Tieber's cheeks drained away.

"What happened?" Her question was barely audible.

"We're going to find that out, ma'am," Sam promised the distraught woman.

"Just spit it out," grumbled Mr. Tieber.

"The body we think is your son's experienced some trauma," Adana said, putting the grim situation as delicately as possible.

Mrs. Tieber looked beyond worried.

"This isn't happening. This isn't happening," she mumbled, gripping her head hard. She slumped against her husband.

Sam sprang up and called in the nurse who recognized the signs of shock and had the men stretch Mrs. Tieber out on the examining table.

"She'll need to rest a while," the nurse reported, once the initial excitement died down. "Try again in a half-hour."

Names and faces started to blur, but Sam took copious notes during the interviews so he could keep his facts straight. The other two families were informed of the three bodies found. Based on the descriptions he received from them, the boy shot on Red Rock Mountain was Matthew Nelson and the one he'd lowered from a tree this afternoon was Todd Clements. He gave them the information to contact the medical facilities holding the bodies.

By the time Sam made it back to his car, mental and emotional energy levels skimmed rock bottom. Sitting in the driver's seat, he ripped off the tie and wrestled out of the suit jacket. As he moved to fling it onto the passenger seat, Sam felt something stiff in the right pocket. A moment later, he pulled out a lottery ticket and remembered Mel slipping it into his pocket as thanks for sacrificing Saturday to paint with her. He held the ticket tight in both hands and tried to imagine Mel holding that same ticket.

Still not ready to tackle the two-hour drive home yet, Sam turned on the overhead light, dug out a quarter, read the game rules, and started scratching off the ticket. He didn't play scratch off lottery tickets much, but he knew the basic gist. Wild Card Winnings had two columns, one for the Dealer and one for the Player. If the player's two-card hand beat the dealer's two-card hand in any round, they won the prize associated with that round. If the player's hand revealed a "wild" card, they won the prize automatically. If the player's hand revealed two "wild" cards, they won all ten prizes.

Top prize was ten million dollars. Sam idly wondered if he'd quit the FBI upon winning that much money.

Lacking the energy to even let those dreams go far, Sam swiped his quarter over the prize boxes first. Since the first three prizes were $5000, $500, and $250 respectively, he doubted he had a winning hand on any of those rounds. He confirmed this by scratching off the player's hand and the dealer's hand. His first round looked good with a queen and a five, but the dealer had two aces. As the game continued, Sam found his spirits lifting as his competitive nature got into the game.

He lost on every single game, but he didn't feel bad about it. It had been fun to dream big for a moment.

As he moved to fling the card aside, the sight of his hands made him freeze. The tips of his fingers were nearly black. Speckles of gray dust floated down from the ticket onto his lap. He blinked and watched another few flakes fall. Plucking up a few of the specks, Sam held them close and squinted down at them. His slow breaths sent a few tumbling from his hand. As the significance sank in, Sam frantically searched for something to hold them in. Remembering the medical gloves he kept in the car, Sam reached into his glove compartment and found the Ziploc bag of gloves. Dumping out the gloves, Sam gathered as many of the specks as he could and funneled them into the bag. For good measure, he placed the whole ticket inside.

Holding up the bag containing his precious discovery, Sam experienced several emotions. Elation and caution clashed within him. If he was right, the investigation had just leapt a few lightyears ahead of where it had been. He didn't even consider being wrong. His gut was rarely wrong when it felt like this, twisted tight with anticipation.

"Got you," he whispered, reaching for his phone.

Chapter 25:
Guild Power

Dr. Nikhil Kumar's Apartment
Stafford Courthouse, Virginia

The cheerful sounds of an incoming call roused Nikhil Kumar from a deep sleep. He glared at the phone then quickly snatched it off the end table so it wouldn't wake his wife. Struggling free of the sheets and blankets, he glanced at the screen on his way to the bathroom where he could turn on some lights. The caller ID showed him a number but no name. The phone also showed him the time which was just after midnight. Trying not to slam the bathroom door, he accepted the call.

"Hello?" he mumbled.

"I'm sorry to call so late, Dr. Kumar," a male voice said quickly.

"Who is this?" Nikhil asked.

"It's Sam Kerman with the FBI. We met a few weeks back when you showed me the evidence from my case."

"Parkside Killer," Nikhil said, as his brain awoke enough to make connections. He pictured the eager young agent and wondered why the man sounded so excited.

"Don't think the name will fit much longer," said the agent in a rush. "I found it!"

Found what?

"What can I do for you, agent?" Nikhil asked, trying to get the man to focus.

"The gray dust. I think it's from a scratch off lottery ticket. If I'm right, it's the scratch off stuff itself. It gets everywhere."

The announcement blasted through the weariness clinging to Nikhil. His mind started churning through everything he knew about lottery tickets, which wasn't much. He'd never bought a ticket in his life, but once in a while, he'd get one as a gift.

"Can you test it tomorrow?"

It took a second for the agent's question to sink in.

"Today, I mean," the agent corrected.

"Can you get it to me today?" Nikhil wondered.

"I'm headed to my apartment now. I'll catch a few hours of sleep then hit the road again. I can be there by nine."

"Guess I'll see you at nine," said Nikhil. He tried to hang on to caution, but the agent's enthusiasm was infectious.

Without much else to say, the men ended the call. Nikhil tried to go back to sleep, but the best he could manage was a restless dozing state. Around 4 a.m. he gave up and rose to make coffee. Turning on his computer, he checked on his *Empire of Destiny* city. With players from around the world, it wasn't unusual to see the world chat conversation lively. He watched it for a while, letting the inane banter relax him.

Thoughts of lottery tickets intruded regularly, so Nikhil started researching scratch off material. The more he learned, the less he truly knew. Chemically, he could guess at some of the elements involved in making the scratch off stuff, but he wouldn't know for sure until he could test the agent's theory.

By 10 o'clock in the morning, Nikhil had the gas chromatography results laid out next to the ones taken from each crime scene. While the expensive machine had done its business, he'd also thrown a small sample onto a glass slide and peered at the substance under several magnifications. It looked very similar to the gray dust specks found on the victims.

The agent had been right.

The readouts matched.

The agent's eyes darted anxiously among the papers then fixed on Nikhil's face, trying to read his expression. Nikhil idly wondered if the young man would explode if he didn't get answers soon.

"They match," he reported.

Agent Kerman's face lit up with delight and relief, but his expression quickly turned thoughtful.

"Does it prove anything?" asked the agent. "I mean, are they unique? Could we tell which ticket it came from?"

"I doubt it," Nikhil said, dousing some of the man's excitement. "Before you arrived, I did a little background research. The substance making up lottery scratch off material is a closely guarded secret, but I believe most states' formulas differ. I can look into that angle if you wish."

"Please do," said Agent Kerman. "I can try to get a warrant to help."

Nikhil shook his head.

"I have an easier way."

"What's that?"

"Guild power," Nikhil replied.

The agent looked baffled, so Nikhil explained.

"I'm part of an online gaming community that has a guild." Nikhil saw that the agent still appeared glassy-eyed. "Never mind. I know people who will send me lottery tickets if I ask."

Finally, Agent Kerman's expression said he understood. Some of the man's excitement returned and was replaced yet again by thoughtfulness.

"Could we appeal to the media?" he wondered. The tone said he was mostly talking to himself. "That might be faster, but it would also show our hand. This is the most unique thing we know about the killer. I don't think we should reveal it yet."

"I can make up a reason for wanting the tickets," said Nikhil, "but where should I have them sent? It won't be much of a secret if we have them mailed here."

"The Bureau keeps some P.O. Boxes for random things like this," said the agent. "I'll see if there's one in this area. If not, I'll think of a different plan. You can have them mailed to me for all I care."

Nikhil disagreed.

"Your name is linked to this investigation."

"Something will work out," said the agent. "I'll open a new box if I have to."

"Let me handle that," said Nikhil, taking pity on the man. "Nobody knows of my involvement."

Agent Kerman started to argue but changed his mind, settling for simple thanks.

"I appreciate that," said the agent. He held out his hand for Nikhil to shake. "If you need any money to track down this lead, let me know. I have some discretionary funds."

A bargain was struck, but the money didn't matter. Nikhil had heard through the rumor mill what the monster had done to those college kids. If he could help catch the guy, any price would be worth it.

As soon as the agent left, Nikhil logged on to his personal laptop and accessed the *Empire of Destiny* website. It felt weird to be doing so on work time, but this was definitely a work-related request. A plausible story formed in his head as he worked. Before he finished composing the message though, Nikhil remembered he needed a P.O. Box.

Ten minutes later, he was the proud owner of a brand new P.O. Box in Fredericksburg, Virginia. He didn't think it wise to get one in Quantico since most of the world knew it hosted the FBI lab. Fredericksburg was close, but it was also a small city, which afforded some anonymity. He'd hesitated a moment over using one of his credit cards, but the paranoia passed.

Once those details settled into place, Nikhil returned to his partially composed message and read it over a few times. Not quite satisfied, he made some tweaks and read it again.

Topic: Seeking Lottery Tickets
Hi. My mother's 75th birthday is coming up. She's a huge collector. I'd like to surprise her with scratch off lottery tickets from every state. If you can help, please mail a ticket of your choice to P.O. Box 22401-3452. Thanks! (I'll return the favor if you wish.)

After posting the message in the off-topic forum as well as the world chat box, Nikhil spent a half-hour privately messaging a few of the people he knew better and put in a personal plea. He felt bad about lying to them about his reasons but reminded himself of the end goal: catching a killer.

When only waiting remained, Nikhil decided to get back to

his normal work. As he moved to clear the gas chromatograph reports, Nikhil looked at the numbers again. The readouts were eerily similar. He'd check tickets from other states and hope they differed enough to let him conclude a match mattered. Still, if his gut instinct panned out, they now knew one more piece of information: the killer bought New Jersey Lottery tickets.

Chapter 26:
On the Prowl

Streets near the World Trade Center
Manhattan, New York City

This was it. He could feel everything click neatly into place. The late hour made yellow cabs harder to find, which in turn made Convcars more attractive. Andrew assumed the name was a lazy abbreviation for "convenient cars," but since there had been no interview for the job, he had never asked about the name. Anybody with an internet connection, a driver's license, and a name could sign up to be a Convcar driver. Apparently, one didn't even need a vehicle, as the company would happily rent you one.

Though he was loath to leave his precious van, Andrew bought a used Toyota Corolla from a private owner sight unseen. The man had balked at not meeting the intended owner, but Andrew had soothed him with an extra $200. The bum had been late to the drop off location, but the car worked as advertised. If it hadn't run, Andrew would have had to think of an appropriate punishment. That would have been annoying.

Tonight, wearing a baseball cap and some prosthetics, Andrew had picked up and dropped off several fares. None of them struck him as good targets. He needed another high profile but random target to get the media attention away from the college kids. They'd been milking the story for a week. The hype would die down soon, but Andrew knew the FBI would be looking more closely at the three boys Andrew had culled from the pack.

These young ladies would do. They wanted him to take them to some place in northern New Jersey. So the direction and distance was on his side. The late hour meant they were tired. He could hear that much in their voices as they chattered about their long day.

"Feel free to drink the water. There's more in the cooler up here." Andrew handed back a third water bottle. He silently questioned the wisdom of abducting three victims at once.

The spiked water bottles had taken him many attempts to perfect. First, he needed to find the best needle and syringe to insert the liquid GHB. Many of the ones he tried were either too big or didn't hold enough liquid. Next, he experimented with various insertion points. The best place turned out to be the bottom because he could turn the bottle over, stick the needle in, deliver the drug, and seal the hole with a dab of superglue. Most water bottles had natural ribbing that hid the work, but even that part had taken some practice.

The women politely thanked him. The blonde was an inch taller than her two companions. She seemed to be the one in charge. As she had also ordered the car, Andrew knew her name: Layla O'Malley. Only one of the girls sipped at a water, but she didn't drink much.

By the time they crossed over the George Washington Bridge into New Jersey, Andrew concluded he would have to change plans. He stuck with the prescribed GPS route while he thought. Layla could follow the route on her phone to check his progress and keep track of the time, but in his limited experience, most people never bothered.

Pulling over and forcing them to drink the tainted water would be the quickest option, but it carried a lot of risk. He needed to get rid of their phones quickly. Waiting until they got closer and hoping they drank the water on their own was safest but also unlikely to succeed. Simply driving them where he wanted to go would be foolish. They would catch on and call for help minutes after he deviated course.

Deciding to be direct, Andrew simultaneously searched for a likely spot to pull over and ran more scenarios in his head. He weighed the risk of jumping out and simply turning around. As long as he moved quickly, everything would be fine. A glance back showed him that Layla was on her phone, likely texting somebody. He drove five miles over the speed limit so he wouldn't be pulled over for speeding.

A traffic signal turned from green to yellow ahead. The stretch of road was momentarily empty. If he exited the car, the overhead light would come on. The red signal gave him an excuse to slow down. At the last moment, he swung the car onto the shoulder and slammed on the brakes. Three startled cries rang out, but Andrew ignored them. Throwing the car into park, he reached down and released his seat belt at the same time as he moved the driver's seat back into the legs of the girl sitting behind him. One of the surprised cries changed pitch to include pain.

Drawing his gun, Andrew whirled, leaned over, and shoved it into Layla's forehead.

Sometimes, he loved being ambidextrous.

"Give me your phones," he demanded.

Since Layla's phone was close, he snatched it away and tossed it onto the front passenger seat.

The young ladies were speechless.

"Phones. Now," he prompted, emphasizing the point by increasing the pressure on Layla's head.

"Do it." Layla's words could barely be heard. As she pushed past the shock, cold anger took its place.

Numbly, her two friends reluctantly handed over their phones.

"Good. Now purses." Andrew kept several phones. He wouldn't put it past these kids to keep multiple devices as well.

"You're robbing us?" asked the girl behind the passenger seat. She sounded almost hopeful.

"Quiet!" He let the order hang in the air until he had their purses piled on the passenger seat. Light from a streetlamp cast enough of a glow for him to see the girls. "Now, open the water bottles and drink them."

"Or what?" Layla challenged. Contempt entered her tone. "You'll shoot us? Right here. In your car."

Andrew had about a second to regain control of the situation, but he really didn't want to kill her in the car. He started to withdraw the gun like he was taking her words to heart. Then, he lashed out with a lightning quick blow, using the gun as a blunt force object. The strike didn't knock the woman out, but it threw her against the back seat. Andrew leaned forward and gripped her neck hard so she'd concentrate on breathing instead of talking.

"Any more questions?" he asked, directing the query to the other two women.

Trembling, they drained the water bottles.

"Help her," he ordered the woman sitting to Layla's right. He nodded toward the remaining water bottle.

The woman spilled a lot of the bottle, but some of it made it into Layla.

"Rest now," he said.

A car passing by reminded him he needed to get going again. Picking up one of the phones, he tapped the power button to reveal a preview of the messages.

The most recent read:

Layla? R u there?

Knowing the three phones probably had a dozen apps blasting their location, Andrew carefully wiped them down with his shirt and tossed them out of the car. He did the same for the phone he'd used to accept Convcar jobs. The police would find them, but that wouldn't help them catch him. The iPhone had been purchased through an online auction and delivered to a P.O. Box he'd opened solely for that purpose before letting the payment lapse. He threw the three purses onto the side of the road too. It would give the cops hope, and that would keep them busy.

Maybe he'd even arrange some bogus ransom demands. He didn't care if they got paid or not so there would be no risk of a trap. This wasn't about ransom. It was about balance. Andrew suddenly realized why it felt right to take these girls. The last three targets were young men paying for their sins. These girls would balance the scales. Nobody could claim true innocence anyway, but they would allow him to continue his experiments. He would find the best way to kill a person.

As the women drifted off into drug-induced sleep, Andrew took the car out of park and turned around. Excitement coursed through his blood. He couldn't wait to get home and begin researching again. He was also happy to have the company.

Perhaps he would break his rule about getting to know the subjects. Layla seemed like a fighter.

Would she help him?

An hour slipped by while he thought about having an apprentice. He couldn't deny the appeal of passing on his knowledge directly. Notes and blogs were good, but they lacked the satisfaction of seeing a pupil absorb and apply the lesson.

What would it take to reshape her?

He'd not considered breaking people part of his job, but it would give him something to do while he laid low. Much as he wished to carry on the noble part of his work, the investigators would be in a frenzy this week. Andrew smiled contentedly. The women would give him a real chance at answering some of his many questions about human nature.

One of them would have to die soon, but he could keep the other two for a while. He needed a body to give to the police. Otherwise, they wouldn't know he was responsible. That would be disappointing.

Chapter 27:
One Will Live

The Killer's Lair
Undisclosed Location

Since he'd stayed out so late, Andrew slept until the middle of the day. Famished, he ate two frozen meals before checking on his prisoners. He made three large peanut butter and jelly sandwiches for them, figuring they must be hungry too. At least one of them was up. He could hear her shouting for help. If he didn't enjoy such space from his neighbors, that might upset him. He imagined the screamer was Layla, but he couldn't say for sure. Loading the sandwiches and three new water bottles onto a tray, he practically skipped down the stairs to the holding cells.

A cry filled with equal parts rage and loathing hit him like a slap when the screamer caught sight of him. As he'd guessed, Layla and the screamer were one and the same.

Setting the tray down, Andrew retreated to his workroom to grab some tools. Pulling the gun belt on gave him a sense of power and authority. No wonder people became cops. Instead of extra gun clips, his belt held a vial of mace, a stun gun, and a Taser in addition to the gun holster. He didn't expect to use the gun today, but the stun gun and Taser were likely candidates, depending on how confrontational Layla wanted to make this.

"Let us out!" Layla shouted, when she saw him again. "You can't keep us like this!" She banged her fists against the bars. She was in the middle cell. "Let us go! What do you want?"

If he let her keep talking, she'd hold the whole conversation with herself. That wouldn't be fun.

"Calm down," Andrew said softly. "Eat something."

Layla looked like she'd rather spit in his face, but the other two appeared intrigued by the notion of food.

"You're him," Layla said, studying Andrew critically.

"Layla," one of her friends whispered in a warning tone. Under the bright fluorescent lights, he saw that this was the woman who'd sat behind the driver's seat. She had shiny black hair and pale skin. Puffy eyes ringed with black said she wore makeup that didn't mix well with tears.

"Who?" asked the third girl. This one had medium brown hair that fell a few inches below her shoulders. The rough sleeping conditions had matted parts of her hair into a tangled mess.

"You may tell them," Andrew said with a benevolent nod. He placed the tray in front of Layla's cell. "But are you sure you don't want to eat something first?"

"He's the Parkside Killer." Layla spat the words like they tasted bad.

Andrew winced. He'd never liked that name. It didn't fit him.

"They didn't die in a park," he said, before remembering the most recent victims. "Most of them didn't die in a park," he amended.

"You're still a murderer." Layla rubbed her head wearily.

Tilting his head curiously, Andrew watched her. He could almost see waves of hatred radiating off her, but something in her eyes had changed. He liked her eyes. They reminded him of Mel. A stab of longing hit him out of nowhere, but he brushed the feeling aside for now.

"I-I don't think I can eat that anyway," said the timid one who'd cautioned Layla. "I'm allergic to peanut butter."

"I'm sorry," Andrew said by reflex. Standing, he addressed the soft-spoken woman. "Can I get you
something else?"

"Stop it!" Layla shouted.

The vehemence startled Andrew and the remaining captives.

"Stop trying to be nice! You can't do it! You're a vicious, murderous—"

"What else do you have?" The timid one raised her voice

enough to cut off her friend's tirade.

Andrew shrugged. He wasn't used to playing chef and waiter.

"Canned soup, tuna fish, crackers. The usual stuff that lasts a while."

The girl requested tuna fish and crackers, so Andrew left them alone to go prepare it. He knew they'd start talking as soon as he stepped out of earshot. The cameras would record the conversation for later enjoyment, but he liked letting them think they had some privacy.

Round one had been intriguing and further cemented their roles in Andrew's mind. Luck would choose his apprentice, but he secretly hoped Fate selected Layla. She had a vibrant spirit Andrew very much appreciated. The timid one allergic to peanut butter was a voice of reason and a practical soul. The girl who hadn't said much might still be in shock. The other two had figured out they would never leave this place alive, though their reactions differed. Layla fought the idea, while the other one accepted it.

After delivering the food, Andrew left them again. He spent the time browsing his collection of lottery tickets, trying to find the perfect one for the first kill. Several appealed to him, but he couldn't make a decision. Something told him to go with a "fives" theme to honor the occasion. This would be his fifth major undertaking. The incident with the boys had been a lot of work, and while he enjoyed the challenge, he was happy to keep this low key for now.

Choosing High Fives, Andrew grabbed the whole roll and a few quarters. His body hummed with anticipation. The temptation to rush through the game gripped him, but he shook it off and forced his hands to release the tickets and quarters. In his mind, he'd already chosen Layla to be his apprentice, but fairness demanded he speak with the other two and give them a chance as well.

A quick check of the cameras told him they needed more time, so he played an online game for a few minutes. After ransacking a few neighbors with his grossly overpowered troops, Andrew checked to see if he had any messages from psycho67. With no new messages, he opened an older one and skimmed it. The man had been a bit of a bore lately, urging Andrew to be cautious and know exactly why he did what he did.

When the cameras told Andrew the ladies had finished

eating, he graced them with his presence again. As expected, Layla started yelling, so Andrew zapped her with the Taser. The move prompted three screams, though Layla's was short-lived. Electricity crackled through her body. It didn't knock her unconscious, but she fell over in a twitching heap, moaning. Andrew unlocked her cell long enough to remove the probes and lay her in a more comfortable position.

"Just rest," he instructed.

The other two appeared too terrified to speak.

Locking Layla's cell, Andrew made a quick trip to the workroom to grab a fresh Taser.

"What's your name?" he asked, kneeling in front of the soft-spoken woman.

"Natasha." The reply could barely be heard even in the stunned silence still dominating the atmosphere. She sat on the ground with her knees tucked close, clutching them like a teddy bear.

"Natasha what?" Andrew pressed.

"Creswell."

"That's a very nice name, Natasha," said Andrew, keeping his tone gentle. "Who's your friend?"

"Layla O'Malley."

"My mistake. I meant the other one." Andrew waved toward the brown-haired woman still staring in horror at Layla's prone form.

"Stephanie Kramer."

"What brought you to New York yesterday?" Andrew couldn't care less, but he wanted to get Natasha focused on him rather than Layla.

Her attention shifted, but she didn't answer his question.

"Was Layla right?" asked Natasha. Her tone held a childlike curiosity. "Are you the Parkside Killer? Are you going to kill us?"

"One will live," Andrew said, choosing to answer her third question.

"Tasha." The soft name came from Layla who was still flat on her back.

"Yes?" said Natasha, thinking her friend meant to catch her attention.

Andrew knew better.

"Why her?" he wondered, directing the question to the outspoken one.

"She … has a daughter," answered Layla.

Natasha gasped like her friend had doused her with icy water.

"Why should that matter?" Andrew stood to peer down at Layla. "People are either children or have children or both. They're still people. They're still evil."

"Tonya's not evil," argued Layla. "She's just a baby."

"Please." Natasha's whole body shook with the effort to contain a grief Andrew couldn't understand.

He didn't know if she was telling her friend to stop talking, pleading for her life, or thinking about her daughter.

"I want to live." This new statement came from the quiet woman, Stephanie. With Layla subdued, she became the strong one. It was fascinating to witness. Her features hardened to a businesslike coolness. "You said one of us will live. How will you choose?"

Andrew found the question irresistible.

"We're going to play a game."

The women listened quietly as Andrew explained the lottery ticket game. Leaving them to ponder the game, he ran for the supplies. By this time, Layla sat against the back wall. Stephanie and Natasha each accepted a ticket from his hand. They didn't appear pleased, but they were willing to play along. Layla crossed her arms over her chest and set her jaw.

Andrew knew what she was attempting, and he admired her for it. He still couldn't let it stand.

"You'll all die if you don't play," he said. "Them first." He let that sink in a second before applying more pressure. "And I won't be gentle."

The last statement elicited a bitter laugh from Layla.

"Is death ever gentle?"

"Play the stupid game, Layla," Stephanie snapped. "Give one of us a chance to get out of this."

Layla's stare reached directly into Andrew's soul.

"He'll never let us go, even if he lets us live," she explained wearily.

"Life is hope," said Andrew. "Nobody knows what tomorrow brings. Would not living another hour be a triumph?"

Layla considered his logic before slowly agreeing. With great effort, she stood up and crossed the cell to accept the lottery ticket.

Andrew found their manner of scratching off the tickets revealing. Layla's strokes were short and firm. Stephanie scratched furiously like her life depended upon finishing first. Natasha worked methodically from left to right across the card.

In round one and two, they all lost.

"This is impossible," muttered Stephanie, throwing down her third card in disgust.

"I lost too," Natasha said sympathetically.

Layla didn't move. She stared down at her finished card with a deep frown fixed in place. Her eyes shut, forcing a few tears out.

Andrew saw a war of wills being waged in her. He patiently waited to see what she would do.

An eternity passed.

Then, unsteadily, Layla crawled over to Natasha's cell, reached in, plucked the ticket from her friend's hands, and slipped hers in its place.

Humans were interesting creatures.

Chapter 28:
Drowning Sorrows

The Killer's Lair
Undisclosed Location
Day 5: Afternoon.

For the first time, I don't know what to do.

The third woman is gone. I drowned her in a plastic kiddie pool. That's not the issue. Layla and her remaining friend have presented me with a moral dilemma.

Before I can wrestle with that, I guess I should speak some about the drowning. This method might work well for small creatures or children, but with a grown woman it's far too much work.

As soon as Layla handed her ticket off to Natasha, I made my decision. Using the Taser, I subdued the third woman. The shock made every muscle in her seize up. She had been seated, so she didn't have far to fall, but still, she fell hard because she could not brace herself. Her head cracked on the cement floor.

From the corner of my eyes, I saw Layla and Natasha clinging to each other, weeping. Why do women weep so much? Death is a natural part of life.

To keep myself from thinking too much, I rushed into Stephanie's cell, handcuffed her wrists behind her back, and dragged her out. The other two might have been screaming. I'm not sure. I was focused on the work. Right before a kill, I get into a zone that's hard to break into or out of. It allows me to be efficient.

Since I hadn't been planning on doing the kill right then, the water wasn't ready. I realized this as I hauled Stephanie to the workroom. Even though not much time had passed, her senses were starting to return, so I put her in the dental chair, released the handcuffs, and strapped her arms down. I used duct tape on her feet. I normally avoid duct tape because it sticks to everything, but this particular woman was headed for a lot of water anyway.

Water is wonderful. It washes away so many sins.

For a second, as I crossed into the workroom, I felt what my brother must feel when holding the burden of life in his arms. It's a heavy thing.

The woman started screaming, so I gagged her with a nearby rag. I'm afraid it wasn't very clean, but she won't have to worry about getting sick from it. She continued to moan, but I don't mind moaning. It's only the high-pitched screams that hurt.

I filled the kiddie pool with water from the hose fixture I'd installed in that room. It's long enough to reach every cell. As I worked, I studied the dimensions. This particular pool is five feet in diameter and can hold about fifteen inches of water safely. If I filled it to the maximum, I could perhaps get a few more inches, but I needed to account for water displacement once the body went in. In theory, fifteen inches should be more than enough.

As the pool filled, I went to the side room and removed my belt. The Taser needed to be recharged anyway. I keep a stable of five Tasers, but I'd already used two in the last hour. I didn't want my gun or stun gun or Tasers getting near the water. I don't think water would damage a gun, but I anticipated some resistance from the victim. In such close quarters, it's better not to mix in guns unless one is fully in control.

Water can be unpredictable.

I wanted to shoot the Taser into the water to see what happened, but a reckless move like that was as likely to kill me as her. That was another reason to remove the belt carrying the Taser.

When the pool filled, I considered what I was wearing. Water had already splashed onto my boots several times by then. For a moment, I thought it would be easier without boots, but the slick floor convinced me to keep the boots. I changed to a long-sleeved T-shirt as opposed to a normal one because the sight of scars along my arms reminded me what motivated victims could do.

A great idea came to me. I had to run up to the bathroom to retrieve nail clippers, but I found some. While Stephanie's hands were immobile, I took a moment to declaw her. I should do this for all victims. It's good as a cleanup ritual, but there's less chance of letting them draw blood if it can be done first.

Her moans had changed to faint whimpers.

Our eyes met. She shut her eyes to avoid me, but we both knew the end drew near.

Releasing the straps on her left arm, I snapped the handcuffs into place. She resisted, but I had better leverage and more strength than she did. Getting her hands secured behind her would have been awkward with her sitting in the chair, so I settled for binding them in front of her. Next, I lifted her out of the chair and dropped her to the ground. Kneeling on her to keep her still while I worked, I released one half of the cuffs, flipped her over, and reapplied them.

She arched her back to hinder me, so I hit her in the head with my fist. That was a mistake. Skulls are very hard. A deep ache moved through my fingers. Angry at myself, I picked up my prize and eased her into the pool as best I could. It wasn't easy. She twisted and bucked like breaking free of my grip would save her life.

Another, more cautious, smack from me stunned her enough to let me place her in the water. She sat up, somehow managing to use the water to rid herself of the gag I'd stuffed in her mouth. Excited, I leapt into the pool. Water splashed over the tops of my boots. I knelt, holding her shoulders down. It was like trying to hold a five-foot fish dipped in grease.

At one point, she got her head above water long enough to draw a quick gasp.

Her bound legs and knees slammed into me as many times as she could bear, each time growing progressively weaker.

I don't know how long our battle lasted.

She pushed up.

I pushed down.

That loss of time is one thing I love about killing. It brings life to a standstill, makes everything more precious and real. There's nothing in the world like that rush.

And now it's over.

I haven't moved the body yet. It still floats in the kiddie pool.

The water fixed her hair. It spread out around her head like a halo. Her eyes are shut as if in sleep. Her concerns and cares no longer exist. She is at peace.

I am tired. It was a great fight, but much work remains. I need to find a suitable park or other location to return her. I suppose I could bury her here, but I've no wish to collect bodies on my land. The dogs are currently well-fed lazy things. They'll be no help. Wildlife's too unpredictable to count on for walking off with the evidence.

I could also try to hide the body forever, but that wouldn't be fair. There's no glory in an unclaimed kill.

Now I return to the Layla problem. Fortune smiled on her, but she gave the winning lottery ticket to her friend. This is pure foolishness. Where did humanity get such notions that self-sacrifice is a good thing? It's as destructive as what I do.

Do I honor her choice?

I'll be busy with arrangements for her friend for a day or two, but eventually, I must come to a decision. I admire her and want to grant her wish, but what good is it? She must know that her friend will eventually die. Why put off the inevitable?

Should I set them free in death together?

Layla would deny the dictates of Fate and Fortune. Dare I let that stand?

Does Natasha get a say in the matter? I should question her about this, but first, I need a conclusion for myself. I can force either action, whether it obeys their wishes or not. Do people given a second chance get to reject the gift held forth? Logic says, yes. By allowing them the chance to choose who dies first, do I relinquish any power, or do I gain by it?

Power must be seized and flaunted where possible.

I know just where to place my drowned friend, but she'll need to wait in the freezer until I need her.

Chapter 29:
Scratch-off Killer

FBI Field Office
Philadelphia, Pennsylvania

"How?" Special Agent in Charge Louis Hatcher's eyes were the locked-on-target, destruction-imminent sort this morning.

Randomly, Sam Kerman's mind flew back to his childhood watching a cartoon version of Peter Pan. He knew what his boss wanted, but he didn't have a satisfactory answer. If he insisted the leak wasn't him, he'd sound pathetic.

"I'm not sure, sir," he said.

A copy of the Philadelphia Inquirer sat on Hatcher's desk between them, facing Sam with the large headline: WHO IS THE SCRATCH-OFF KILLER? He'd read the article. It claimed that "a source close to the investigation" had confirmed that dust from lottery tickets had been found at multiple crime scenes.

"If I find out it's one of my people, I'll bury 'em so far in the basement their ears'll pop from the pressure," Hatcher declared. The man's nostrils flared like a bull about to charge.

"Yes, sir," said Sam. "What would you like me to do?"

Hatcher drew his hands down his face, looking more weary than angry by the time his hands reached his chin.

"Cat's out of the bag," he muttered to the air. Refocusing on Sam, he added, "We're on damage control now. You've got a 1 o'clock interview with Kim Riley."

"Should I confirm or deny?" asked Sam.

"Confirm the detail then help her appeal to the public for information," Hatcher instructed. "Meanwhile, have your people start canvassing lottery retailers in New York, New Jersey, Pennsylvania, Delaware, Washington, D.C., and Virginia."

Sam's eyes widened. The list matched the one he had prepared, but having it spoken aloud drove home the point of how futile it seemed.

"Agent Okiro will help you coordinate with the locals, but I want you to personally follow up on the best leads. Do you have any other angles to follow?" Hatcher's glare lost some of its punch, but that was the extent of his sympathy.

"Dr. Kumar at the lab has been performing some tests to narrow the search," said Sam, happy to have something to offer. "I need to check in with him."

"Good, I'll have a word with him as well, but don't be late to your interview. Anything else?"

"After the cabin incident, I put in a request for the Behavioral Science Unit to put together a profile," Sam admitted. "That should be arriving sometime today or tomorrow."

Hatcher nodded briefly.

"I'll give their SAC a call to light a fire under them. You'll have the report by the end of the day," Hatcher promised. "Is there anybody else you need me to motivate?"

Sam shook his head, unable to think of anybody else, but he liked this helpful side of his boss. As he rose to get back to work, Sam thought of one thing he needed.

"Are any of the small conference rooms free today?" asked Sam. "I'd like to make my phone calls in complete privacy."

"Check with Dawn," said Hatcher. "She'll take care of you."

Within ten minutes, Dawn Hopper arranged for Sam to take over Special Agent Emilio Vega's office. The agent was currently on vacation in the Bahamas and wouldn't need his office for the next few days. It felt strange to sit in another man's chair, but Sam soon got past the awe. He'd refrained from bothering Dr. Kumar since that frantic midnight call-to-action Saturday night, but the news article gave him an excuse to check up on the man's progress.

The scientist answered on the second ring.

"It was not me," he said, before Sam could even blurt out a greeting.

"It doesn't matter who it was at this point," Sam noted, "but it gives us a chance to do a wider appeal to the public."

"That is not necessary," said Dr. Kumar. "The last few confirmation tests are running now. I would have called you soon anyway."

"What did you find?" Sam's question came out in a rush.

"I'd rather not say until the tests are finished," said the scientist.

"If they're for confirmation, you're pretty sure of your theory," Sam pointed out with obvious impatience. Time with Jenn had taught Sam that science people loved to share their knowledge. "Tell me."

"The closest chemical match for the dust found at the crime scenes are tickets from New Hampshire, Texas, Oregon, and New Jersey," Dr. Kumar reported.

Sam's mind mentally smacked down each suggestion then seized upon the last possibility. It had to be New Jersey. He supposed someone could stock up on lottery tickets, drive down from New Hampshire or fly up from Texas, and go on a murdering spree before returning home. But easy answers tended to be right answers.

"Can you narrow it down any more?" Sam asked hopefully.

"I called lottery officials in each state. They would not confirm much, but I believe each state uses the same factory to manufacture their tickets," explained Dr. Kumar. "The four states mentioned have formulas for scratch-off material that is similar to your crime scenes. I have not checked tickets from every state, so I could not tell you these are the only ones."

"Have you checked Pennsylvania, New York, DC, Delaware, and Virginia?" Sam asked. "Those are the other likely places our killer could hale from."

"I did check those," confirmed the scientist. "No match."

After thanking the scientist profusely, Sam checked the time. He still had almost four hours before the interview, so he decided to track down Adana. The lottery ticket retailers in New Jersey would need to be canvassed, but Sam wanted to know as much about this guy as possible before they started asking questions. If they failed to ask the right question, they could miss the chance to identify their suspect. This was inherently a long shot, but the evidence showed this wasn't a casual scratch-off ticket player. He would be a regular somewhere, perhaps several places.

Somebody out there has seen this guy.

One would hope lottery ticket sellers would notice their regular customers, especially those who spent a lot of money on the games. Sam wondered if that part was true. Did the killer spend an unusual amount of money on tickets? The weight of Sam's job landed on him anew. Orders from him would change the day for many agents and policemen across the state next door. What if he was wrong?

He needed a second opinion.

Finding Adana, Sam pulled her into his temporary new digs, brought her up to date, and asked for her thoughts on the matter.

"I agree with you," she said, after letting a long, uncomfortable silence reign a while. "Somebody who plays enough that he's leaving shavings on bodies will be known to the few places he frequents."

"Can you handle the search?" Sam asked, knowing it was a monumental task.

"Yes, but I recommend using the hotline too," said Adana.

Sam made a face. When he'd been a brand new baby agent they'd stuck him on a two-month hotline tour, which translated to time listening to crazy people air conspiracy theories. The disgust had never quite worn off.

"I know it catches a lot of nonsense," said Adana, correctly reading his expression, "but it will be easier than going store to store, even if we could identify every place with a lottery license."

"I'll mention it in my interview," Sam said, letting his tone convey his reluctance.

"Surprise Ms. Riley with that news at the end," Agent Okiro suggested. "She enjoys leaving her readers with a sense of suspense and giving them a chance to help. The paper has enough readers in central and southern New Jersey to help, but I'll also create a press release to distribute tomorrow."

"Why wait?" Sam asked. They would lose a whole day on the search if they put off their public plea until tomorrow.

"Politics," Adana said succinctly.

Sam's face reddened with anger.

Adana held up a hand to delay his reaction.

"I don't like that aspect either, but it's the only reason we received an early edition of the paper they intend to run tomorrow."

"Early edition?" Sam echoed, stunned.

"Didn't you check the date?" Adana asked. She waved the papers he hadn't realized she'd been holding. One was a copy of the newspaper he'd seen earlier and the other was a plain manila folder.

"No," Sam admitted. That explained why Hatcher hadn't chewed him out completely. "Why would they send us a copy?"

"It's a common tactic. The article's vague and full of questions. They know if they ask us nicely, there's a small chance we'll make their day. It doesn't always work, but this time, it got Ms. Riley her interview with you. Speaking of which, I'm told I should prepare you for that, but first, this was faxed from DC." Adana handed Sam the manila folder.

Whipping it open, Sam skimmed the profile. Most of it he already knew: likely a white male age 28-42 with a high affinity for technology. He'd practically told them that much. A statement near the end caught his attention.

Unknown Subject is probably a compulsive gambler. He enjoys taking risks as evidenced by multiple public areas for dumping bodies. He likes games of chance, but needs a sense of control over the game. His gambling may be confined to online opportunities or lottery tickets. If the latter, he will likely buy in bulk, perhaps even purchase a whole roll. He may be using them to make decisions. I.e. Does she live or die today?

When requesting the report, Sam had not known the gambler angle. It felt good to get third party confirmation.

"Did you read this?" Sam asked Adana.

"I did," she confirmed, "and I agree with the conclusion."

Sam read on to get to that conclusion:

Unknown Subject is likely to escalate until caught. Although many serial killers are average and blend well with society, this subject exhibits a high degree of movement. If he has a day job it's either computer based or involves making deliveries that include the body sites. There's a high chance he resides within a 50-mile radius of the affected areas. He may keep an online blog or diary to anonymously gain fame for his deeds.

Head snapping up, Sam stared at Adana.

"How would we check something like that?"

"I've already set the cyber agents on the hunt," said Adana. "Jordan loaned us two agents for the task, Fritz and Keagan, and he promised to keep me informed of their progress."

Sam didn't like delegating so much, but the level of technical expertise needed for that task was far beyond him.

"All right. Let's go beat the bushes to find our gambler," he said.

Chapter 30:
The Apprentice Test

The Killer's Lair
Undisclosed Location
Day 6: Late evening.

I got so wrapped up in the latest moral questions that I forgot to give an update about getting an apprentice. Several days ago, I realized I've been going about this very wrong. My initial hope was to turn one of my captives into an apprentice, but I haven't the patience for slowly breaking down their will.

Of my current captives, only Layla would have the backbone to work for me, but her disposition is completely wrong. Worse, I think she may be religious. The cameras catch her sitting in a corner with her eyes closed muttering to herself or quietly comforting her friend. She's chosen her role as sacrifice, and I respect that. It will buy her friend a few extra days on Earth. The one to live is allergic to peanut butter, but I've enough other options to weather the inconvenience.

It's not quite time to kill Layla. It should go without saying that bodies keep better while alive. The freezer option works, but it can be troublesome, especially when one puts in a soaking-wet drowned body.

What I need is somebody who already appreciates my work and wants to help expand the cause. Normally, this process should take months or even years because rushing in will only lead to trouble. However, I have the advantage in that I already know some likely candidates from years frequenting the same forums.

Psycho67 would be my first pick, but he's not the kind of man to take orders. I need someone willing to learn and grow with me. He must be of a like mind. It amuses me that when I dig deep into the background of those who visit the Dark Web most often, I find them to be from every walk of life. Politicians and law enforcement personnel are well-represented in my world.

The Dark Web has many levels. On the surface, one finds posers and fantasy lovers, those who enjoy the thrill of pretending to indulge their darker impulses. Many "normal" people are attracted to the shadowy cyber world because it breaks up the monotony of their boring lives. A level beneath this, you will find the marketplace, which mostly attracts the shady consumers. Those wishing to buy illegal drugs or guns but who can't or won't get off their sorry behinds to hit the streets and make the proper contacts can be found here.

The third, fourth, and fifth rings down start getting more serious. This is the modern manifestation of a medieval guild, where one must prove their worth before being accepted into the fold. Everyone in the fifth ring must be sponsored by an established member. Psycho67 was my sponsor. I don't know how long he'd been a member before me. I too have sponsored a few worthy individuals, but I've not kept close contact with them.

I'm currently in the fifth ring of the Dark Web. I'm told there is a sixth and seventh ring, but I'm not privy to them. These written accounts are my application essay for the sixth ring. It's not about number of kills. It's about the thought and the appreciation for the craft.

Attracting an apprentice will be a big step forward in proving my worth. One must have a following. This isn't a problem. There are millions in the first and second levels who endorse their favorite stories. I think half the fools think them fiction. The program changes key details and names, of course, and publishes them in regions unlikely to be affected by the events. It even translates them as necessary.

What am I looking for in an apprentice?

He—or she, for now I'll keep an open mind—must have attained the fourth level of the Dark Web. This means the individual has a proven record of ending another life. That's not hard to obtain, for we allow soldiers, mercenaries, assassins, and other professionals to count their government sanctioned kills. I'm sure the other rings have people who would devote themselves to me and my work, but I haven't the time to teach a complete newcomer.

My apprentice must be loyal and willing to take orders blindly. I will not reveal myself for a prescribed time. I'm sure some of the people lurking here have hidden agendas. If he gets caught, I'll not have someone who will rush to a plea deal at my expense.

When I put out the official call several days ago detailing my requirements, I received five applications immediately. Three were worthless, not even meeting the most basic requirements. I've kept the other two to look into further. Since then, I've built up a list of seven more potential candidates. Their occupations range from secondary physical education teacher to police officer to truck driver to rich widow to barista. There's even a prison guard, a professional clown, and two taxi drivers. Many more applications were rejected because they're not working in the same area I am.

I'm inclined to trust the uniformed applicants more than the others, but these nine have earned the right to take my test. As I'm a firm believer in there being more than one right answer, I shall give them several options for passing this exam.

The FBI agent is a little dull as a nemesis, but one does not control such things. I did some research and found out a possible reason he may have drawn a case like this. He's former military. The talking heads just love their soldier boys. Women must dig them too. I'm surprised Mel has stuck around so long. Guess he's okay to look at, but she's got to be on a different plane in terms of intelligence.

Their relationship must end, but I'll handle that part myself. He's not good enough for her. Half the time he ignores her in favor of chasing me. Mel deserves a man who can give her his full attention, and treat her like a princess.

Making the lottery ticket connection was unexpected and a point in Kerman's favor, but I do not know if it was his triumph or something accomplished by the vast resources he can access. The story hasn't officially released but chatter from several news sources confirms it will break tomorrow.

The body in the freezer may need to come out soon. I'm ready to make my next statement. It's good that he does not scare easily, but I do wish he took me seriously. We're drawn together like stars locked in a gravitational embrace. If this keeps on, there will be a crash. That's why I need to get Mel away from him.

It would be lame of me to order the agent assassinated from afar, but it's fair game for the candidates to capture him. Same goes for his sister. Jennifer Kerman reminds me a bit of Mel. They both have brown hair, though Mel's has golden streaks at the tips. My sister's far more beautiful, but pictures of the young woman easily capture a wholesome goodness in her. She wears little makeup and her nose is slightly larger than it ought to be, but instead of making her awkward, they add to the earthy quality.

I may even have Mel brought to me, though I certainly wouldn't harm her. I'd like to see her. It's hard to fight so long for someone who does not know the real you.

In the interest of giving my potential apprentices options, I'll open up the field to include Special Agents Adana Okiro and T.J. Newhouse. I might even settle for dead or alive on the last two. I hesitate to mention that because people are not always bright. They may rush off in a frenzy and accidentally kill those I wish taken alive. Much as I want to see Mel in person, I'll not risk her life. Perhaps she should be barred from the first round. Once I have an established apprentice, that can be his first job for me.

I'd still like to give them five options. The Special Agent in Charge is a tempting target, but I don't wish to draw that much attention. Having them kill any random person for me would be too easy. Now, killing somebody they actually like would be an interesting test of loyalty, but such tasks are not worth mentioning at this stage.

Perhaps the wild card will be to capture one of the park rangers or sheriffs named in the reports. If I go with that, I'll need to put an age limit on this. Can't make it too easy for them. Some of the rangers and sheriffs are old men and women. I'm not against killing old people. Just because one makes it to a certain stage of life doesn't entitle them to an easy road, but I want this to be a fair competition. The FBI agents and Kerman's sister are young or at least capable of physically offering resistance. I believe the oldest agent is forty-three, so that will be my cap. If my would-be apprentice can't even find out the names of their potential targets, they don't deserve the job.

It's about time to post my official assignment. I look forward to seeing what my candidates can do. Even though I'm only offering this to nine of them, I expect with the tight deadline about half will drop out or fail. It'll be very interesting should multiple candidates pursue the same target. Perhaps I should tweak my wording about requiring the subjects alive. There can be no doubt of that being optional. These people are vying to be my helpers. The kills are mine.

Chapter 31:
Convenience Store Canvass

FBI Field Office
Philadelphia, Pennsylvania

The interview with Ms. Riley lasted much longer than Sam would have liked, but in that time, Agent Okiro pulled off an organizational miracle. SAC Hatcher loaned Adana the use of half a dozen new agents for the task. Sam didn't ask her for details since he trusted her judgment, but she reported anyway.

"I wrote the press release, then contacted the New Jersey Lottery Commission, the governor's office, the FBI offices in Trenton and Newark, and a few friends in the press. After the standard runarounds, I tapped a few favors and had the cyber agents help with posting notifications on various police forums."

"Did you fax them to the various law enforcement agencies?" Sam asked. Knowing how notorious some of the fax machines could be, he didn't think that would be possible, even if she'd started the second he stepped away for his meeting.

Adana flashed Sam an amused grin.

"There are over five hundred such agencies," she pointed out. "And nobody uses faxes anymore. I had people call the state's Association of Chiefs of Police and work from the top down. Agent Fuller warned the hotline agents to expect an influx."

"Any hits yet?" Sam wondered.

"I don't expect much until tomorrow," said Adana, "but yes, some of the quieter municipalities have checked in to say they'll dispatch officers as soon as possible."

"Great." Sam couldn't think of anything she'd forgotten. "So, what do you need me to do?"

"I thought you might want to participate in the canvass, so I mentioned that to the nearby towns and cities. We have official invitations to join officers in Cherry Hill, Haddonfield, Camden, and Deptford. Agent Newhouse is already headed to Camden, and Fuller's from Cherry Hill so she'll head there. Do you have a preference on the remaining two?"

"Not really," said Sam. "I'll take Haddonfield if you don't care either. Do you have an address for me?"

"I'll text it to you."

Sam wasn't certain of the wisdom in having his entire team pursuing this one lead, but he couldn't deny any of them the opportunity. The investigation had crawled for weeks. They needed the morale boost of actually pounding the pavement if nothing else. In the last few meetings, he'd felt their growing restlessness.

Grabbing his gear and hustling out to his car, Sam tried to hang on to the good feelings, but it was difficult. The killer's last rampage had been more disturbing than usual. Sam had lost the beginning of this week going through photographs and painstakingly piecing a timeline together for those incidents.

He thought as he drove, making use of the twenty-five minute drive.

Why those boys?

His people agreed with the initial assessment that Matthew Nelson, Jacob Tieber, and Todd Clements had been the primary targets. The college kids who had died from the gas attack simply chose the wrong party that evening. Adana dug up the information about the earlier attack that implicated the young men as assailants. Sam believed her about the connection, but he wasn't convinced a relatively small case of justice being denied would call down the killer's wrath.

The increased brutality even within that incident bothered Sam. Autopsies confirmed that Clements had died from the knockout gas, and Nelson had been shot three times. Those were tragic but normal deaths Sam expected in this line of work. He'd never heard of a case involving fireworks as the murder weapon. Who would bother? As weapons, they were as dangerous to the man wielding them as to the victim. The killer hadn't simply been murdering Tieber; he'd also been punishing the young man.

Does this guy care if he lives or dies?

Sam saw evidence for both in the series of crimes. The lottery ticket leavings seemed to be a genuine mistake. Other than that, useful physical evidence was scarce. The lack of fingerprints told him the perpetrator took some measures to avoid detection. The notes and messages said he wanted acknowledgment for his deeds.

The methods of murder varied widely. There had been a knife attack, a shooting, a strangling, and death by fireworks. This told Sam the killer wanted to experiment, but he didn't know to what end. Most killers found a method they preferred and stuck with it, changing only in small increments to improve the craft.

Inevitably, Sam's mind poked at the next logical question.

What will he try next?

***

Pit Stop Shop
Haddonfield, New Jersey

Three hours into the search, Sam was less enthusiastic about this lead, but he enjoyed the company of Officer Adam Hearn. The twenty-year veteran originally from the Bronx had never lost his accent or his instincts for being a beat cop. He took the time to know the people who crossed his path on a regular basis.

"If you're hungry and don't mind hotdogs, the ones in here are great, but skip the chili," Hearn advised.

"What's wrong with the chili?" Sam wondered. Mention of food made his stomach grumble at his neglect.

"Ahmed cooks up fresh hotdogs upon request, but I think he gets the chili in the beginning of the week and leaves it there. Most guts ain't up to that sort of workout if ya know what I mean."

"No chili, gotcha. Anything else I should avoid?" asked Sam.

"Pretzels are like cardboard in here, but they won't kill ya," Hearn reported.

"How's the coffee?"

"Not my favorite, but Ahmed keeps enough sugar packets and creamers to make it passable."

Armed with this insider information, Sam climbed out of Hearn's patrol car and made his way to the double doors. Hearn headed for the coffee station while Sam perused the hotdog selection. They looked good, but then again, anything looked juicy and wonderful when one hadn't eaten for hours. A lanky teen who looked like a younger version of the heavyset man sitting by the front cash register wrapped up four hotdogs and put them in a plastic bag for Sam.

"Do you want a fountain soda for $0.99?" asked the kid, pointing to a sign on the counter.

"No thanks," said Sam. "I'll grab a coffee in a moment. Actually, go ahead and charge me for two. I'll have what he's having." He waved over to Officer Hearn, who held up his large coffee cup so the kid could see the size.

Shrugging, the kid tallied Sam's order. Once the appropriate change was dispensed, Sam strolled over to the front counter where Hearn chatted with the store owner. The officer handed Sam a large cup of coffee filled to the brim.

"Forgot to ask if you wanted milk or sugar," said Hearn apologetically.

"This is fine, thanks," Sam replied.

Hearn handled quick introductions before jumping into their main purpose.

"Sam here is with the FBI. He's got some questions for you about your lottery customers. Do you have a moment to talk?"

The bell above the door rang, announcing the arrival of new customers. Ahmed didn't look happy with the notion of chatting with law enforcement, but he called his son over to man the counter while they stepped off to the side.

"We're not investigating you or your store, sir," Sam assured the nervous man. "The case I'm working on has a person of interest—a man—who may purchase a lot of lottery tickets. Do you have any regular customers who spend an inordinate amount on scratch-off tickets?"

The man looked at Sam like his brain was decoding a foreign language.

"Do ya know anyone who rolls up in here and drops hundreds on a single type of ticket?" asked Hearn.

Sam didn't take offense to Hearn translating for the locals. It had happened several times in their brief partnership. For the life of him, he couldn't figure out what he was saying wrong, but when Hearn said almost the exact same thing, lightbulbs flashed over people's heads.

"Ah, yes, I know such a man," said Ahmed.

A thrill ran through Sam, as it had the last twenty-two times he'd heard similar phrases. He braced for a letdown. Apparently, there were a lot of people obsessed with unloading hard-earned money on the small chance at quick riches. Most of the time, the proprietors missed the part about the tickets of interest being scratch-offs only, not the ones spit out by a machine that involved some sort of daily or bi-weekly drawing.

"What's he look like?" Hearn asked cautiously.

Ahmed's right shoulder lifted in a shrug.

"Average height, white."

"What color hair does he have? Is it long or short? Does he have any distinguishing marks? Does he buy anything else?" Sam consciously stopped the flow of questions to let the man answer.

The man squinted in concentration.

"I believe he has light hair. Short. And he usually only comes in for the tickets."

"Did you notice his eye color?" Hearn inquired.

"I am sorry," said Ahmed. "I do not remember anything else about this man."

"Does he have a favorite type of ticket?" Sam asked. "Does he come in often?" He kept mental fingers crossed that it would be a predictable pattern they could use to set a trap for the guy.

"I am sorry," Ahmed repeated, looking like he wanted to help more.

"He buys a lot of $5.00 tickets," said the younger version of the store owner.

"How many?" Hearn asked, narrowly beating Sam to the question.

The kid's shrug unconsciously mimicked his father's earlier movement.

"Unused rolls," said the kid. "They're all worth $300, so he speeds up the transaction by taking the new ones."

"Does he have a favorite day of the week or month to stop by?" Sam pressed.

Ahmed and the teenager considered the question, shrugged again, and shook their heads.

"No. He's only come by two or three times," said Ahmed.

"We remember because very few people buy tickets by the roll," said the young man.

Sam's heart leapt within him.

"Thank you," he said quickly. "You've both been very helpful." Handing over a card to each of them, Sam asked them to call if they thought of anything new.

Reaching for his phone, Sam strode with purpose toward the exit.

"Wait, sir!" called the teenager. "You forgot your hotdogs!"

Sam waved to acknowledge the news but kept on heading for the door.

"I'll take them to him," said Hearn.

Finding Adana's number, Sam put the call through then tapped his foot impatiently while it rang.

"Agent Okiro speaking."

"Adana, I need your help spreading the word," Sam said in a rush. "I've got a lead on a guy who buys tickets by the roll. That's unusual enough that the owner remembered him. Can you add that to the press report?"

"Yes, sir," Adana said, picking up on his excitement. "That would be very helpful."

"If he does this enough places, we can narrow the search," Sam continued.

"It's a big 'if,'" Adana cautioned, "but it's worth pursuing."

After hanging up with Adana, Sam's enthusiasm dropped a little, but his heart still raced.

"You think it means something?" asked Officer Hearn, handing Sam a foil-wrapped hotdog.

"I do," Sam answered.

I definitely do.

As he munched on the hotdog, Sam's gaze swept over the colorful displays in the convenience store. At some point, the killer had looked upon these same displays. He could feel it.

Chapter 32:
Calling Card

Samuel Kerman's Apartment Building
Narberth, Pennsylvania

Since dating Mel, Samuel Kerman had come to enjoy morning street runs. He wished he could see her more often, but phone calls and emails composed the bulk of their communication thanks to both their crazy jobs. This serial killer case was taking over his life, but now that they had solid leads, he didn't dare back off and risk losing the momentum.

After warmup stretches, Sam jogged down the stairs, sailed out the front door, and paused for a few last quad stretches. Force of habit made him scan the immediate vicinity. The morning sun shone down cheerfully. Part of the borough looked like a transplant from a 1950's tiny town. It made him feel good to come back to a sleepy place like this after dealing with death and destruction in the big bad city.

A figure sat on the ground leaning back against a tree, looking down at something. From the angle, Sam couldn't tell if it was a man or a woman, but he called a friendly greeting anyway. He didn't want to startle the person by barreling past in a moment. The figure said nothing in return. In this day and age, with the prevalence of earbuds, that wasn't unusual, but Sam didn't see the telltale white or black trail from ear to waist that would indicate earbuds. In another step, his senses automatically kicked into overdrive.

The figure was unnaturally still.

Sam stopped stretching and stared for a five-count. If sniper training years ago had taught him anything, it was how to wait and watch well.

No movement.

A moment of indecision seized him. The impulse to return to his apartment for his phone and gun butted up against the need to step closer and check on the figure. He delayed the decision a moment by scanning the street in both directions. Not a soul stirred. His legs brought him forward, so Sam knelt next to the body and gently checked for a pulse. The pasty complexion, blue lips, and empty eyes told him the effort would be wasted, but he had to check anyway. As his hand dropped away, his eyes fell upon the object the figure had been staring at.

He recognized it instantly.

A lottery ticket.

His breath stuck in his throat. The interview with Ms. Riley took place three days ago, and the article announcing the lottery ticket angle came out yesterday. A killer keeping close tabs on the media wasn't unusual, but one who knew his home address was highly worrisome.

"Good morning, Master Samuel," called Mrs. Heathcliff. "What have you got there?"

Sam sprang to his feet and positioned himself between his elderly neighbor and the body. He did not need her having a heart attack on him right then.

"Mrs. Heathcliff, how nice to see you," Sam said, striving desperately to keep his tone normal. "The sun's awfully hot today. Here, let me fetch your paper so you don't have to come outside." Seeing she was without glasses this morning, Sam held out hope Mrs. Heathcliff might not guess the figure leaning against the tree within twenty feet belonged to a dead body. Scooping one of the papers off the ground, Sam sprinted to the front door to complete the delivery.

"How sweet of you," said Mrs. Heathcliff.

As gently as possible, Sam herded his neighbor back inside. Crossing the threshold, they nearly crashed into Jenn who was on her way out.

"I thought you went running," Jenn commented.

"He stopped to do his civic duty," announced Mrs.

Heathcliff, beaming up at Sam.

"Jenn, go grab my things, will ya?" He flashed his sister a look that told her not to argue.

"What do you need?" Jenn asked, picking up on his tension.

"The trio will do," Sam replied, trying to lighten his tone. "I'll take Mrs. Heathcliff up to her apartment and meet you back here in a minute."

Getting Mrs. Heathcliff safely delivered into her apartment stretched Sam's patience, but he returned to the doorway as his sister stepped out onto the stoop. She stiffened upon seeing the reason for his strange behavior.

"Sam." Jenn dragged out his name. "Is that what I think it is?"

"Yeah," he replied. Gingerly, he took possession of his gun, identification badge, and cell phone. His hands were full since he didn't have any pockets. The trio definitely clashed with running shorts and a ratty T-shirt. "Do you want to check the body or call 911?"

"Body."

Sam knew she would say that, but actually hearing it still hit him with a shot of unease. The image didn't fit his memories of the annoying kid sister who used to nearly blind him by wearing pink everything.

"Fine. Stay here, try to block the door, and keep people away from the body," Sam instructed. "I'll go change and make some phone calls."

By the time Sam morphed into work mode and made it back downstairs, Jenn was fully gloved and taking pictures from every conceivable angle.

"I called Doc Mira," Jenn announced, still lining up new shots. "She's on her way."

"I know. She told me," said Sam. "She also said you found something."

Jenn straightened and let the camera hang from the neck strap. Walking over to her purse, she plucked out a plastic bag.

"Doc said I could bag and tag as long as I got good picture coverage first," said Jenn. Her steps were stiff as she made her way over to Sam. Her voice stayed steady, but the rest of her exuded anger. "I wanted a look because I saw lettering on the back of the card during one of my first shots."

Sam accepted the lottery ticket from his sister and flipped it over. Blood-red letters delivered the killer's message in all capital letters.

HER LUCK RAN OUT.
DO YOU FEEL LUCKY, AGENT?

Yes, I feel lucky because you're desperate.

"How does he know where you live?" Jenn demanded.

"I don't know," said Sam. "It's not widely known, but he could have followed me home one day." He shrugged. "I haven't exactly been taking counter surveillance measures."

"Well start," Jenn said. Her voice started out strong but hitched as she continued. "Don't you dare make me explain to mom and dad how you got yourself killed."

Sam thought about teasing her, but he could see she was shaken. Drawing her into a hug he rested his chin on her head. He didn't speak until releasing her.

"Guys like that are all talk, Jenn. Don't worry about it."

The hard look returned to her. By this time, cops, curious neighbors, and paramedics crowded the scene. Jenn leaned close so she wouldn't be overheard.

"This guy has been dropping bodies left and right for months," she hissed. "Forgive me if I think he's a little more than talk."

"I'll be careful," Sam promised, knowing he wasn't going to win the argument.

Jenn spun away and returned to her work.

One of the local police officers came over to take Sam's statement. Introductions took place, and Sam walked the officer through the brief story of discovering the body. When the official interview ended, Officer Curtis Gallagher closed his notebook and handed Sam a card.

"Call me if you remember anything else," said the officer. "And watch your back. This perp seems to have it in for you."

"He's unravelling," said Sam. "In a way, that's good because it means he's going to make a mistake sooner rather than later."

"Guess so," agreed Gallagher, as he shook Sam's hand

firmly. "I don't envy you, sir, but keep up the good work." The man's eyes swept over the busy scene, pausing briefly on Jenn and Dr. Stratham. "I should go see if I can be of use."

Sam figured he ought to do the same, so he stepped to the side and called his boss, Agent Okiro, and Agent Newhouse. They needed to identify the woman as soon as possible.

To his surprise, Jenn came through with a tentative identification before Sam finished with his first call.

"Her name is Stephanie Kramer," Jenn reported. Her voice stayed low so they couldn't be overheard. "She's one of three women who went missing from New York City last week."

Sam vaguely remembered seeing the headline in his browser's newsfeed, but he'd had no reason to connect it to his case until now.

"How do you know that?" Sam wondered. He'd barely begun to grease the official wheels.

"Social media," Jenn answered. She held up her phone as if to prove a point. "The face looked familiar so I searched for recent missing persons cases. The first article about these three women had links to their social media profiles." Jenn looked upset. "Each one has dozens of pictures of the three of them together. They must have been close. It's not official, but it's definitely her."

"Thanks," said Sam, truly meaning it. "Send me the article link. I'll look up their home town and get somebody on the official notification right away." Noticing a far-off expression on her face, Sam touched Jenn's arm. "Hey, what's wrong?"

Her concerned brown eyes met his.

"I can't stop thinking about them," Jenn said. "If Stephanie's here, where are the other two?"

Oddly, the question gave Sam some hope. Not having their bodies meant the other two could still be alive.

Chapter 33:
Dark Web

FBI Field Office
Philadelphia, Pennsylvania
Finding a body outside his apartment put Sam in a working mood. He called Mel and begged off of their lunch date. She seemed to understand, but he still felt bad. There would always be more work to do, but somehow, it didn't feel right to enjoy a leisurely Saturday afternoon with his girlfriend while a young woman's family was getting notified of their daughter's murder.

A round of calls confirmed Sam would be the only task force member pulling Saturday hours. Adana Okiro had a birthday party for her son to run, and T.J. Newhouse was visiting his daughter in New York City. Adana asked if he wanted her to check with the other three agents who had done some work with the task force over the last few months. Sam turned her down. The reminder that most people spent weekends with their families increased his guilt. Jenn would be thrilled to help him, but she too had a day out planned.

Finding the main office area strangely quiet, Sam decided to seek the company of the cyber agents. He couldn't remember who had told him that cyber agents pulled the most weekend hours, but Sam believed it. Enough of his friends throughout high school and college kept weird hours in favor of participating in certain online games. He doubted the agents played games from their work computers here, but they might be pulling some flex hours so they could sleep in late on other days.

As expected, Sam found Jordan Berkowitz and several cyber agents in their crowded corner of the world. The enthusiastic welcome he received was not expected.

"Agent Kerman! You're just the man we need to see," called Jordan, waving Sam over.

"I am?" asked Sam, heading toward Jordan. "How exciting and nerve-wracking."

"Agent Kerman, this is Rob Gillman," Jordan said, pointing to a young man who looked about eighteen. "He's one of our special contractors, and I think he found something you need to see."

"Hi, I'm a hacker," said the kid, barely taking his eyes off of the screen.

Jordan smacked the kid's shoulder.

"What'd I say about the 'h' word?"

Gillman rolled his eyes.

"There are no cameras in here, and everybody else knows what I do." Turning to Sam, he added, "Call me Gill."

"It's nice to meet you, Gill," said Sam. "You can call me Sam if you like. What'd you find?"

The young man's first attempt at an explanation contained so much technical jargon that he lost Sam in about fifteen seconds.

Jordan sighed.

"Stop talking," he said, tapping the kid on the shoulder. "Just show us, and I'll translate." Jordan sat in a rolling chair to Gill's right and pointed to an identical chair near Sam. "Pull up a chair. The show's about to begin."

Following the instruction, Sam sat to Gill's left and wheeled the chair over enough so he could see the young man's screen. To Sam, it looked like a black screen with a bunch of random numbers and symbols rapidly appearing and disappearing in concert with Gill's flying fingers.

"Nothing big's going on this second," said Jordan. "He's just getting into the Dark Web."

"Never heard of it," Sam noted, earning strange looks from both Jordan and Gill.

"It's an area of the internet where less-than-legal transactions can take place with a reasonable expectation of privacy," Jordan explained.

"If it's illegal, why doesn't somebody shut it down?" Sam

wondered.

"Can't," said Gill. "It would pop up somewhere else. The hubs already shift regularly to keep casuals to a minimum."

Sam quirked an eyebrow at Jordan.

"You don't get in the same way every time."

"If you can get in at all, you should be able to take some action," Sam insisted.

"Web jurisdiction's a mess," said Jordan. "It's not illegal to talk about buying drugs, only to have money and product actually exchange hands. That's harder when the money exchange is untraceable and the product is shipped from out of state or out of country."

"What kinds of things can be bought and sold?" asked Sam.

"Anything," said Gill, still typing.

"We track what we can to keep an eye on the really bad stuff, but it's tricky because millions of otherwise upstanding people also use the place to blow off steam," said Jordan.

"They lie to make themselves feel better about their boring lives," Sam murmured, testing his own powers of decoding cyber-agent-speak.

"Exactly," Jordan confirmed. "There's freedom in being able to create a separate persona online."

"I have a tough time keeping up with real-life, let alone maintain much of an online one." Sam shook his head to emphasize his bewilderment.

"I'm in." Gill tilted the screen toward Sam.

"What am I looking at?"

It appeared to be some sort of forum, but Sam figured it would be faster to ask for an explanation.

"This is a brag blog." Gill's explanation didn't help much.

"Sometimes it's hard to tell the lies from the truth in here," said Jordan, "but basically, it's a place for people to post about something they've done so others can comment on it."

Why bother? Sam barely held the question in.

"In addition to his infiltration skills, Gill's a decent programmer. He came up with a program that gives a statistical probability for whether a story's true by comparing it to articles from major news networks." Jordan paused for Sam to absorb the information. "This time, I had him go the other way."

"I was with you to 'networks' before you lost me," Sam admitted.

Jordan's words flowed faster as his excitement grew.

"I had him scan the brag blogs for keywords from a bunch of articles written about these murders. He got a hit on this particular post."

Leaning forward, Sam skimmed the post Gill had pulled up. It looked like an insane person's idea of a fun mad lib puzzle.

"How can you get anything out of that?" he inquired.

"Put it through the filter," Jordan suggested.

Gill tapped out a few commands, and the screen blacked out for a second. When it came back, the post was written in English but still had some words in odd places.

"Every name is replaced with a random animal," said Jordan, reading the confusion on Sam's face. "That's why his program needed to isolate other keywords, not names."

The post resembled a rambling diary, but it didn't take Sam long to key in on the relevance. The entry started with a claim to having killed somebody for the first time.

Sam straightened.

"How many of these are there?" he demanded.

"Six, but only five are readable right now," said Jordan. "The program caught another one this morning, but it's taking longer to translate because it doesn't seem to be linked to any news articles."

"Why would that matter?" asked Sam.

"This guy's good," said Gill.

"He protects the entries with encryption programs to keep them private," Jordan said, elaborating slightly. "I'm guessing he has a group of dedicated fans with the key to slip in any time. Everybody else has to physically break in every time."

"What do you mean 'every time'?" Sam was getting tired of asking questions, but it beat clinging to his confusion.

"If we closed out the browser, we'd have to start over," Jordan explained patiently. "In other words, you've got to prove your worth before you can even read about his exploits, and they're definitely the murders, at least the first two."

"Can you print them?" Sam inquired.

"Not easily, but we'll work around it and get you a copy

ASAP," Jordan promised. "You can go back to your office if you want. I'll run them up when we're finished."

Sam thanked them for the information and took his leave. He wanted to wait until the fully translated versions became available. Squinting at the screen would only give him a headache.

Returning to his borrowed office, Sam started reading through the mountain of police reports related to this case. He'd been over them a dozen times, but there was always a small chance something new would jump out at him during a fresh read. Five files in, he took a break to fire up the coffee machine. Usually, Sam tried to only drink water when reading important files, but sometimes, he just needed the comfort of a hot mug in his hands as he read.

As he walked back with coffee in hand, Sam saw Jordan knocking frantically on the door.

"Miss me already?" he greeted.

Whirling, Jordan pierced Sam with a sharp look.

"I called twice," he said, a note of disapproval clear.

"Just stepped out for coffee," Sam said. "What's up? You look agitated."

Drawing near, Sam saw that Jordan's T-shirt was almost soaked through with sweat. His face glowed with a nervous sheen.

"Grab your phone and call your team," Jordan ordered. He brandished the papers clutched in his hands. "The sixth entry came through with a link to an ad. If we're right about what it says, he's made it open season for kidnapping the task force agents."

Sam snatched the papers from Jordan and stumbled into the office to grab his phone. He wanted to call his people right away, but he needed to read the papers first to know what exactly he was warning them about.

Why would he want to kidnap my team?

Chapter 34:
Open Season

Agent Okiro's Residence
Flourtown, Pennsylvania

The man watched as droves of small children and their parents milled about, wandering in and out of the Colonial house. The kids seemed to be playing an intense game of tag while the adults attempted crowd control or stood off to the sides, drinking punch from large cups. He only caught glimpses of his target, but he knew almost immediately that getting to her would be extremely difficult. Still, if he didn't grab this agent, odds were good that somebody else would once the party died down. He couldn't wait that long.

Since cars were coming and going regularly, he pulled out of the parking space and drove a few blocks to gain some thinking time. This target lived closest to the drop off location. If he left her and pursued another one, he could potentially lose the race even if somebody waited until late evening to take her. On the other hand, he needed to be doing something now, not waiting ten hours for a convenient time.

According to the online calendars he'd hacked, one of the male agents was in New York City and the other would be heading up to Hillsborough, New Jersey. The only other semi-convenient target was the lead agent's sister. She had a lunch date with some friends in Philadelphia. After that, he had no way to predict her movements unless he could tail her directly. To be on the safe side, he needed to remove the female agent from the equation.

The game rules specifically said the victims couldn't wind up dead, but it said nothing on the matter of wounding. The man had no wish to anger his new boss during this phase, but he had options. Sending the agent to the hospital would likely earn her a protective detail, taking her out of play. For a moment, he considered shooting one of the children. Since most of the other children were white, finding Agent Okiro's son or daughter shouldn't be too difficult. She would never leave their side in that case, but he wasn't keen on testing his boss's creativity threshold yet.

By the time he arrived back at the correct house, the best parking spots were taken. The man parked illegally near the fire hydrant and reached over for the large gift bag he'd brought for the occasion. After a short debate, he decided to leave the engine running. Time would be of the essence once he made his move. He wore a tactical vest under a windbreaker just in case. The agent wouldn't be carrying a weapon at her kid's birthday party, but the bulky vest would change his looks. Wraparound sunglasses, a baseball cap, and faded jeans completed his outfit.

To any onlookers, he was simply another father here to drop off his kid at the party. Adrenaline soared through him, but he kept his gait unhurried. Although the bag held nothing but more bags, the man held it in such a way that it looked heavy.

"Need help with that?" asked a friendly stranger. He started to hand the woman next to him the drink in his hand.

"I got it," grumbled the man. The response came out gruffer than he'd intended, but he couldn't dwell on it. He needed to find the target now. "Where's Mrs. Okiro?"

"I think she's inside cutting the cake. You're just in time," said the friendly man. "Say, what's your name? I don't think we've met."

Without responding, the man entered through the front door. The sunglasses made everything dark, but his eyes adjusted after a brief pause. The kitchen lay directly ahead. He couldn't see most of it, but the part that mattered was framed by the doorway leading from the entry room to the kitchen.

Agent Okiro stood with a large cake-cutting knife in her hands. Two other women stood near her, handing her small paper plates as she carefully parsed out a massive sheet cake. Causing collateral damage could reflect poorly upon his performance, so he needed to be closer. If everybody stayed in position, this would work without a hitch, but the helpers were moving back and forth across his path.

Drawing even with one of the women helping, the man swept his left arm out batting her aside.

She screamed, causing everybody in the room to freeze for a fraction of a second.

The agent turned toward him, still holding the massive cake knife.

Their eyes locked through his sunglasses.

For a moment, he considered altering his plan and walking out with the agent. Then, her grip tightened on the knife, and people started to come out of their shocked stupor.

His gun centered on the agent's chest.

The onlookers held their collective breaths.

Adjusting his aim to high on her right shoulder, he fired.

He waited only long enough to watch her stumble back and hit the far wall, the knife falling from nerve-less fingers.

Whirling away, he fled.

The helpful couple entered the house as the man tried to leave. He barreled straight into the woman, sending her flying back into the man. They temporarily blocked his path until he finished knocking them over and jumped over their fallen forms.

Screams, shouts, and conflicting orders followed him as he sprinted to his idling car. Leaping in, he peeled away, nearly sideswiping a passing car in the process.

Both drivers leaned on their horns, exchanged curses, and sped away.

***

Toni's Café
Philadelphia, Pennsylvania
The man wished he'd taken the time to grab something to eat, but the drive to Philadelphia from Flourtown went over its projected half-hour. Kidnapping someone in broad daylight pretty much never happened, which is why it would work. He'd parked at the train station and used public transportation to get to Toni's Café. Leaving his car behind wasn't easy, but he didn't have time to switch to something unconnected to him.

The wait for the woman to come out went on forever.

204

Eventually, the man went in and ordered a soda and a sandwich, making sure to be seated far away from his target yet close enough to keep tabs on her. He laid twenty-five dollars on the table to cover the meal in case he needed to leave in a hurry. Thankfully, the café's service lived up to its stellar reputation, giving the man a chance to eat during his interminable wait.

The target sat with two other young people. They'd clearly finished their meal long ago, but nursed along watery sodas, ignoring the anxious looks from the wait staff. Laughter rang out from their table on a regular basis, drawing annoyed stares from nearby elderly couples. The man wished the target kept a lower profile. At this rate, the entire restaurant would remember everything about her.

Finally, midway through his second cup of coffee in addition to the soda, the target and her friends paid their bill and left. He frowned when he saw them leaving together. The scenarios he'd planned for did not involve multiple people. If the woman left with her friends, he'd have to scrap the plan and try again later. He really didn't want to do that. Hasty plans rarely worked as well as ones he had time to plan for problems.

Luck favored him. Just outside the main entrance, the target hugged each of her companions and reached into her purse for car keys. She'd been fortunate enough to find a parking spot close to the entrance. He waited impatiently for some distance to open between the woman and her friends. They were still uncomfortably close as she unlocked the car and started walking around the back toward the driver's seat.

He'd have to improvise.

"Ma'am!" he called, rushing out the café's front door. "Did you forget this?" He jogged casually toward her, holding up his cell phone.

The woman paused and glanced around to make sure he was talking to her. Then, she shook her head to let him know that the phone didn't belong to her.

By this time, he'd closed the distance between them. Thinking fast, he pretended to trip, knocking the woman's keys out of her hands as he stumbled forward.

"I'm so sorry," he murmured, as they both knelt to retrieve the keys. "I have no idea what happened."

"It's fine," she assured him. "Don't worry about it."

In that time, he'd traded his phone for a small gun that fit in the palm of his right hand. As the woman's fingers gripped the keys, his left hand clamped around her forearm. Their bodies and the bulk of her car shielded the move from any passersby on the sidewalk. He held out his right hand palm up so she could clearly see the gun. Her expression rapidly changed from surprised to shocked to horrified.

The car chose that moment to relock itself.

The woman sucked in sharply to let out a scream, but he released her arm and slammed his hand across her mouth. His palm covered the entire lower half of her face. The only sound to escape her was a surprised squeak.

"Leave the keys. I'll take them and unlock the car. You stand quietly and get in the driver's seat. I'm going to climb into the back. Once we're settled, you get the keys back and you drive where I tell you to. Nod if you understand."

She nodded but anger glittered in her eyes, telling him she'd do something stupid at the first opportunity.

"You try anything, and I'll track down Chris and Dana." The man hoped he'd remembered the names correctly from her appointment calendar.

The tension in her shoulders and the fear in her eyes convinced him his memory was accurate.

The second nod was slower and more sincere than the first.

He left his hand in place a second longer, drilling his sincerity into her with his eyes.

"Get up," he ordered, using his grip on her face to urge her to rise.

Midway up, he let go and spun around behind her, making sure she felt the gun's muzzle touch her back.

"Stand still," he said quietly. Bending down, he retrieved the keys and unlocked the car. "In."

Opening the back door, he paused and waited while the target climbed in. Once both doors shut, he tossed the keys onto the front passenger seat and spoke in a normal volume.

"My gun is still leveled at your back."

"Who are you? What do you want?" The woman sounded numb, like the questions only came out of her because they were hardwired into every kidnapping victim in history.

"Never mind that. You want to live, you buckle up and

drive," said the man. "Start by taking this street four blocks and making a left at the light."

A long silence fell as the woman contemplated her options. As the man opened his mouth to voice more threats, she leaned over and picked up the car keys. For a second, he thought she'd choose the hard way and toss the keys out the window, but she merely slipped the key into the ignition and started the vehicle.

A slow, sad country song filled the air.

With shaking fingers, the woman poked the off button on the radio and a new silence took over.

The man started to relax. He had his prize. Now, he just had to deliver her.

Chapter 35:
Dying Wish

The Killer's Lair
Undisclosed Location

Andrew Novak frowned. He should be excited. Seven apprentice candidates had posted genuine interest in working with him. Although he hadn't requested it, they often privately messaged him their top target choices. Everybody had at least one person after them, so it would be interesting to see who won the race. Despite this, his thoughts dwelt on the two women staying in his holding cells.

Layla O'Malley and Natasha Creswell spent most of their time talking so quietly the cameras couldn't pick up on it. Any time he walked in, they fell silent, hands clasped in a show of unity. Silence usually didn't bother him, but for some reason, their quiet hostility hurt.

Tucked in his chair before the bank of monitors, Andrew watched his captives. He'd muted the sound since it didn't help anyway, but subtle movements told him Layla was doing most of the talking. During the past few days, the women spent hours sitting side by side in their cells, heads tilted toward each other. It was sickening.

Layla's the problem.

Once the tiny thought formed, Andrew felt its truth immediately. If he wanted to enjoy the anticipation of the day, he would need to deal with the Layla issue. He'd avoided making a decision thus far by keeping busy with the search for an apprentice and good memories from the last kill. Stephanie's murder no longer excited him, and his would-be apprentices were busy with their final exam.

He had nothing to do.

Slaughtering online characters held no satisfaction now that he could have any weapon he ever wanted. Lack of challenge meant boredom, a horrible fate.

Determined to seize control, Andrew stood and stared hard at Layla through the monitor screens. If he dealt with her, perhaps he could enjoy the anticipation of the apprentice competition.

Leaning back and closing his eyes, Andrew pondered the ways he could kill Layla. None of the methods tried already seemed right for her. He admired her courage in giving her friend the ticket that would delay her fate. That deserved some consideration. Guns were too impersonal. Knives had the opposite problem. He needed something easy to clean up today. His apprentice candidates could call at any minute with news of success.

Electrocution would be fun, but he ruled it out as too complicated to set up at the moment. Drowning was out because he'd done that to Stephanie. Pushing Layla off a tall building would be new, but he'd need to do some heavy duty research before attempting such a thing. The logistics of getting into and up a high enough building to kill her then getting safely out were enormous. He could go old fashioned and hang her, but most of the trees on his property were too flimsy to bear the weight. Suffocation and lethal injection were also viable options.

Perhaps Layla would have an opinion. Who was he kidding? Of course, she'd have an opinion. The woman bled opinions left and right. Still, it pleased him to let her choose the manner of death.

Wandering into the workroom, he grabbed a small stack of the chosen lottery ticket: Quick Six Riches. He wasn't sure of the wisdom in using tickets to count his kill incidents, but it felt right so far. Once he got past ten he might have trouble finding appropriate tickets, but he'd deal with that problem if and when it arose. He might just start over with one again in a new location. Every state had some form of lottery, and even if they didn't he had enough tickets in his stock to see him through a good decade's worth of work.

As expected, his two captives stopped talking when he entered. Something about the way he strode in must have alerted them to this visit being different. Both women stood up. Layla's grip on Natasha's hand increased, causing the other woman to wince.

He stopped in front of Layla's cell and reached for the Taser. To his satisfaction, fear forced Layla to drop her friend's hand and shrink back into the corner.

"Please. Don't," said Natasha. As he started to line up the shot, she spoke faster, sounding winded. "You don't have to do this."

"But I want to," he said. "It'll be fun."

Remembering the lottery tickets in his other hand, Andrew lowered the Taser and tossed in the six loose Quick Six Riches tickets. Drawing out a quarter from his pocket, he flipped it neatly onto the haphazard stack.

"Pick one," he instructed. "If you win, you get to choose how you die. If you lose, I'll make the decision."

"What are the choices?" Layla asked. Her tone lacked much inflection, but the tightened fists showed him her struggle to keep calm.

"Suffocation and lethal injection," he answered. "Those will be easiest to clean up. Do you have a preference?"

"Which is less painful?" she inquired. This time, fear softened her voice to a whisper.

"Not sure," he said honestly. "I don't have the official combination states use in their injections, so I'll be improvising, but that will likely be quicker."

"Go with that then," she said, fighting to force words from her dry throat.

"You're not going to try to win?" he asked.

Layla only shook her head briefly, sliding down the wall until she sat curled in the corner. Resting her head against the back wall, Layla blinked rapidly to contain tears. Natasha knelt beside her and gripped her left shoulder. For a second, it looked like Natasha would speak, but her mouth shut and she bowed her head.

"Are you going to let her die for you?" Andrew demanded, surprising everybody with the force behind the question.

Natasha was speechless, but her eyes drifted to the fallen lottery tickets then up to Andrew again.

The idea struck him at the same time as it must have occurred to her, for she started to stand. Picking up on the shifts around her, Layla stared up at her friend then glanced over at Andrew. Moving faster than he thought possible, Layla dove for the tickets, scooped up the entire stack, and started ripping them to pieces.

"Stop!" Andrew ordered.

Layla responded by tearing another ticket to shreds.

The Taser prongs leapt out and caught Layla in the chest, knocking her over backward. Twin screams sailed through Andrew, giving him a thrill. Unlocking the door, he slipped into the cell and rescued the remaining tickets. After removing the prongs from Layla, Andrew tossed the momentarily useless Taser out of the cell and kicked the quarter over to Natasha.

"You win; you get to decide who lives and dies. You lose, and her decision stands," Andrew explained, tucking the remaining tickets into Natasha's cell.

Four tickets remained.

Natasha wasted no time in furiously scratching the tickets clear. Her eyes devoured the tickets, as hope and fear flickered across her expression.

"Let me see them?" Andrew doubted she'd understand what she was reading in her current state of mind.

A thorough review of the tickets revealed them to be losers. Given the statistics of winning lottery tickets, that many losers in a row meant Layla had probably torn up a winner. Meeting Natasha's eyes, he shook his head. She cast a worried look at her friend. Scrambling as close as the bars would allow, Natasha addressed her friend.

"Layla, listen to me. You don't have to do this. You have so much to live for."

Struggling to sit up, Layla avoided her friend's intense gaze.

Andrew enjoyed the drama unfolding between them. He waited anxiously for a final decision.

"Layla?" he asked. "Do you have anything to say?"

The renewed flare of agitation pleased him.

"You're wrong, but I stand by my decision."

Andrew wanted to preserve the moment, but it vanished.

"So be it," he murmured, trying to think what movie he'd heard that in. "I'll go make some preparations then bring you and your friend some food. Then, we'll do this."

The plan proceeded as predicted. He found some off-brand drugs that would paralyze her and put her to sleep. Then, he found some amphetamines that would overload her heart. In theory, she should die of a heart attack in her sleep. The last meal was a frozen pizza, but Layla barely touched it.

He thought he'd have to use the Taser again in moving her to the dental chair, but she followed directions without protest. She didn't even cry until he held the mouthpiece up for her to bite down on.

"Don't be scared," he whispered. "It'll be like going to sleep."

"I may not be your first victim," said Layla, conviction coming through clearly. "But I hope I'm your last." She looked like she wanted to say much more, but she bit down on the mouthpiece.

The simple last words echoed in his mind as he prepared the injections. The distraction was so complete he nearly missed her arm with the first shot. Somehow, he finished, but he walked away before the drugs completed their deadly task. He needed some fresh air.

Chapter 36:
Special Delivery

Abandoned Parking Lot
Chester County, Pennsylvania

"He'll be here soon," the kidnapper promised.

Jennifer Kerman ignored him. They'd been parked in this weed-filled lot for almost an hour. The drive from Philly had taken about an hour and fifteen minutes. A dozen half-baked plans tumbled through her head. She would have tried one of them ages ago if she didn't believe the man would carry out his threat to go after Dana and Chris. She also had the nagging feeling she'd met him before.

Why me?

The tiny question wouldn't leave her alone. The endless litany of assurances that someone would be here soon told her this guy had no intention of keeping her. That was both comforting and disturbing. Putting a few hundred miles between her and this guy would certainly be good, but the idea of being handed over to somebody else frightened her deeply. Nobody kidnapped people for free, so it followed that the "somebody" they were meeting had paid for this pending meeting. To her knowledge, she hadn't made any career enemies yet. Forensic scientists, especially ones right out of college, rarely generated the sort of enemies that prompted paid kidnappings.

Sam?

Her brother's only major case was the Parkside Killer, and

that had been dragging on for months. The body showing up outside his apartment had caused a brief surge in media attention, but by now even that had waned. Sam never babbled about case progress, but Jenn could usually read his moods. If he were close to breaking the case open, he'd be practically bouncing on his toes.

Ransom?

She dismissed that reason right away. Part of her wished her folks were rich enough to tempt kidnappers, but middle-aged, semi-retired librarians and civil engineers did not earn enviable money.

Random?

That was by far the scariest possibility. Psychopaths who targeted random people tended to do their own dirty work. She was too old for most types of sicko, opportunistic predators.

A white van pulled up alongside her red Elantra.

"Get out," ordered the kidnapper.

Not wanting to get shot, Jenn opened the car door, got stuck on the seat belt, freed herself, and tried again. Force of habit made her take the car keys with her. The kidnapper leapt out of the back seat and trained his tiny gun on her. His ease with the weapon told her she probably wouldn't die by accident, but he could always change his mind about handing her over and kill her on purpose. As the doors slammed shut, she remembered leaving her purse on the front passenger seat. It felt weird to not have the bag's reassuring weight in her arms.

"Give me the keys."

Jenn wished the guy would learn to phrase things as requests. The snippety orders were annoying. Nevertheless, she held out her keys then crossed her arms since having them close offered some psychological comfort.

A blond young man walked around the back of the van. His youth shocked her. Judging people's ages had never been her strong suit, but he couldn't be more than a few years older than her twenty-three years. His face bore patches of scruff that made him look even younger. He had pretty blue eyes and a curious, puppy-dog-eager nervous energy about him.

"Who are you?" demanded the kidnapper. His posture had stiffened, and he looked ready to choose a new target for his gun.

"The man you came to meet," said the stranger with a small smile.

Disgust and disappointment washed over the kidnapper's face.

"You can't be him," he muttered. "You're barely out of diapers."

"I take it you've changed your mind about working for me?" The stranger's inflection turned it into a question. He appeared disappointed but resigned, as if he'd expected this might happen.

The kidnapper's whole face twisted into an angry mask, but before he could speak, the stranger moved. Jenn had noticed his right hand hovered slightly behind his back and thought little of it. Now, the stranger's right hand swung forward holding a bulky, awkward-looking gun. Yelping, she pressed her back against her car as the weapon emitted a noise like a thousand bugs being zapped simultaneously.

Twin prongs leapt forward and latched onto her kidnapper, delivering a massive shock that locked all his muscles. He fell back against her car and continued toward the ground. Terrified, Jenn stepped to the side, ramming her lower back into the side mirror. Before she could gather enough wits to run, the stranger spoke.

"Please don't go anywhere."

His eyes stayed on her, but his gun—a real gun this time—pointed down at her kidnapper. With barely more than a casual glance, the stranger shot the man three times, twice in the chest and once in the face.

Jenn's hands flew to her mouth, but she was too shocked to scream. Her stomach twisted inside her like a live thing. Spots danced before her vision, and she worked hard to control the urge to throw up.

"It's nice to meet you, Jennifer," said the stranger. His gun now pointed directly at her gut.

She'd read about what bullets could do to flesh, but seeing it done was overwhelming. Try as she might, she couldn't move her gaze.

"Please get in the van."

The stranger's instruction seemed easy enough to follow, but Jenn's entire body had been thrown into neutral.

With a sigh, the blond man stepped over the kidnapper's body and touched Jenn's right arm. She tried to back away but between the car, the body, and the stranger, she had nowhere to go.

"What—"

"I'll explain later," interrupted the stranger. "We need to go."

"You're just going to leave him there?" Jenn asked, not liking how winded she sounded.

"There would be no point in moving his body," the stranger pointed out. "You're not dead yet, and I'd rather not hurt you here. Please don't make things more difficult than they need to be."

"You want easy, let me go," said Jenn.

A crooked smile and a head shake were her only answers. He motioned again toward the van. Somehow, the order held a lot more weight when emphasized by the handgun.

I don't want to die.

With those words unhelpfully scrolling through her head on loop, Jenn finally forced her body to move. The stranger scrambled ahead to open the door for her, revealing another body.

For the second time in less than two minutes, Jenn leapt back, covered her mouth, and tried not to scream or retch.

"Don't mind her," said the stranger. "We're going to leave her here."

Now that she looked closer, Jenn saw that the body belonged to a young woman. Like the dead guy who'd kidnapped her the face evoked vague feelings of familiarity.

"Who was she?" she asked softly.

"Doesn't matter now," replied the stranger. "Get in and stay out of the way while I move her."

The thought of him tossing the body out of the car like a trash bag bothered Jenn.

"May I help?" She would have gone ahead and reached for the body if the example of his explosive temper didn't lie a few feet away.

The stranger shrugged. Together, they tugged on the plastic sheet under the body. As the head reached the doorway, Jenn slipped her arm underneath to support it. Through the plastic, the body felt warm to her touch. That made the situation even more heartbreaking. A day ago, maybe even hours, this woman had been alive.

"Hold her while I pull the sheet free," said the stranger.

At least he wasn't referring to the dead woman as an "it."

Jenn looped her hands under the woman's armpits and leaned back as the sheet pulled free. Without the sheet, the body felt even warmer, almost feverish. A crazy thought occurred to her, but she forced it from her mind before it could show up on her face. If she lived long enough, she'd dwell on it later.

"Would you like to leave something for your brother to find?"

The man's question managed to surprise Jenn.

"Like what?" she asked, standing in the hopes of keeping his attention on her.

If the woman still lived, letting this man know would be akin to killing her.

"The necklace," he answered.

With fumbling fingers, Jenn removed her simple cross necklace and dropped it into the man's outstretched hand. Her neck felt strange without it. The stranger studied the jewelry for a few seconds before turning his hand over and letting the necklace drop onto the woman's chest.

"What do you want with Sam?" Jenn asked, fearing what the man might discover if he looked at the body too long.

"I want him to know what failure feels like."

The answer made Jenn shiver. She climbed into the black box that was the van's interior and huddled in the back left corner, as far from the man as she could get.

Chuckling at her reaction, the man bunched up the plastic and threw it in after her. Then he closed the door. As he walked around the van, Jenn scrambled back to the door and tried to open it.

Nothing happened.

Time would tell what this madman truly wanted with her. A lifetime of mysteries and thrillers in movie and book form as well as a handful of criminal justice classes tormented her with the terrible truth. Odds were good that she would die in the next twenty-four hours.

Chapter 37:
Messages

Melissa Novak's Private Residence
Hillsborough, New Jersey

The week couldn't get much worse. One of Melissa's patients had died on Wednesday, and somebody had rear-ended her car yesterday. Hospital policy changes thanks to the national insurance nightmare meant less money, longer hours, and more work for her. Josh went fishing with his buddies, and Josie and the kids were visiting with a college friend. Sam had canceled yet another date, leaving Melissa alone in her nice house.

Painting or wallowing in self-pity were viable weekend options, but even those took effort Melissa wasn't sure she wanted to spend. The news highlighted the tragedies due to weather, conflicting ideologies, and random acts of stupidity. The few hundred other TV channels offered nothing that remotely interested her. Out of desperation, she checked the local movie theaters to see if anything good was playing. The only two possibilities were ones she'd rather see with Sam someday.

Deciding to declutter her email, Melissa signed into her Gmail account. Nine hundred and two new emails greeted her, letting her know it had been a while since she had checked the account. The spam folder was worse, but she simply hit the delete-all button for that. The others, she decided to at least skim on the off chance it held something good. The volume didn't surprise her since she used this account to sign up for store promotions, donate to charities, and subscribe to newsletters. The nearly mindless activity of sorting emails soothed her.

Nearing the end of her task, Melissa flipped over to trash and emptied it. The move felt good until she noticed her inbox number jump up from forty-four to forty-five. Navigating back to the inbox, Melissa saw it was a notification for a Matchmaker Miracles private message. She frowned at that because she thought she'd turned off the ability for others to communicate with her.

The message turned out to be from Sam's account, but it didn't sound like him. It rambled on about how wonderful she was but that things just weren't working out for them. Melissa read it three more times before the words started sinking in beyond her disbelief.

He's breaking up with me.

Try as she might, Melissa couldn't fathom a legitimate reason for this stunning move. Their busy lives made time together scarce, but she always enjoyed hanging out with Sam. The affection that had grown between them over the last few months felt genuine. Certainly whatever they had warranted more than an impersonal "we should go our separate ways" message. The more she thought about it, the angrier she got. She needed to talk to Sam. A face-to-face conversation would be best, but phone would have to do for now.

After finding her phone, Melissa pulled up Sam's number, but her finger hesitated over the call button. She didn't want to interrupt him if he was busy with a case crisis. Then, she remembered he had taken the time to compose a breakup message. If he had time for that, he could spare a moment to level with her. Resolve renewed, Melissa stabbed her finger into the call button. It rang and rang, which meant he was probably using the phone. When it finally gave her the chance to leave a message, Melissa froze.

"Call me," was about the extent of words she could manage and not break down into a raving mess.

Ending the call, Melissa tossed her phone onto the couch. She needed to run. The sun would be high and hot this close to midday, but she didn't care. Changing took only a minute, but Melissa took the time to put on some sunscreen. Part of her felt that maybe a painful sunburn would help her forget the other misfortunes in her life, but she'd treated too many cases of skin cancer that got out of control not to take precautions.

Melissa usually tried to stretch first, but right now, her body simply wanted to move. A swift jog for several blocks warmed her up sufficiently. After pausing for a brief stretch, she continued the workout. Generally, she preferred to work to a time not a distance, but today, she wasn't keeping any track. Her jog turned into a full run. The beautiful scenery failed to move her. The ache in her heart only intensified as her body strove for speed and distance. Tears joined the sweat pouring down her face. She'd forgotten to tie back her hair. Most strands flapped behind her like a flag, but some clung to her face and neck, making her miserable.

When she paused to deal with the hair issue, Melissa realized she wasn't immediately sure of her location. Seeing a street corner ahead, she jogged over to it and got her bearings. Since she wasn't wearing a watch today, Melissa couldn't tell how long she'd been running, but if she remembered the intersection correctly, she was about two miles from home. Surprised, she turned around and picked her way back at a more reasonable pace. She'd slowed to a walk by the time her house came within sight. The view reminded her how much work remained, but that wasn't something to address today.

A short cool shower followed by a longer, hot shower put Melissa in a slightly better mood. A light lunch of cold cuts on toast also helped. Thus fortified, she felt ready to call Sam again. The call reached his voicemail, but now that she wasn't quite so upset, she left a calmer request for a return call. Curious to see if she had any new emails, Melissa woke her computer and saw that she did.

The one from Josie made her laugh, but she marked it as unread so she'd remember to reply to it later. Josie had a funny, sarcastic way of describing the most mundane events. The temptation to dump her problems on her friend was strong, but Josie deserved a stress-free weekend. Melissa didn't recognize the most recent address, so she clicked on the box next to it and sent it over to trash.

A second later, a new email popped up from the same address. The subject line said: MEET ME.

She might have trashed this second email too if curiosity didn't get the better of her. Hoping it didn't contain a virus that wiped her computer clear, Melissa opened the email. The message within was short and to the point.

Mel, I've missed you. Meet me at the farm at 9
o'clock tomorrow.
A.

"A." had to be Andrew, but why would he send an email to
set up a meeting after all these years. What if she'd had other plans?
She didn't, but that wasn't the point. Andy could be self-centered
sometimes, but he had never struck her as completely lacking in
social niceties. Should she go or pretend to have better things to do?
The possibility of seeing her brother excited her, but he could have
had the decency to call or at least phrase the meeting as a request.

The farm was an odd meeting choice too. Their grandparents
used to own a farm in Florence, New Jersey. Upon their deaths, the
deed had passed to her parents, but health problems had prompted
them to sell quickly. She hadn't thought about that place in years. It
held great memories for her. If she ever had a ton of money she had
no other use for, Melissa would look into buying the farm back, but
she saw no point in regretting what couldn't be changed right now.

Melissa couldn't believe she was considering going.
Likely she'd drive over an hour only to meet the strangers who'd
bought the property decades ago. That was a long way to go to
trespass on a patch of land. The rational half of her admitted this was
crazy, but the impulsive side wanted to seize the moment.

It'll be an adventure.

With the afternoon suddenly free, Melissa decided to answer
Josie's email. She'd likely be out and about with the kids right now,
but they could have an evening chat. They had much to discuss, and
Melissa could certainly use some laughs. She debated whether she
should tell Josie about the breakup and decided to leave the final
decision until later.

Chapter 38:
High Stakes

The Killer's Lair
Undisclosed Location
Day 7: Early evening.
The thrill for the job is fading, and I'm still without an apprentice.

I'll need to work up a new ad and post it tonight. The parameters will have to be different because most of the agents are on high alert now.

Officer Curtis Gallagher successfully kidnapped the lead agent's sister, but when he met me, he showed only contempt. He could never willingly take orders from me. I'd always be waiting for a betrayal, so I killed him. I felt nothing doing it, except for a vague sense of disappointment. Usually, there's a thrill or fear of being caught to enhance the situation.

I think Gallagher shot the female agent. I never said they couldn't wound the agents, so his move was within the task guidelines. Still, in my new ad, I'll have to be much clearer.

I don't need them for Mel. She'll come to me. Having her disappear will likely give law enforcement the final clue they need to discover my identity, but I don't care.

I'm done with this area. I need to move on.

The agent's sister is resting in the cell formerly occupied by Layla. Her appearance tells me she spent some of the ride home crying. As I moved her to the cell, I felt her eyes absorbing everything. I should have blindfolded her, but it's too late for that now. I gave her a sedative. She'll be out for the night. She knows my face, so she must die. Natasha too, though for Layla's sake, I'll leave those details until the last moment.

If I leave in the night, nobody will ever catch me. Eventually, they'll find this place and the remaining bodies and they'll know it's me, but it will be too late to stop me.

Leaving will be difficult. I grew up in this small state. Mel will come with me. She may not want to, but she'll have no choice. She's a smart woman. She will find a way to start anew any place we land. If I play my cards right, maybe I can fake her death and pin it on Josh. His shiny reputation could use a few more visible spots. He has a private gambling problem, but so far, he's hidden it from Mel and Josie. The numbers don't lie. I've been floating him some money through various sources because I can, and it amuses me to have him in my debt. Maybe I'll let him get deep enough that he'll take the fall for these murders to pay the debt. It's worth considering.

I would never hurt Mel, yet I'll secretly admit the appeal. She's perfect, but the only way to truly preserve perfection is to freeze it in time. The only way humans stop growing and changing and disappointing their loved ones is to die.

With all the awful things happening in the world, does Mel wish to be free?

In death, Layla's worries ceased to matter.

In death, the young men paid for their crimes.

In death, the homeless woman found a home.

Do I wish to be free?

Yes, but there's too much work to do. I must carry the burden for others.

High stakes are irresistible. My brother could tell you more about that. His gambling takes place online. He hardly ever plays the lottery. I should send him some tickets so he can remember what it felt like to win that way.

Maybe I'll kill Josh before disappearing. If he goes, Josie will want to go with him, but she needs to raise my nephew and niece without the corrupting influence of their father. One should never gamble with more money than they have. It's foolish and leads to trouble. What if he'd taken a loan out with the wrong sort of people? He was more than ready to do so before I intervened. They would have gone after Josie and the kids. They deserve better than

Josh. Maybe I can find her a good man on Matchmaker Miracles. The matching algorithm is quite good.

The agent's sister will make the game high stakes for him, but she has no value to me. Therefore, killing her has no appeal. I can use her to get to him, but what would that prove? If he comes to me, what then? Killing him would be a small triumph I suppose, but would it really change the world?

The agent may need to die to let Mel forget him, but other than that, I don't see much reason to bother with him. His sister was on the list just to give my apprentice candidates more targets.

Nobility only goes so far as a motivator.

The stakes must matter.

The only thing that matters to me is Mel.

I stare at that statement and know it's true.

It means she alone can give my life meaning now. I must test her luck. If she wins, then she'll come with me and we'll leave as planned. If she loses and dies, then I'll know fickle Fate had turned its back on me.

I need to feel again.

I don't want to hurt Mel, but if her time has come, who am I to argue with Fate?

I don't matter. Only the work matters. It must continue. If I am no longer the one chosen to carry it on, then I too must cease.

I haven't time to get an apprentice to do this work. The FBI agent will realize his sister is missing by tomorrow. That will get things rolling much faster. It will probably take them a while to track down her car, but once they do, he will know I have her. By that time, I may reach out.

I needed to break the agent and Mel up today so he's not thinking about her and she's not thinking about him. I left her a message to meet me at nine tomorrow morning. I think she'll do it. I also put a filter on their phones so their messages come through me. I don't want them communicating without my permission.

Getting Mel to come alone might be trickier. Josie was her shadow in the old days. She has the kids to worry about now, but she'll want to see me too if she knows Mel plans to meet me.

I know Mel's been following the case in the papers. I see her come back from work with stacks of newspapers, sit at the kitchen table, and clip out articles. I don't think she suspects me, but her interest isn't healthy. Would she turn me in if she knew? If I denied it to her face, would she believe me? I'd like to think so, but I hardly know her anymore.

The only way I get answers is to ask her. To do that, I must bring her here. She probably remembers this place better than I did. The three of us spent carefree childhood days wandering the woods around here. I think even Josie came a time or two. Guess sentimentality runs in the family. What Mel and I have is stronger than blood. She was always my rock as a child. I need to know if I can still count on her for inspiration and hope.

The work I do is difficult. The physical aspects were predictable, but the emotional strain is far worse. Self-doubt and uncertainty are the biggest enemies.

Am I supposed to punish the guilty or free the innocent? Dedicating myself to doing both is taking a toll.

I am at a crossroads. Two paths lie before me.

It becomes clear to me that Jennifer Kerman must participate when I test Mel. She will be a substitute for her brother. Maybe the good agent will be decent enough to join us too. If he does, I might be tempted to participate as well. Having my life as a stake would also heighten the excitement.

Do I bring Sam here? He would come if he thought I held his sister here, but agents don't often come alone. They bring SWAT guys and their gear along. Would he come alone if I asked nicely? He never answered my question about how much he values his sister's life.

It's late, and I have plans to finalize. Jennifer, Sam, Mel, and I are going to discover a lot about ourselves tomorrow. The anticipation's still not what it used to be, but it's an improvement over the last couple of days.

Chapter 39:
Slightly Illegal

FBI Field Office
Philadelphia, Pennsylvania

Samuel Kerman officially filed the weekend under the category "worst days ever." The bulk of Saturday went into warning his team to watch their backs and updating his boss. As he started to believe everything would work out, he'd received the call about Adana being shot in broad daylight at her kid's birthday party. Understandably, the kid was a wreck and the husband had looked like he wanted to punch Sam. Many more hours were spent pacing the Chestnut Hill Hospital waiting room and making more phone calls.

At least Adana wasn't dead. Either the shooter was a horrible shot, or he hadn't intended the wound to be fatal. Sam wasn't sure which option would be worse: a competent nutcase or an incompetent one. The doctors seemed decent, but the flow of information had some serious kinks in the system. Sam despised feeling helpless, but he couldn't do much besides arrange for local police officers to guard the hospital room to prevent a second incident.

Sam's throat hurt from being on the phone so long. Adana would have done a much better job of coordinating the moving pieces, but since she was temporarily out of commission, the task fell to Sam. He checked in with Newhouse who once again assured him he was fine. The other agent's daughter was less than pleased about having her Saturday plans royally interrupted, but they were in a safe house being guarded by agents from the New York field office. Sam wasn't pleased about having Agent Fuller or Agent Hill watching his back constantly, but he could endure a day or two. He decided to work Sunday so he wouldn't need babysitters.

When his phone rang at 9:00 a.m. Sunday morning, Sam didn't bother checking for the caller's ID. About a dozen people were slated to call him back for one reason or another.

"Agent Kerman speaking," he answered.

"Sam, it's Josie. You'd better call Mel." The woman sounded both worried and furious.

"I'm a little busy here—"

"Don't give me that!" Josie snapped. "You owe her an explanation after the cowardly way you broke her heart yesterday, you slimy, poisonous toad!"

"Wait. Back up. What'd I do?" Sam had been ignoring Mel's calls to deal with the other crises popping up, but that wouldn't put such anger into Josie's voice.

"You not only had the nerve to break up with her, you did it in the most impersonal, callous, stupid way possible!"

"I didn't break up with Mel," Sam said. "I canceled lunch with her yesterday. That's it. Something came up at work. Why does she think I broke up with her?"

Stunned silence fell across the line.

"You didn't send her a message from Matchmaker Miracles?"

"No, I haven't been on that site in months," said Sam.

Josie squealed like an excited child.

"This is great!" Sobering immediately, she gasped. "Oh, no! If you didn't send that message, who did? If somebody's pretending to be you, then they could also be pretending to be Andy. Mel could be in trouble."

"Slow down, Josie," Sam said, affecting his lion-taming tone. "Who's Andy? Where's Mel? Why do you think she's in trouble?"

"You need to call her," Josie said, repeating her earlier order. "Andy's her brother, but she hasn't seen him in years. She's meeting him now at their grandparents' old farm in Florence."

"Where's that?"

"South Jersey somewhere. I don't know the exact address.

Maybe my husband remembers. I'll give him a call. Get back to me after you've smoothed things over with Mel. And Sam?"

"Yes?"

"Don't wait." Josie ended the call before Sam could respond.

He stared at his phone and tried to make sense of the odd conversation. If his Matchmaker Miracles account had been compromised, he needed to know what else had been broken into. The timing was too convenient to be a separate incident.

A call to Mel went immediately to voicemail. Sam left a rambling message and said he'd try again later. As he moved to put the phone down, it rang and showed him his mother was calling.

"I can't talk long, Mom. What do you need?"

"I'm sorry to bother you, sweetie. I know you're working hard," said his mother. "Have you heard from your sister?"

"No, last I talked to her was Friday. She said she had a lunch meeting with Chris and Dana Saturday, but I've been busy with work stuff."

"She missed a hair appointment this morning. You didn't notice if she came in or not?" his mother sounded incredulous. "She's living with you!"

"Yes, but she occasionally stays out too late and crashes with a friend," Sam said defensively. "Did you call her?"

He silently admitted that Jenn was typically good about telling him when her plans changed drastically.

"Of course, but it just keeps ringing. You know she never empties her messages. I don't think I could leave one if I wanted to."

Sam wasn't sure what gave his mother the impression he could get through to Jenn any better than she could, but he promised to look into the matter when he had a chance. As he wound the conversation with his mother to a close, Sam mentally added "call Jenn" to his list of things to do.

No time like the present time.

He dialed his sister's cell phone as he headed for the computer lab where he hoped to find Jordan Berkowitz and Rob Gillman. Finding Gill working alone, Sam realized this was better than finding Jordan.

"Where is everybody?" Sam inquired, pausing just inside the door.

"Late breakfast," replied the young man.

Locking the door and pulling down the shade, Sam crossed the room and sat down beside Gill.

"I know we just met, but I need you to do something that might be slightly illegal."

The young man looked intrigued.

"What's that?" His hands kept typing even though his attention moved to Sam.

"Can you track a phone's GPS from the number?" Sam wasn't sure why his mind went there, but once formed, the idea wouldn't leave him alone.

"Sometimes. Is the GPS active or do I need to activate it remotely?"

"I'm not sure," Sam admitted.

Reaching down next to him, Gill picked up a sleek black laptop.

"Can't do it from these clunkers," Gill explained, logging into the new machine. "What do you need this for?"

"A hunch," Sam said, not wanting to go into the whole Melissa saga. Telling the kid he was tracking down his girlfriend made Sam feel like a creep. "And my sister's missing." He meant it half in jest, but the idea wasn't completely bad.

Gill gave him an odd look and finished his typing.

"You're gonna break the law to check on your sister?"

"I need to know if it can be done," said Sam. "Can you do it without being caught?"

"Give me the number."

Sam gave him Jenn's phone number, and Gill opened a new window and entered more commands. Trying the easy way one more time, Sam placed calls to both Mel and Jenn. As expected, Mel's reached voicemail and Jenn's did not. He waited through the whole "leave a message" spiel on Jenn's phone before hearing the mechanical voice tell him the mailbox was full.

"That's weird," said Gill. "You sure the number's right, man?"

Squinting at Gill's screen, Sam compared the number to the one from his phone.

"That's the one. What's wrong?"

In answer, Gill tapped out some more instructions and pulled up a satellite image of the phone's location.

"This isn't a live image, but it was taken within the week," said Gill.

The picture showed tall grass, scattered trees, an overgrown parking lot, and nothing else.

"Can you pull up a live image?" Sam wondered.

"Can and will are two different things. The only reliable satellite images are owned by the military and billion-dollar companies. Their security is a lot tighter than phone companies, and the penalties are way more than fines."

"Okay. Give me everything you can on that location, and I'll call the locals to look into it further."

In seconds, Sam held a glossy photo of the abandoned lot with the coordinates and county information printed on the back. After thanking Gill for the first information, Sam pressed his luck and gave the young man Mel's number.

"Who are we stalking this time?" Gill asked.

"My girlfriend," Sam admitted.

Gill's hands stopped typing.

"Should I be worried?"

"Somebody hacked into one of my accounts and sent Mel a message supposedly from me," Sam explained. "Her friend told me she's meeting her estranged brother at a farm that's been in her family. If somebody's been impersonating me, I've no doubt they could do the same for her brother. I need to know where she's going so the locals can look in on her."

The explanation satisfied Gill enough to get him working again.

While he waited, Sam contacted the Chester County sheriff's office. After explaining his story about ten times to various parties, he received a promise that somebody would check on the abandoned lot in question. Sam considered updating his mother, but the scant information he had would only worry her more.

"Got it," Gill announced. He handed Sam another printout. "You sure know how to pick places in the middle of nowhere. This place is massive, but I don't think it's an active farm. The ownership's a mess. If my workload stays light, I'll look into it later."

Sam agreed with the assumption of abandonment upon seeing the overgrown grass and patches of woods.

"How far away is the farm?" he asked.

"Address is on the back," said Gill. "Should take you about an hour to get there if you leave now. Are you going?"

Hatcher had told Sam to lay low. He couldn't get much farther off the grid than an unscheduled trip to farm country in New Jersey. He should tell his minders, but they probably wouldn't even miss him. He could be there and back within three hours.

"Yeah, I'm going," said Sam. Since they seemed to be losing track of people this weekend, he added, "I'll have my phone on. Do me a favor and keep an eye on it. I'll check in when I get there. If you don't hear from me in two hours, text me. If I don't answer in a reasonable time, send backup."

"What's a reasonable time?" asked Gill.

Sam had no idea what to tell the kid.

"Seconds? Minutes? Use your best judgment."

Chapter 40:
End of the Line

The Killer's Lair
Florence, New Jersey

Jennifer Kerman awoke the next morning feeling very alone. Hunger pains told her a lot of time must have passed. Her arm ached from whatever he'd drugged her with. While she'd slept, a new figure appeared chained to the wall over by the scary chair, but she wouldn't be much of a conversationalist since she was unconscious. The young woman sleeping in the cell to Jenn's left might have some answers, but she didn't want to wake her. Even in sleep, the woman looked haunted. Having absolutely nothing else to do, Jenn watched the woman and tried to place where she'd seen her face before. Despite long black hair obscuring part of her face, the sense of familiarity was overwhelming.

Sometime later, the answer sailed into Jenn's mind along with a memory. She thought hard, trying to remember the relevant details. Three friends went missing after visiting New York City. One body had been found outside of Sam's apartment. Recalling that hectic day brought random images flashing into her mind.

The cop!

The thought caused Jenn's heart to skip. She gasped. The man who kidnapped her had been one of the cops helping at the scene outside Sam's apartment. Try as she might, no names came to mind, though Jenn clearly remembered his uniform and the notebook he'd been scribbling in as he talked to Sam.

Is he a real cop? Why would a cop kidnap me?

After letting those questions spin on the hamster wheel in her head, Jenn gave up on them and studied the woman next to her with renewed interest. She tried to remember how long ago that kidnapping had taken place. It had been before Dana and Chris's baby arrived, so at least two and a half weeks ago. If she'd been down here the whole time, that would explain the disheveled state. Not having a watch suddenly bothered Jenn. Seeing the seconds slowly tick by would probably be awful, but not knowing was even worse.

Her stomach growled, but since she had nothing to fix the problem, Jenn tried to ignore it. The poor woman looked like she hadn't combed her hair since her kidnapping even though a brush lay next to the tiny sink built into the wall beside the toilet. The cells weren't much to look at but they would keep somebody alive indefinitely as long as food was delivered regularly. Jenn wasn't desperate enough to try the water yet, but she assumed it would be passable.

The toilet occupied a good amount of the cell's back left corner if one were standing outside looking in. The back right corner where Jenn currently sat held two dirty blankets. The front half of each cell was blank. Each floor sloped inward at an angle leading to a drain set into the floor. If she could pry it up, she'd have a hefty chunk of metal to use as a weapon, but an experimental tug on the drain ruled that out.

The prison held three cells like the one she was in and a slightly larger area that featured wall chains and a dental chair. Jenn tried very hard not to think of what the crazy guy used those for. The drains made more sense when she spotted the giant hose hooked near the wall chains. Her lodgings consisted of the second of three cells. The first was empty and her slumbering neighbor currently occupied the last cell in line.

He holds 'em, he kills 'em, and he cleans up. How efficient.

The lumpy blankets didn't provide much comfort, so Jenn stood up and paced the cell for a while. The movement felt good. It reminded her she still lived. To pass the time, she counted her steps, the woman's breaths, the tiles along the back wall, the number of bars making up the cells, and anything else she could think of.

As she started on the number of spokes in the drain, her

captor arrived bearing a tray. The impulse to spring at him and shrink back into the cell canceled each other, leaving her stranded over the drain. She watched his approach with the suspicion of a rabbit eyeing an approaching fox. The tray held several sandwiches on paper plates and two water bottles.

"Are you allergic to peanut butter?" he asked, pausing outside her cell.

Jenn shook her head slowly.

Kneeling, he slipped a peanut butter and jelly sandwich under the door and rolled a water bottle after it. She stared at the food longingly, trying to decide if he'd poison her for kicks. His earlier actions showed he was nuts enough to pull something like that, but the woman one cell over proved he also kept some captives alive. Picking up the sandwich and the water bottle, Jenn retreated to the blankets at the back and sniffed at the food. Her brother always made fun of her for smelling things before she ate them, but the ritual calmed her. Grape jelly wouldn't be her top choice, but right now, anything sounded good.

As she took her first bite, Jenn watched the man slip a paper plate holding a different kind of sandwich under her neighbor's door. After completing the delivery, the man picked up the tray and stood. Then, he ran the tray over the bars like a giant musical instrument, creating enough of a racket to rouse the woman.

"Breakfast," he announced. Without waiting for a response, the man walked out.

Alternating bites of sandwich with sips of water, Jenn watched the woman slowly sit up and stare listlessly at the food sitting by the cell door.

"He's not much of a cook, but it's not bad," said Jenn.

The woman's eyes filled with tears. She pulled the blankets further onto her lap and wrapped her arms around them. When she blinked, tears began the trek down her cheeks toward her chin and plunked onto the blanket. Her blue eyes were full of misery.

"You should try to eat something," Jenn encouraged.

Shaking her head, the woman only tightened her hold on the blankets. As Jenn started to doubt she'd ever get the woman to speak, a whisper reached her ears.

"I want to die."

"Don't say that." The plea came more out of reflex than

thought. Jenn set down the last quarter of sandwich and scooted closer to the other cell.

"Why not? It doesn't matter. This is the end of the line. We're never getting out of here."

"You don't know that," Jenn protested. She wanted to stop the flow of depressing words. "Cops could be on their way to get us this second." Jenn didn't believe it, and from the woman's expression, she didn't either.

The woman's tears dried up, and she stared hard at Jenn.

"I came here with two friends. One of them was in that very cell hours ago."

Jenn thought about the body she'd helped to unload from the van. She opened her mouth to share her impressions but reconsidered. They had no way of double checking the truth. If the woman believed her, it might pull her out of the funk, but she didn't seem the sort to take much on faith anymore.

"I'm sorry," Jenn murmured. "You don't have to tell me what happened, but I'm here to listen if you need it."

"There's nothing to tell," said the woman. "She's dead."

"Where are we?" Jenn asked, desperately trying to change the subject.

The question brought forth a bitter smile.

"Hell on Earth," replied the woman.

"Besides that." Jenn mentally kicked herself. She should have seen that answer coming. "Come on, think. If we can figure out where we are—"

"Then what?" challenged the woman.

With effort, Jenn held in an exasperated sigh.

"I don't know," she admitted. To give herself a moment to think, Jenn shoved the last part of the sandwich into her mouth and chewed. Her mother would be horrified, but Sam would laugh. "We can't give up."

"Layla used to say that." The statement had a flat, emotionless quality to it.

Mention of the name reminded Jenn that she had no name for her neighbor.

"Name's Jenn," she said, sticking her hand through the bars between them. "Jennifer Kerman."

After staring at the hanging hand for a long time, the woman briefly shook it.

"Natasha Creswell."

"It's nice to meet you," said Jenn, manners asserting themselves. She indulged in a small, humorless laugh. "I'd prefer it not be here, but I'll take what I can get."

"Your name is familiar," said Natasha. Her curious expression conveyed the obvious question.

"You're probably thinking of my brother. Sam's an FBI agent working the Parkside Killer case."

"Is that how you ended up here?"

"Probably."

"Are you going to eat?" demanded their captor.

Jenn flinched. She hadn't even heard him approach this time.

"I'm not hungry." Natasha's stomach contradicted her.

"Leave it a little longer," said Jenn. "I'll try to get her to eat something."

Grunting, the man collected Jenn's empty plate and stormed off.

"That dude is seriously scary," Jenn muttered.

Natasha giggled then laughed, releasing some of the tension in the air.

Although pleased to hear her laugh, even if it bordered on hysterical, Jenn hadn't meant to be funny. Several seconds of silence fell before Jenn attempted to coax Natasha into eating.

"I'm sick of tuna fish," Natasha declared. "It's been most meals for over two weeks."

Jenn grimaced. She liked peanut butter and jelly well enough but subsisting on it didn't sound appealing.

"Eat it," she said diplomatically. "We'll ask him for something else when he collects the plate."

Natasha shot her a grumpy look but crawled over to the plate and bit into the sandwich. She ate in silence for several minutes. Not wanting to disturb her, Jenn spent the time rearranging the blankets. Trying to keep down the thought that these blankets were last used by the woman she'd unloaded from the van was like playing whack-a-mole.

When the man returned to collect the garbage and empty

bottles, Jenn brought up the subject of meal variety. He didn't say anything, but he nodded and shrugged.

Time passed with excruciating slowness. Several attempts at conversation fell flat. After the meal, the other woman curled up on her blankets and slipped into her own thoughts. The weighty sadness settled on her again.

"How do you do this?" Jenn shouted, louder than she needed to just to break the oppressive silence. "I'm so bored!"

Natasha slowly turned her head to regard Jenn.

"Be grateful he's ignoring us. Sometimes he stands outside the cell and watches."

"I can see that being worse," Jenn admitted, "but please, tell me about yourself. I'm going crazy here just thinking."

"If you don't know me, it won't hurt if I die."

The grim statement shocked Jenn into speechlessness for several beats.

"It's not true," she whispered at last. Forcing her stiff, sore body up, Jenn knelt by the bars and reached as far as she could into the other cell. "We need each other. We need to stay strong, and we need a plan. I am not waiting around for that man to kill me, but I may need your help."

Natasha stared at the outstretched hand like it would bite her, but eventually she clasped Jenn's hand and squeezed hard.

Chapter 41:
Reunion

Andrew Novak's Private Residence
Florence, New Jersey

Melissa Novak didn't need the GPS to guide her through the last few miles. She remembered the way well. As she pulled down the long, narrow driveway, she marveled at how big some of the trees had grown. The frequent notices against trespassers shook her resolve a bit, but she pressed on. Maybe if she knocked on the door, the owners would be kind enough to let her stay a while and reminisce. She was ten minutes early. Andy had never said where they should meet, but she assumed it would be near the main house. The familiarity in seeing the big house drove away some of the week's frustrations and heartache.

The narrow driveway opened up into a large lot that could accommodate several trucks or a few dozen cars. Melissa parked near a large white van, noting that a dirty Ford Explorer and slightly less dirty Dodge Ram also occupied the lot. Somebody had to be home. Gripping her slippery courage, Melissa tucked her phone into her purse and hiked up to the door. The sound of several barking dogs filled her ears, but she didn't see a dog pen out front. As she lifted her hand to knock, a yellow sticky note caught her eye.

In neat block letters, the note said: COME IN.

Sticking the note back where she found it, Melissa considered her options. She could assume the note was meant for her and follow the instruction or she could be on the safe side and knock anyway.

A ding from her phone startled her. Confining her reaction to a slight jump, Melissa rooted around in the purse until she found the phone. She'd received a text message consisting of one word: Enter.

How does he know I'm here?

The Andy she remembered hadn't been so mysterious. Questions about him and this house filled her head. The note could have been left for anybody, but the text message was clearly aimed at her.

"Guess I have permission to enter," said Melissa, still hesitating.

Despite the invitation, the whole situation struck her as highly unusual. Visions of horror movies sprang to mind. Lonely houses in the middle of nowhere never held good things for female sojourners.

Get a grip!

Before the last of her nerve could drain away, Melissa twisted the door handle and stepped inside. The shift away from sunlight momentarily plunged her into darkness. As her eyes adjusted, she became aware of another presence in the room. The darkness didn't line up with her memories of the place. Someone had rigged heavy drapes across every entrance, creating a cave-like atmosphere.

"Hello, Mel. Thank you for coming." The voice belonged to Andy but the first words sounded sad and far too formal. "I have a Taser pointed at you. Please don't make me use it."

The last statement made zero sense.

"Andy?" The name sounded shaky. "What are you doing? Why do you need a Taser? I came here to meet you." Melissa took a step toward him.

"Stop!"

The cold tone as much as the order halted Melissa's forward progress.

"Don't move!"

"Tell me what's going on," she demanded. Anger helped overcome the fear keeping her feet cemented in place. She stepped carefully back toward the door.

"I warned you," said Andrew.

A loud pop and a strange crackling sound reached her ears as pain unlike anything she'd ever felt coursed through her entire body. Everything turned rigid. She was completely aware of falling but helpless to brace or prepare in any way. The pain cut off, but her muscles were still on strike. She lay on the ground not quite remembering how she got there.

"Why didn't you listen?" Andrew cradled her head and righted some strands of hair that had landed across her face. His fingers traced her jaw and then continued stroking her hair in a comforting manner.

Eventually, the ability to speak returned, but Melissa couldn't think of anything to say that wasn't a repeat of earlier questions.

"Mel? Please say something." Andrew's fingers brushed aside a few fresh tears.

"I'm … trying to understand," Melissa began. Her voice caught on a sob, not letting out any more words until she swallowed the painful lump. "But I can't."

"I'll explain later. I promise. Just relax. I'm going to move you now. Don't fight me, or I'll have to hurt them."

"Who?" The one-word question conveyed her confusion. "Andy, you don't have to hurt anybody. Please, tell me what's going on."

"Shhh. I'm going to cover your eyes just for a moment. Close your eyes and rest. When I get you situated, I'll explain everything." Leaning down, he kissed her forehead.

A silky sleep mask settled across her eyes. The material absorbed the new round of frustrated tears. She started to reach for the mask, but he caught her hands.

"Leave it on," Andy instructed. "I'm going to help you stand now. Let me lead and everything will be all right."

Prior to the Taser encounter, Melissa would have denied Andrew possessed the ability to harm a person. The shock had been a rude awakening in many ways. The news that he had other captives made her heart and head hurt. She wanted to turn back time and ignore the message to come to a meeting. While on the subject of wishing impossibilities, Melissa hoped Sam would come. She quickly pushed that thought away for many reasons. One, she had no idea what would happen. Two, they were finished, according to him. Three, right now, keeping everybody she cared about far away from Andy seemed like a good idea.

Survival instincts told Melissa to flee, but a small, curious side of her wanted the answers Andy held. There was a chance the whole cloak and dagger business could be explained as a prank gone too far. She was having a difficult time reconciling this new Andy and the sweet kid from her memories. If anything, she would have guessed Josh coming to this before Andy, since he'd always been the bossy one. Having no other choice, Melissa let her brother lead her through the expansive house. She didn't remember enough to be able to track their movements throughout the house, but when they started descending stairs, she knew they were headed for the basement.

As they reached the bottom, it occurred to her that he might actually hurt strangers. The thought made her stumble, but Andy righted her balance and continued leading. She stiffened as he started to turn her. His grip on her arms tightened.

"Remember what I said before about hurting them," he whispered. "Turn around and sit down."

"This would be so much easier if you just told me what you wanted," said Melissa. She let him spin her around and press her shoulders against a rough surface. Gentle but consistent pressure, lowered her to a kneeling position. Feeling for the ground, Melissa eased her body down on the hard surface.

"Lift your arms above your head."

"Why?"

"Stop questioning everything!" Andy shouted, driving a fist into the wall near her head.

The blow came so close Melissa felt the wind of its passing.

He grunted and ripped off the blindfold. Clutching his right hand, Andy stared at her with anger and contempt.

Melissa blinked up at him, hardly recognizing him as her brother. The shout had torn yet another layer off of her nerves. Much of her effort went into not trembling.

Reaching down, Andy yanked her left arm up and snapped a metal cuff around the wrist. He repeated the move with her other arm. In less than four seconds, any chance of defending herself disappeared.

Closing her eyes, Melissa rested her head against the wall, trying to imagine anything but this nightmare. The snap of the cold metal cuffs echoed loudly in her mind, driving off the last scraps of hope the explanation would make sense.

"I'm doing this for you."

The statement brought Melissa's eyes open and her head forward. The ridiculousness put her on surer emotional footing.

"No." The protest was short and firm. "There is nothing you can say that would ever justify this." She moved the chains so he understood her meaning. "Or keeping them," she added, tilting her head to indicate the three cells lined up to her left.

Both the middle and the last cells held the prone form of a woman curled up under several blankets.

"It's not their time to die yet," said Andy. His factual tone chilled Melissa.

Realization washed over her like cold rain.

"You're the killer Sam's been after." The heavy truth pressed down upon her chest, and she started hyperventilating.

A ding from his phone announced a new text message. When he read the message, Andy's whole face lit up.

"We can continue this conversation later. I need to make a phone call. You're not ready for the whole truth anyway." Andy reached into a pocket and withdrew a hypodermic needle. Flicking off the safety cap, he pressed the needle into Melissa's left arm. "Just rest."

Melissa felt the cuffs being tightened right before her senses completely abandoned her to darkness.

Chapter 42:
Everybody Gets a Turn

The Killer's Lair
Florence, New Jersey

When Melissa Novak woke up her situation hadn't improved. In fact, it got worse because now her left arm ached and her head felt fuzzy. As before, tight metal cuffs secured both wrists to the wall above her head. Pain shot through her lower back from sitting on the unforgiving floor.

"I think she's awake," said an unfamiliar female voice. "Hey, are you awake?"

"Shhhh," scolded another voice. "If you wake her, he'll come back."

"She's been out for hours," said the first voice. "Besides, the sooner he comes back, the sooner the suspense will end. It's doing bad things to my nerves."

"When he comes back, one of us will die," noted the second voice. She sounded more resigned than worried.

Though her eyelids felt like they weighed a ton, Melissa forced them open. Her gaze took in an odd sight. Two young women sat in wooden chairs, one to her left and one to her right. The awkward bent to their shoulders told her their wrists were likely bound to the spokes making up the back of each chair.

"What's your name?" asked the woman on Melissa's right. "I'm Jenn."

The simple question tugged at Melissa's heart as she recalled

Eddie asking it incessantly.

"Why do you bother?" wondered the cynical one sitting to Melissa's left. "We're all going to die." Anger lent strength and volume to the words.

"Mel."

Jenn's attention snapped into sharper focus.

"Is that short for Melissa or Melanie?" Her tone said she already knew the answer.

"Melissa. Why?"

The woman's face registered shock.

"You're her," Jenn mumbled.

"Her who?" asked the other woman impatiently. "There must be a million people with that name."

"She's my sister." Andy's soft answer made all three women tense.

"I've wanted to meet you, but this wasn't what I had in mind," said Jenn.

"Me neither," Melissa whispered. She kept her eyes on Andy as he circled around the far end of the dental chair and sat on it sideways, facing them.

"What's the game this time?" asked the woman to Melissa's left.

"First things first. Have you met each other?" Andy looked at each of them briefly. Receiving no answer, he performed quick introductions. "As I said, Mel's my sister. Jenn is Sam's sister, and Natasha's the survivor from the three I came across in New York," he concluded.

Natasha snorted.

"Kidnapped. The word you're looking for is 'kidnapped.' And who's Sam?"

"Andy, why are you doing this?" Melissa suffered no illusions he'd give her a straight answer, but she had to try anyway. "Let them go."

"Sam's an FBI agent," Jenn explained. "He's been investigating these cases. He's also Melissa's boyfriend."

Melissa shook her head wearily.

"Ex-boyfriend," she corrected. "He sent me a message yesterday with that news."

Jenn shook her head emphatically.

"I don't believe it. He's crazy about you, and I would know if he planned on breaking up. He stinks at keeping stuff like that in."

Melissa wanted to believe her, but she was having a hard time wrapping her mind around anything.

"I'll bet he did it," Natasha said, glaring at Andy.

It took several moments for Melissa's brain to catch up to the implication.

"Andy?" Melissa emphasized the question with a pleading stare, not knowing which answer she wanted.

He nodded once.

"He had to go, Mel. If this goes our way, we're leaving this place. We'll start over somewhere else. I'll find you somebody new."

Her head reeled from the influx of information.

"You don't simply find people like Sam," Melissa said.

Andy tilted his head in a thoughtful manner.

"I suppose we could bring him too, if you want."

"No!" The protest sprang out with force from both Melissa and Jenn.

"Forget about him," Melissa urged her brother. She would never forget Sam, but the less Andy thought about him, the better. "Where are we going?"

Andy held up a hand in a stopping motion.

"We have to win first," he announced.

"And if you lose, you die," said Natasha. Her tone was as cold as deep space.

"Not necessarily," Andy countered. He stood up to begin his explanation. "I'm going to release you one at a time. You're going to each receive a Spectacular Sevens lottery ticket. The winner chooses who sits out the round. If nobody wins, everybody gets a turn."

"Even you?" asked Natasha. "I think you should play. It's only fair."

Andy ignored her and carried out his plan of distributing lottery tickets. Melissa couldn't fathom why the ticket ritual meant so much to Andy, but it kept everybody alive a few moments more. She used the time to compose arguments and sort options. She wanted to survive this, but part of her felt guilty for Andy's actions. Fighting him would likely get all of them killed. Going along with his game would only doom one of them supposedly. If she could get him to leave with her, the other two might have a chance. The devotion in his eyes looked genuine.

"Your turn, Mel," said Andy.

He unlocked the cuffs and lowered her arms down to her lap. His touch was light and gentle. A lottery ticket appeared in her hands along with a quarter. Melissa read the directions as slowly as possible. It had a slot machine theme. If one obtained three like symbols, they would win the prize for that row. Getting three sevens in a row would net the top prize of ten million dollars. Feeling Andy's intense gaze linger, Melissa moved the quarter across the ticket, carefully scratching every corner until the entire thing was clear.

She lost. A glance at the other two said they'd lost too.

"Guess everybody gets a turn," said Andy, as he returned Melissa's hands to the cuffs attached to the wall. "Except me. I have to run the game."

Melissa was absolutely certain she didn't want to know the game he had in mind. That feeling intensified when he reached into one of the cargo pants pockets and pulled out a small revolver and a single bullet.

Chapter 43:
Trespassing Triumph

Farm
Florence, New Jersey

Sam Kerman's heart leapt when he saw Mel's car parked at the end of the massive driveway. Several other vehicles occupied the lot as well. He'd spent most of the drive rehearsing things to say. The two messages from Mel made it clear she was upset, and he felt bad about that even if none of the trouble was his doing. Before getting out, Sam took a moment to get into his Matchmaker Miracles account and find the message sent from there. It made him want to punch something, but first, he needed to speak with Mel.

He also remembered to call Gill. As he pulled up the kid's number, another call came in. The caller ID said Easttown Police Department. Sam couldn't think of an immediate reason for that particular department to call him, but he decided it must be important for them to bother on a Sunday. Accepting the call, Sam identified himself and inquired about the caller's purpose.

"Agent Kerman, this is Lieutenant Owen Marsh of the Easttown Police Department. I received a request from the county offices to look into an abandoned parking lot in my jurisdiction."

"Yes, I made that request," said Sam. "That was fast." For some reason, that told him the news wouldn't be good.

"My officers found an abandoned Elantra in the lot that traces back to a Jennifer Kerman. Any relation?"

"My sister."

"They also found a young woman pumped full of drugs and left for dead, but she doesn't match your sister's picture. That was confirmed when they broke into the car to retrieve the purse on the front passenger seat. They thought it might have a clue as to what the unconscious woman took."

Sam's heart lurched as the news washed through him. Guilt, relief, and anxiety flooded him with adrenaline.

"One of my officers thought the woman looked familiar. I don't have a positive ID yet, but she looks an awful lot like one of those women kidnapped from New York a few weeks back. I'm only telling you this because I'm aware you're working on that case."

"Thank you. Would you like me to call the Tenafly PD, and can you get an all-points bulletin prepped for my sister?"

"Already done on both accounts, sir," said Lieutenant Marsh. "The parents and husband are on the way to Paoli Hospital now, but before you go, there's one more thing. A witness thinks he saw someone get into a white van. He was on a bike too far away to see much, but he reported it because he thought kids might be drinking in the abandoned lot again."

After thanking the officer a second time, Sam double checked that the man had posted a competent guard on the survivor and ended the call. He debated who to contact next. His mother would want to have the update about Jenn, but he also needed to alert his people of the latest development. SAC Hatcher wouldn't be pleased that he was so far out of pocket, but he'd get things done.

"What now, Kerman?"

It wasn't the warmest welcome, but Sam spilled his news anyway starting with Jenn being missing, tracking her phone to the lot, and the police finding a half-dead woman there.

"If you're asking me to watch over things here, that means you're not available to do it," said Hatcher. "This begs the question: why aren't you here?"

"I'm following another lead, sir," Sam said, wincing at how pathetic that sounded. His eyes fell on the white van parked on the other side of Mel's car. Inspiration slammed into him. "It's a long shot, but I have some license plates for you to check."

His boss growled at that announcement but barked out an order to read him the numbers.

Exiting his car as fast as physically possible, Sam jogged to the van. The slamming car door prompted a chorus of furious dog barks. Sam filed the information in the back of his mind. The back license plate was caked with a thick layer of mud, so he checked the front plate. That too wore a coat of mud.

"Kerman?"

"One moment, sir," said Sam. Wishing he'd worn something besides dress shoes, Sam kicked at the front license plate until clumps of mud thudded to the ground. When the prize revealed itself, Sam rattled it off to his boss. On a hunch, he checked the Dodge Ram and the Ford Explorer. After giving them the same kicking treatment, he conveyed these license plate numbers to his boss as well.

"Who do you think they're going to come back to?" Hatcher inquired.

"Don't know, sir," Sam admitted. His eyes swept over the paved lot. Although many cracks spoke of neglect, he saw no immediate explanation for the mud.

"Where are you anyway?"

"I'm at a farm in Florence, New Jersey," said Sam. Knowing Hatcher, he was standing over a computer screen displaying his phone's GPS. "My girlfriend's around here somewhere. When you told me to lay low for the rest of the weekend, I figured I'd come here and smooth out a misunderstanding."

Hatcher's grunt managed to be neutral.

"Where are Fuller and Hill?"

"This was a spur of the moment trip. I didn't tell them." Sam felt slightly guilty over that now.

"Well, get back as soon as you can. I want you at Paoli Hospital interviewing that survivor the second the doctors can get her lucid."

"Will do, sir. This shouldn't take long. I'll call you when I'm on my way."

Having covered everything he needed to, Sam closed out the conversation and pulled up his mother's number. Before he could touch the button to place the call, a male voice spoke from behind.

"Put the phone down and get your hands up."

Sam started to turn.

"Eyes straight ahead," snapped the man.

Without knowing if the man had anything to back up the

order, Sam followed the instruction. He placed the phone on the ground and raised his hands.

"I'm an FBI agent," Sam said evenly. "I can explain my presence."

"I know who you are." The bitterness in the tone sounded like it had deep roots.

Sam knew he was being given too much credit, but he kept his mouth shut figuring he ought to try to learn something before getting shot.

"I'm here looking for someone."

"Mel's inside," said the man. "We can go meet her as soon as you give me your gun."

"Everything to this point can be explained as a misunderstanding," Sam said, "but if I hand over my gun based on a threat, you'll have broken half a dozen federal laws. Do you really want to do that?"

The question earned a derisive snort.

"If we don't hurry, he's likely to kill Mel, so if you want to speak with her again, give me your gun right now."

Sam reluctantly followed the directive.

"Good. Now, walk into the house, nice and slow."

Turning, Sam stepped on his phone as he moved toward the front door.

"Get away from the phone," ordered the man.

When Sam was a few paces from the phone, he heard a crunching noise. He winced. The bean counters were going to love the explanation for this expense. He hoped he lived long enough to tell them the tale.

Sam and his escort made their way inside with the man calling out directions from a safe distance away. As they turned a corner, his peripheral vision showed him the man's gun, which was different from the one Sam surrendered. Strangely, knowing the threat was real made Sam feel better. It cleared up a lot of the indecision about how to treat this guy.

"Go down the stairs to the basement."

"I'm going to give you one last chance to change your mind, then all bets are off," Sam said with a false sense of calm.

A shove in the back answered his offer.

Sam nearly took the stairs headfirst, but he caught his

balance at the last moment and eased his way down. The sound of Mel's voice made him rush down the final three steps.

"Let them go, Andy. This isn't right."

A hand caught his shoulder and hauled him to a stop.

"Wait," ordered the man. "I want to hear this."

Sam listened hard.

"It has to be this way. I need to know if I'm called to continue this work. Psycho67 said this would be a definitive test. If you live, I'll have my answer and can continue the work."

Sam couldn't place the male voice Mel had called Andy.

"And if I die?" asked Mel.

"I'll move on," said the man.

"What does that mean?" The question sounded like it came from Jenn.

The realization moved through Sam like ice water. Forgetting the man behind him, he rushed forward into the next room. The strange sight brought him up short next to a large dental chair. Mel sat against the far wall with her hands caught in metal cuffs above her head. Jenn and a new woman flanked her in stiff wooden chairs. Sam recognized the new woman as one of the three victims he'd just been discussing with Lieutenant Marsh, but he couldn't remember which one. A man whose features sort of matched that of the guy behind him whirled and leveled a revolver at Sam's gut.

"Look what I found lurking outside," said the original captor.

Mel's expression could have been the dictionary definition of unpleasant surprise.

"Get on with it." The man kept close to the wall, stepping around Sam. His gun moved from Sam to the man holding a gun on Mel. "Or better yet, step aside. I know you don't have the guts to kill her."

These must be Mel's brothers, the twins.

"What are you doing here?" The man with the revolver looked bewildered.

Dark laughter burst out of the one Sam decided to dub "Evil Twin."

"Isn't it obvious? I'm here for the millions you've hidden away."

Chapter 44:
Brother vs. Brother

Andrew Novak's Private Residence
Florence, New Jersey

Melissa Novak's heart crumbled to dust within her as she watched her two brothers point guns at each other. Having Sam near gave her some hope, but she could see he was as much a prisoner as the rest of them. Reasoning with Andy had gone nowhere, but she had to try again.

"Josh!"

"Stay out of this, Mel," said Josh.

"Don't do this," Melissa pleaded. "Think of Josie."

"What about her?" asked Josh. "I'll send her enough money to get by."

"What now, brother?" asked Andy in a mocking tone. "Are we going to die together?"

"If I know you—and for the record, I do—you've only got one bullet, and if you use it on me, you'll never get the answers you seek," Josh pointed out. "How lucky are you feeling?"

"Very." Andy's back was to her, but he sounded far calmer than a rational person ought to feel. "You need me alive to get the money. As you've mentioned, it's hidden away."

"Well, let's go get it," said Josh impatiently.

"I need to finish this."

"Fine. Do it quickly." Josh's tone conveyed boredom.

The revolver's barrel brushed Melissa's forehead. She closed her eyes and waited for the end. Gasps rang out from either side of her.

"No!" Sam's shout was accompanied by scuffling noises.

Melissa's eyes flew open and locked on Sam. He looked dazed but determined. Josh had forced him to his knees and pressed the gun to the base of his neck.

"Keep still. It'll be four quick shots," said Josh. "If none of them strike, you'll all live to see another day."

Andy rolled the revolver's barrel and once again focused on Melissa.

"I hope it works," Melissa whispered, "because I won't have to face what you've become." For a second time, she squeezed her eyes shut.

"I hope you're wrong," said Andy. "You're the only thing I love."

A loud, empty click greeted her ears.

Her eyes flew open. Despite her earlier words, Melissa wanted to live. The triumph in Andy's eyes sickened her. He swung the gun to his right and pulled the trigger. Another empty click cracked through the air. Natasha sagged with relief, tears streaming down her face. The gun swung back the other way, headed for Jenn.

"Wait!"

"Sorry, Mel, everybody has to play," said Andy.

"Spin the barrel again. You're not giving them a fair chance if you don't."

Natasha looked like she wanted to murder Melissa until Andy nodded, did as asked, and pointed the gun at Jenn again. Melissa fervently hoped she didn't just get Sam's sister killed.

The empty click was a welcomed sound.

As Melissa started to breathe again, Andy turned to Sam.

"Don't do it. Don't do it." The words tumbled from Melissa.

Andy lined up the shot then stopped.

"Would you take his turn?" he asked.

"Yes!" Melissa and Jenn gave the answer simultaneously.

Josh chuckled.

"This is an interesting moral question. Who has more right to spare Sam his chance to die, the sister or the girlfriend?"

"Everybody faces Fate today," said Andy. Without hesitation, he fired at Sam.

Another click sounded.

Tears of relief blurred Melissa's vision.

"What are you doing?" Josh roared the question.

"I told you. Everybody faces Fate today, including me," Andy explained. "If I live, the money's yours. If I die, you were never meant to have it."

"Put that gun down," Josh ordered.

"Or what?" Andy challenged. "You'll kill me? That'll end your chances of getting my money."

Josh's eyes bulged. Sweat made his face shiny. His nostrils flared, but when he spoke, the words held deadly promise.

"No. I'll kill her."

The gun in Josh's hands boomed, sounding like a cannon in the small room.

Multiple screams rang out.

Pain ripped through Melissa's left shoulder. Her arms had gone numb from hanging above her head so long, but the bullet's abrupt passage slammed her hard against the wall. At first, it felt like being hit with a really fast baseball, but then the burning, aching pain took over. She couldn't make heads or tails of anything else going on in the room. The world had been reduced to fiery pain and deep sorrow.

***

The instant Josh fired at Mel, Sam made a snap decision. He always wore a pocket pistol strapped to his right ankle but getting to that would take time he didn't have. In most situations, it would simply be a matter of going for the crazy guy with the gun, only this time, there were two such targets. Screams filled the room, adding to the confusion. Blocking out the distractions, Sam tackled Josh.

The blow drove the younger man into the wall. The gun clattered to the ground. Josh had youth, speed, and bulk on his side. Sam had desperation, fear for Mel, and actual hand-to-hand combat training going for him. They fell over in a tangle of arms and legs. Sam tried to keep his arms wrapped around Josh, but the young man thrashed like a cornered bear. The back of Josh's head met Sam's chin, splitting his lower lip and giving him a massive headache. Heaving up, Sam used the leverage he had to slam Josh back to the ground, hopefully knocking the wind out of him. The thrashing continued but with less vigor. Encouraged, Sam changed his grip long enough to throw a short, quick punch into his opponent's head.

Knowing he had to end the fight quickly, Sam flipped Josh over and smashed his left fist into his cheek. At the same moment, the air whooshed out of him as Josh's fist crashed in from the side. Not sure how long the victory would last, Sam looked frantically about for the gun.

He spotted it over by the dental chair. If he dove, he could have it in a second.

"Stop." The order wasn't loud, but it seemed so in the absence of screams.

Still climbing off of Josh's prone form, Sam didn't need to look to know Andy's gun would be pointed his way. Stopping his efforts to rise, Sam shifted his body so he'd have easier access to his backup gun. His eyes moved past Andy's gun to Mel. Mercifully, she'd passed out, but blood still soaked the left side of her shirt.

Tearing his gaze away, Sam looked at Andy. The young man looked more like a lost little boy than a threat, but he still held a gun with a bullet in it.

"Help her!" Jenn pleaded, addressing Andy.

If Sam drew now, he had a good chance of taking down Andy, but in the close quarters, he also had a good chance of hitting Jenn, the other woman, or even Mel. Besides, insane or not, Andy was Mel's brother. Shooting him would have to be a very last resort. He drew his gun anyway but kept it out of sight by his ankle. His knees began to burn from crouching, but he didn't want to break the uneasy calm that had fallen.

Something nagged at Sam, but his weary brain refused to define that feeling with any clarity.

"Andy, she's going to bleed out," Jenn said urgently. "You love her. You said it yourself. Don't let that happen. Let us help her or save her yourself, but do something!"

My gun!

The thought burst into Sam's mind. His gaze whipped down in time to see Josh pull the gun free of his pocket. Desperately, Sam slammed the butt of his gun down on the man's head.

The gun went off.

Everybody froze.

In slow motion, Andy dropped to his knees before Mel. A neat hole appeared in his back. Then, blood trickled down.

Whipping out his handcuffs, Sam secured Josh's hands behind his back and double checked that he was still unconscious. Searching the man's pockets, he found a cell phone and used it to call 911. After a short, tense conversation to relay the facts, Sam dropped the phone and rushed to Andy.

The man had fallen to his hands and knees, sobbing. Sam stretched him out on his stomach, trying not to disturb the wound. This time, he conducted a thorough search for weapons. Riffling through Andy's pockets produced a ring of keys. In a moment, Jenn, the other woman, and Mel were released from their chains. Sam applied the handcuffs that Jenn had worn to Andy and one of the support slats on the chair she'd sat in.

"Go watch Josh," Sam instructed his sister. "Make sure he stays quiet."

An animalistic growl from the other woman warned Sam a second before she lunged at Andy. Catching her around the waist, Sam threw her back into the chair she'd just exited and reapplied the handcuffs.

She rained down curses on him, but he ignored her.

"Ma'am, this is for your safety and mine," Sam said calmly.

"Let me kill him!" she screeched.

"Natasha, please," said Jenn. "We don't have time for this. We need to save Mel."

Leaving the beast-taming role to his sister, Sam gently lowered Mel to the ground. Stripping off his rumpled dress shirt, he wadded it up and pressed it over Mel's shoulder.

She groaned at the renewed pain.

"Lie still. Let me stop the bleeding," said Sam.

Her head lolled to the side and she caught sight of Andy. Mel tried to sit up, but Sam held her down.

"Please." She didn't get any further, but Sam got the gist.

"Jenn, see if there's something you can do to stop him from bleeding out." Sam didn't look at his sister, but he could imagine the look she was giving him.

Natasha loosed another curse-laced rant until Jenn threatened to duct tape her mouth shut and stomped off to get a cloth or bandage to help Andy.

With the worst of the crisis over, Sam leaned down and kissed Mel's sweaty forehead. The move hurt his split lip, but he didn't regret it.

"I know my timing's terrible, but I love you." He had a whole lot more to say, but it would have to wait until she woke up again.

Chapter 45:
Psycho67

Andrew Novak's Private Residence
Florence, New Jersey

A haze of pain carried Melissa Novak along in a state somewhere between consciousness and unconsciousness. Someone nearby held one of her hands and spoke in a low voice, but her mind refused to make sense of the words. Instead, one word forced its way through the haze and blazed within her mind.

Psycho67.

Because she'd been fully convinced she was about to die, Melissa had paid attention to every nuance of the conversation with Andy before things went from bad to worse. Andy had spoken the name with a childlike, trusting tone. The numbers told her the name probably doubled as an online handle. Who would choose a name like that though?

A devoted fan.

Connections clicked together almost faster than Melissa could follow. To organize her thoughts, she listed the facts she had, regardless of how much they hurt her to think about. Andy was a murderer many times over. He might come across as crazy, but he followed logic that made sense to him. According to her fellow prisoners, he rambled a lot about fate, destiny, and being called to clean up the world. That sort of crazy usually didn't spring up in isolation. It required a following.

Psycho67 meant something to Andy, so whoever owned that

moniker was either a mentor or a fan. The tone used had her leaning toward mentor.

As kids, Andy, Josh, and Mel had played games exchanging letters in words and substituting numbers.

Hitchcock's movie *Psycho* had been a family favorite when they were kids.

They'd vacationed in California one year when the boys were very young and seen a 49ers game together as a family at Candlestick Park. Despite concerted effort from their father, the boys had been 49ers fans ever since.

The only book in high school they hadn't whined about reading was *Catch-22*.

Josh is Psycho67.

Melissa couldn't fathom everything that meant, but it opened up a new, soul-deep ache within her.

He loved playing with numbers. Psycho67 would make perfect sense to him if he combined the things he enjoyed. Most people used numbers from their birth year, but 1967 was way before Josh and Andy's time. If one took the number 49 and brought the first digit up by two and the second digit down by two, they'd end up with 67.

Forcing her eyes open, Melissa tried to sit up. She needed to get to a computer.

Sam's concerned face loomed above her.

"Don't move. The EMTs will be here shortly."

"Josh!" Melissa tried to put the urgency she felt into the name.

"The police will deal with him. He's fine," said Sam, not understanding her meaning.

Groaning with the effort, Melissa shook her head.

"He's ... responsible." She swallowed hard and drew some quick breaths. She didn't remember talking being this difficult in the past.

Sam smiled down at her sympathetically.

"Mel, Josh has a lot to answer for, but Andy's the killer. You're the only one Josh shot, and I think you'll live."

"No. Yes." Melissa let out a noise that somehow hit both groan and growl. Gritting her teeth, she said, "Get me to a computer."

"Slow down, woman," said Sam. "Your email can wait."

Melissa gripped Sam's hand as hard as she could with her rapidly depleting strength.

"Must ... show you something."

"Can't it wait until after we get that hole in you patched?"

She shook her head and tried to sit up yet again.

"Hang on. You're not going anywhere, Doc," said Sam. "Let me check the wound. If it's not too bad, I'll help you sit up." He turned his head to look over his shoulder. "Jenn, see if you can find a laptop." Cradling Melissa's hand between his, Sam grumbled a question. "Why do doctors make poor patients?"

Not having the energy to offer an answer, Melissa closed her eyes and tried not to pass out.

Jenn soon returned with a laptop.

"It's password protected," she warned.

"Is Andy conscious?" asked Sam. "He'd know the password."

"He's still out cold," Jenn said, sounding tentative. "And there's an awful lot of blood."

Forcing her head up, Melissa looked at Jenn. "Help me, please."

"Let him rot," said Natasha.

They collectively ignored her.

"He got hit saving her, and he's still her brother," Sam said, speaking to his sister but still looking at Melissa. "If you don't want to help him, come sit with her."

"I'll do it." Jenn clearly wasn't happy, but her voice held sincerity.

Since Sam still wouldn't let her get up, Melissa had him hold the laptop while she tried a few passwords. On the fifth try, the computer unlocked.

"How'd you know?" asked Sam with an annoying amount of surprise.

"He's good with computers; lousy with passwords," Melissa explained.

The one that had worked had been a combination of her nickname and Josh's name in alternating letters.

Typical Andy.

Sam moved the laptop so he could type but angled it so

Melissa could watch the screen.

"What am I looking for?"

"Search for 'psycho67.' I think it's Josh."

The search yielded dozens of hits. Sam whistled after reading a few entries. He looked to the opposite side of the room and glared. Melissa assumed his target was Josh.

"Got anything to say about this?" asked Sam.

"He knew," Melissa whispered. "He wanted it to happen."

The truth of the words made them harder to bear. How could her brothers have strayed so far from right? How could she not have seen it? She wanted to stop thinking, but her mind conjured one more terrifying thought.

If I'm so bad at judging character, what does that mean for Sam?

This new pain was distinctly different than the others she'd felt today. Melissa looked up into his handsome face and knew what she had to do. She had to protect him from the fallout.

"Sam."

He met her eyes.

"I'll have my people dig into this computer later," Sam assured her. "They'll find out how much Josh was involved."

"Sam," she repeated. Melissa clung to slippery scraps of courage. "I—"

Sam placed a finger over her lips.

"Oh no, you don't. We already broke up once this weekend because of them. It's not happening again."

"But—"

"You're not them, Mel. You haven't made their choices."

"But all those people, those families ...." Melissa let that sentence end unfinished. There was no easy answer.

"I know," said Sam, "it's going to be messy and difficult, but we'll face it together."

His words weren't particularly profound, but she believed him.

"Sam? I love you."

He grinned.

"Finally, you're talking sense!" Leaning down, he gently kissed her lips. "And just for the record, I said it first."

Melissa didn't remember if he had or not, but once again, she believed him. The love wrapped around her heart and gave her hope that she could face the future.

Epilogue:
Old Bet, Fresh Start

Four Months Later ...
In a Plane
Somewhere over Eastern Pennsylvania

"One hundred bucks. Pay up, Kerman!" shouted Sergeant First Class Neil Cunningham.

Melissa watched as Sam nodded solemnly and handed over a crisp bill.

"What was that about?" she asked, when he came up beside her. She'd already paid their fees for the jump.

"Old bet," said Sam. He spoke directly into her ear to be heard. "Told him I'd never skydive again."

"Knew I'd get my money back with interest someday," said Neil, slapping Sam on the back. "So, you two love birds ready to fly?"

Melissa nodded, knowing her expression betrayed her terror.

"Ladies first," said Cunningham.

Shortly thereafter, Melissa was strapped securely across the sergeant's chest, ready for the tandem jump. Her eyes sought Sam, but he only waved.

"Don't worry, princess. Prince Charming'll be right on our heels."

Melissa didn't have time to reply because the soldier chose that moment to leap from the plane.

She screamed.

The first ten seconds were among the scariest of her life, but then, she peeled her eyes open and saw the stunning view. From up here, one could see for miles. The land stretched in a beautiful, multicolored ribbon punctuated by large swaths of green and gold. Bodies of water sparkled like fine gems. Her breath jerked out of her as the parachute deployed, giving her a moment to enjoy the rush of wind. Their descent slowed but continued as Neil used the steering straps to head toward an open field.

Once he brought them to a safe landing and set her loose, Melissa thanked him for the thrilling experience. The air down here was warmer than up in the plane or descending through the air but not by much. Melissa didn't mind. Fall was her favorite season. Her jeans and sweatshirt kept her warm enough under the flight suit. Her left shoulder ached, but she appreciated being alive too much to care. The surgeon who'd removed the bullet had cleared her for the jump, though she didn't sound pleased with the notion.

"Fun's not over. K-man's got one more surprise for you." Neil's voice took on a serious quality as he held out a hand for her goggles. "I can just show you, but it'll be more fun if you close your eyes and let me lead you there. Totally up to you."

The concern told her that Sam must have shared some of her recent experiences with his friend. The memory shot fear through Melissa, but she pushed it aside and handed over the goggles.

Andy's not here. This isn't his basement.

Things with her brothers were far from settled. Sam's task force had linked Andy to a number of horrific crimes. His lawyer was talking about trying for an insanity plea, but he didn't sound optimistic about getting it. One of Melissa's psychiatrist friends had started seeing Andy in prison. Josh had already been charged with attempted murder and kidnapping. The task force considered several other charges and conspiracy-to-commit charges, but she wasn't sure what became of them.

Josie and the kids had moved in on a semi-permanent basis.

Thankfully, Sam's team member, Agent Okiro, had made a full recovery.

Andy's healing was slow. He might end up permanently paralyzed from the waist down from the bullet meant for her. He'd expressed some remorse, though transcripts of the conversations between him and his lawyer, which he let Melissa see, showed some serious gaps in logic. There might actually be some grounds for declaring him mentally deficient, but she didn't know which way to wish that would go. Thankfully, such decisions were out of her hands.

He'd surprised her early this past week by granting her use of several large bank accounts. An entire team of lawyers and accountants had been over them with fine-tooth combs and concluded they were legitimately earned through a variety of online business ventures, including Matchmaker Miracles. She hadn't told Sam about the money yet. When the lawyers got done salivating, they'd help her anonymously use some of the funds to support the victims and their families. She gave silent thanks that both Natasha Creswell and Layla O'Malley had recovered physically from their close encounters with death. To a man—or woman—the lawyers had advised against public support of the victims, for fear of backlash and to avoid sparking a slew of gold-digging civil lawsuits.

Realizing she'd been silent too long, Melissa forced a smile, closed her eyes, and held out a hand for Neil to lead her.

"I trust you," she said.

"Brave lady," quipped Neil, "but I already knew that since you date K-man."

The soldier's grip was steady enough to offer guidance without making her feel threatened. He kept up a running commentary about the beautiful scenery she was missing.

"And here we are," Neil announced. "One safely delivered lovely lady. K-man, catch ya later. Three's a crowd and all. Oops, almost forgot this. Do me proud, brother."

"Out," ordered Sam.

"Righto. Best of luck. It was nice meeting you, Mel. Anytime you wanna skydive, you know who to call. Bringing the K-man's totally optional." The words carried the essence of a jaunty farewell.

She thanked him again for everything.

"Can I open my eyes now?" Melissa asked, once certain they were alone.

Another set of warm hands picked up hers.

"Yes." Sam's voice held a nervous energy she couldn't place.

Opening her eyes, she saw Sam looking dapper in a dark suit with a bright blue tie. Mel suspected Neil had led her in a few wide circles before stopping here beneath a canopy of tall trees. She had to admit, Sam's choice of location was superb. A gentle breeze moved through the trees high above them, allowing the sunlight and leaves to create a dazzling light and shadow show.

One second, she stared up into Sam's smoky, gray-green eyes. The next second, her gaze was drawn downward as he knelt, still holding her hands. Her mind went blank.

Sam smiled and let a moment pass in complete silence before attempting to speak.

"I know I have timing issues, and I know this might seem fast or wrong in some other way. But I love you, so I have to ask." He stopped long enough to draw a box out of his right pocket. "Dr. Melissa Novak, will you marry me?"

A dozen reasons to turn him down clamored for attention right alongside her heart doing triple-time in her chest. To buy a moment to think, she tugged him to his feet and wrapped him in a tight hug. When she thought her voice might work again, she cleared her throat, leaned back, and looked deep into his eyes.

"Are you sure you want the trouble?" she asked hoarsely.

Resting his forehead on hers, Sam said, "I've never wanted anything more, but if—"

She cut him off with a very long, satisfying kiss.

"Yes," said Melissa when the kiss concluded. Leaning back, she poked him in the chest. "But you should have warned me. I'm feeling underdressed here."

Sam grinned.

"I thought you might say that." He changed position and offered her his elbow. "My sister's waiting just over that hill in her toy car with some wardrobe choices Josie picked out."

Melissa laughed.

"You thought of everything," she said, looping her arm through his.

He shrugged.

"We tried, but I think we forgot appropriate shoes," Sam explained. "If you'd prefer, I can use the car to climb back into the plane-jumping monkey suit, so you won't feel out of place. By then, Neil should have our picnic ready."

"How'd you get Neil to agree to that?" Melissa wondered.

Sam's grin had a slightly evil quality to it.

"By agreeing not to punch him when he asks Jenn out

sometime today."

"What a good brother," said Melissa.

The statement sobered her by bringing up thoughts of her own brothers, but with Sam by her side, she refused to let regrets steal the day.

THE END

Thank You for Reading:

Each book is a labor of love that I enjoy sharing with people.

Many of my previously published books are free.

Please visit my website: **www.juliecgilbert.com** to find a link to the current free works. If you still wish to show support, there are combination books and other formats to purchase. The audiobooks have fantastic narrators, and the paperbacks have a nice, crisp feel to them.

Join the Facebook group "Julie C. Gilbert's Special Agents" for monthly book discussions and giveaways.

I would love to connect via email:
devyaschildren@gmail.com
juliecgilbert5steps@gmail.com

Other Contacts:
www.facebook.com/JulieCGilbert2013
www.instagram.com/juliecgilbert_writer/
https://twitter.com/authorgilbert
www.bookbub.com/authors/julie-c-gilbert

Love Science Fiction, Fantasy, or Mystery?

Choose your adventure!

Visit: **http://www.juliecgilbert.com/**

For details on getting
Free ebooks.

www.ingramcontent.com/pod-product-compliance
Lightning Source LLC
Chambersburg PA
CBHW070859180626
46817CB00003B/828